PRAISE FOR SPARKS

"*Sparks* is stunning and visceral, alive with the journey of self-discovery and the emotional imperatives of loss, first love, fear, and friendship. This absolutely unique novel pushes the limits of creative imagination, illuminating what it means to be different in a world consumed with conformity."

- Alex Poppe, award-winning author of *Girl, World, Moxie, Jinwar and Other Tales from The Levant*, and *Duende*

"I devoured *Sparks* in one sitting. I simply could not put it down—and you won't be able to either."

- Ian Lewis, author of *The Ballad of Billy Bean*

"Ancient mysticism, Nazi atrocities, and unspeakable evils in our time set the stage for this dark and disturbing tale. Readers will find themselves cheering on a pair of unlikely heroes racing to discover the truth about Wolfgang Law's Great Home for Good Girls and Boys."

- Heidi Marie Ayarbe, award-winning author of *Freeze Frame* and *Compulsion*

"*Sparks* is an ingenious blend of adventure, mysticism, and teenage self-discovery. This is a unique orphan's tale, boasting a vibrant cast of misfits and some truly nasty villains. The story zips along with clever twists, culminating in a dazzling display of sci-fi pyrotechnics. David Michael Slater will enthrall readers with this witty, exuberant tale."

- Natalie Pinter, author of *The Fragile Keepers*

"Wildly imaginative, often poignant, and on occasion, delightfully profane, *Sparks* is a thrill ride that leaves the reader breathless at the end."

- Steven Mayfield, award-winning author of *Treasure of the Blue Whale* and *Howling at the Moon*

SPARKS

David Michael Slater

Fitzroy Books

Published by Fitzroy Books
An imprint of
Regal House Publishing, LLC
Raleigh, NC 27587
All rights reserved

https://fitzroybooks.com

Printed in the United States of America

ISBN -13 (paperback): 9781646031733
ISBN -13 (epub): 9781646031740
Library of Congress Control Number: 2020951629

Interior and cover design by Lafayette & Greene
Cover images © by C. B. Royal

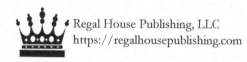

Regal House Publishing, LLC
https://regalhousepublishing.com

Printed in the United States of America

For Jay Lender

— DMS

For Annika, the light of my life.

— F. Becker

I don't know what to do and I'm always in the dark
We're living in a powder keg and giving off sparks

— Bonnie Tyler

2008

SPARKS, NEVADA

PROLOGUE

CHINA, THE UNBAGGER

Someone left the back door open, so I can see the metal monsters that live behind Headquarters with my very own eyes for the very first time. They're all sleeping now. Rusty cars and trucks and motorcycles and refrigerators and signs and piles and piles and piles of old machine parts. I know what some of them are because Charlie tells me everything. Charlie's a Suck, but a special one. She's allowed to learn all about the Shit Show to help us pass its tests. I'm the only one that listens to her lessons, so the other Sucks say she's my mom. I pretend it bothers me so they'll keep doing it.

I have to wipe my hands on my trousers because the Wolf says if any of us steps ONE FOOT into the yard, the junk monsters will wake up and give us the OLD TANGO UNIFORM. Which means kill us dead. But I know the Sucks go in there at night to see who's brave enough to stay the longest. The record is fifty-two seconds. I can't show how brave I am, though, because I'm not allowed to step so much as one foot outside Headquarters. Under any circumstances. Period. LAW OF THE LAND.

But I am eight years old, and I am brave, and I want the Sucks to stop teasing me.

My feet climb out of my clogs all by themselves, and one bare foot steps through the door like it has its own brain.

Fifty-three seconds is its plan.

Snap!

My foot steps back into the kitchen, but it's too late. A little bit of pee comes out all by itself.

'Cause it's the Wolf.

I turn around and see him staring at me with his black, black eyes that are dark caves, where wolves want to rip me to ribbons with sharp white teeth. The scars that reach up onto his cheeks from under his wild beard slither around like snakes because he's angry, and his yellow rubber glove thumbs hook under his suspenders, stretching and stretching them away from his scratchy white shirt. *Snap!* He lets them go and they snap back against his bulgy chest. The Wolf's as big as a bear and almost as hairy.

I hate the Wolf's eyes and the Wolf's gloves and the Wolf's scars, but his hat—the real head of a real dead wolf—is the worst. It sits on his head like it died there, with its fur hanging down his cheeks like two hairy arms. I hate it the most 'cause I feel like its yellow eyes follow me even when the Wolf's black ones don't.

The Wolf drops a Bag from his back, and I start breathing so fast like I am running. Which I am not allowed to do. I can never run. Ever. Never. Ever. But I'm breathing and breathing and breathing and everything is going fuzzy.

"AT EASE, CHINA, YOU LITTLE OXYGEN THIEF," the Wolf yells. "YOU KNOW IT'S NOT FOR YOU."

He calls me China because I break easily—I have a problem with my bones—but my real name is Felix.

"HEY, SUCK!" he shouts, looking down the hall where a boy a little bit older than me was trying to hurry by. "LINE UP FOR MANDATORY FUN!"

The boy does as he's told, but he walks like his clogs are on backwards. He's looking down at his shirt and trousers because he thinks they're dirty and that's why he's in trouble. It's easy to get a Headquarters shirt dirty because they are white, but the trousers are brown, like the girls' dresses. The girls make all of our clothes out of wool. I never get my Headquarters uniform dirty. I slip my clogs back on.

"CHINA HERE BROKE THE LAW OF THE LAND," the Wolf says when the boy comes close. "WHAT HAPPENS AT HEADQUARTERS WHEN SOMEONE BREAKS THE LAW OF THE LAND?"

The boy looks like he drank spoiled milk. I see blobs of sweat dripping from his nose. Right when he barfs up the word *Bagged*, the Wolf's yellow hand whips out his Hotshot and jabs him in the chest with it.

ZAP!

The boy's eyes roll back in his head. Then he falls to the floor, his whole body shaking and shaking and shaking.

The Wolf hates electricity and won't let it in Headquarters—except in his Hotshot, because he says it's a good teacher. It's a mean teacher. But the Sucks listen to it.

"BAG," says the Wolf.

Snot and boogers are coming out of the boy's nose. And even though he's still shaking, he climbs inside.

"ZAP ZIP," the Wolf says, and I know he's talking to me.

My hands are wet, so it's hard to work the zipper right. But I do it. I see one of the boy's eyes through the little space I leave open so air can get in. The eye hates me so much. It hates me twelve times forever.

When I'm done, the Wolf yells, "IT WOULD BEHOOVE YOU TO REMEMBER, CHINA, THAT WHEN SUCKS VIOLATE THE LAW OF THE LAND, SUCKS GET BAGGED. AND WHEN CHINA VIOLATES THE LAW OF THE LAND, SUCKS GET BAGGED."

Spoiled milk is in my stomach too, so I can't say I do behoove.

"DOES THIS MEAN YOU'RE SPECIAL?"

Spoiled milk says I can only shake my head no.

"NONE OF YOU IS SPECIAL! FREAKS AND SUCKS—YOU'RE ALL TEN POUNDS OF SHIT STUFFED INTO FIVE-POUND BAGS. DO YOU COPY?"

I nod my head to say I copy.

"BAG!" the Wolf shouts, "DO YOU SEE THE LIGHT?"

The shaky lump inside the Bag is allowed to answer the Wolf. The only thing a Bagged Suck is allowed to do is answer the Wolf.

"Yes, sir!" the shaky lump shouts. He has to shout extra loud through the Bag leather.

"AND WHAT DO YOU SEE IN THE LIGHT?"

"Discipline!"

"TAKE NOTE, CHINA," the Wolf tells me. He pushes my helmet up so he can see my eyes better. "HOW THE HELL ARE YOU GOING TO SURVIVE THE SHIT SHOW IF YOU CAN'T SEE THE LIGHT?"

I don't have to say I don't know because the Wolf is already going away, shaking his head. I want to unBag the boy, but I can't do that until tomorrow morning. No one is allowed to get out of a Bag until they are unBagged. Sucks can get reBagged for doing that. Bagged and Dragged even, right to the Brig. The Wolf doesn't want to bother with the unBagging, so he gave the job to me. Because I never get Bagged. I never get Bagged because at Bed Check the Wolf goes around kicking Bags to make sure they are still full. If I got Bagged, he'd never remember which one I was in. And if he kicked my Bag, he'd have to call Doc, and if I wasn't dead, I still wouldn't be able to unBag probably for a long time, and then he'd have to do it himself.

So I'm the unBagger. China, the UnBagger. Even though my name is Felix and I hate my job so, so much. I hate it twelve times forever.

I stare at the Bag Eye because it's staring at me. I can't look away and so I have to cry. I'm crying because I never got anyone Bagged before. My hands decide to unBag the boy, so my clog slides toward the Bag. But then it slides back because the boy won't want to come out before he's allowed to. But then it slides forward again, because it's still my fault he's in there. And now I'm breathing again. Breathing and breathing and breathing and the Bag is starting to spin.

But then something good happens. Charlie is here for Kitchen Patrol, wearing her apron and bonnet over her Headquarters dress. She is so pretty. So, so, so pretty. She squats down and looks me right in my crybaby eyes and says, "It's okay, Felix."

But now she's spinning and spinning and I'm going to faint—which I'm not allowed to do.

Then Charlie breaks a Law of the Land.

She touches me.

With both hands.

She holds my shoulders but so, so gently. Her face stops spinning. It goes soft and sad and her brown eyes are so big I want to zip myself inside them and never come out.

Then she does worse! Charlie picks me up and lets me wrap my arms and legs around her middle. I can breathe better now, but I'm crying harder because I'm going to get her Bagged too! Charlie! Who is unBaggable. Because she is pretty and perfect and she has Discipline. She's the oldest in the house because she's almost eighteen, which means she'll be Discharged soon. Tomorrow! Her birthday is tomorrow and she will leave me here alone, and now I am crying the hardest. I will miss her the most because she is the only one at Headquarters who doesn't hate me.

Charlie takes me out of the kitchen. There's a full Bag on the floor out here too. She doesn't kick it like other Sucks sometimes do because she would never do that.

"Shhhh," Charlie says, turning into another hall to escape the Bag. I am playing with her long ponytail. Which is my favorite thing to do in the whole world. It makes me breathe even better. But I can't stop crying. I will cry forever. Twelve times forever.

"Shhhh," Charlie says again. There's no Bag in this hall, but there's something just as bad. A Tango Uniform machine. The Sucks say it came from a fun house, which can't be true because I know a fun house is a place full of fun games for children to play. This game says EXECUTION on top in blue letters on green glass. There are always pennies in the coin return slot to make it go. I made this one work once, but never ever again. Inside the machine is the front of a tiny castle with tall wooden doors guarded by a tiny soldier. When I put a penny in, the doors creaked open. And then I could see a tiny man in a chair with a bag on his head and a rope around his neck. I heard a click, and all of a sudden the floor under him opened, and he fell through, dead. I've never put a penny in the other Tango Uniform machines. I won't even go in their halls. But I've heard Sucks say they all have tiny men getting The Old Tango

Uniform. Some get their heads chopped off. One has a man in an electric chair that shakes and shakes and shakes.

Charlie stops at a door—but it's a Bag Room door! Bag Rooms all have a Bag hanging from a nail on their doors. The hanging Bag means AUTHORIZED PERSONNEL ONLY, KEEP THE HELL OUT. Which means OFF LIMITS.

But Charlie opens it anyway! My heart is booming like drums.

What is Charlie doing?

She takes us inside!

Then she shuts the door behind us!

I squeeze my eyes shut. But they open themselves because they want to see what's inside even if I don't. The room is full of dusty old radios and TVs piled up on wooden tables and on the smelly mattresses of broken bunk beds. But then I notice a big glass bubble on a red shiny base. The bubble is full of candy! I want some even if it's old. The only candy I've ever had is the taffy we make once a year. But Charlie carries me through the room fast, toward a tall clock that's also a tower next to the bunk beds. She opens the front of the clock.

There's a door inside! And behind the door are skinny stairs that go up into shadows!

"Shhh," Charlie whispers, carrying me into the clock and up the Clock Steps. Her breath is warm on my neck. "There are lots of secret stairs at Headquarters," she tells me. "And besides the Wolf, I'm the only one who knows about them." I wonder how she knows. But I know she knows because she is special. I am very scared and very excited, all at the same time. But I am still crying like a Bug Company Suck, which means a brand new dumb-dumb who doesn't know SHIT FROM SHINOLA.

At the top of the stairs is another door. And behind it is the inside of another Clock Tower, and through that is another Bag Room. This one is full of toys! Old toys, but beautiful toys. They are rusty and beat up, but I love them so much. There are cars and trucks I could hold in my hand, but also big ones a boy like me could sit on and pedal. Metal fire trucks, police cars, and trains fill up plastic tubs on the table. Another tub is full of a million plastic dolls. Why can't we play with these toys? Why can't we even know they are here? I reach out to grab a fire truck, but Charlie says, "We can't, Felix. But it's okay. I have something even better for you." She carries me out of the room and into another hallway, while I look over her shoulder at the fire truck.

Charlie shuts the Bag Room door behind us, and I see that we are on the third floor—my floor. Then she takes me into her room! I've never been in anyone's else's room before, and I don't understand what's happening or why we are breaking so many Laws of the Land. What if I get Charlie Bagged and Dragged? That would be the worst thing ever to happen in twelve million years. I would never ever forgive myself. Ever never ever. Charlie is my friend! I'm the only one who knows her real name is Charlotte.

Her room is just like mine. She has a bed and an oil lamp hanging from a nail in the wall, just like I do. Charlie carries me into her closet, whispering, "Shhhh. Shhhh. You poor baby. Shhhh." She closes the door and puts me down. I think maybe we are hiding and will have to hide forever because of all our violations. That would be scary because what would we eat? But also good because Charlie would be with me.

Charlie reaches up to a board on the ceiling and pushes on it. It moves! She pushes it more until a ladder made of rope falls down into the closet.

I want to ask why all these strange things are happening, but I can't. I'm still crying. I will cry until my eyes make a flood, and maybe we can swim away from Headquarters together. I don't know how to swim, so Charlie will have to teach me.

"Shhhh," Charlie whispers. She climbs the ladder and disappears into dark. Before I cry out, her face looks down at me from above. "Come up slow!" she tells me. I'm scared, and even though I'm not allowed to climb, I do what she asks because she's Charlie. One step at a time. Slowly. Slowly. Up and up, while my heart beats like drums again. When she can reach me, Charlie gently takes my arm and helps me through the hole.

We're in a giant attic. A whole extra floor! Only, it has no halls. It must be the biggest room in the entire world! I didn't know this was here, and I don't think anyone else knows either, or the Law of the Land would be Authorized Personnel Only! Keep the Hell Out! The walls reach up to high, high ceilings under a curved roof. I wonder if bats live up there in the cobwebs. The floorboards are piled high with boxes, stacks and stacks of them. And the boxes are filled with books! I know about books because everyone at Headquarters has a Bible and Charlie has other books she uses for teaching. But I have never seen this many books before—and magazines too!—spilling out of the boxes.

I want to rush to the stacks and start reading everything, but Charlie says, "Come here, Felix." She takes my hand and leads me over to a stack of boxes that make a mountain, with book stairs that lead all the way up to a diamond-shaped window under the roof. She helps me climb up to the top, where it's flat like a shelf and we both sit down.

And then Charlie shows me something even more amazing than Bag Rooms and Clock Steps and a secret attic full of books. A spyglass, like the one from Charlie's stories about Captain Hook. It's the most beautiful thing in the world that isn't her. It's silver and shiny and has swirly whirly decorations all around it.

Charlie puts the big end of the spyglass into a circle of string that's hanging in front of the diamond window, then she presses it to the glass and says, "Put your eye to the little end like this." She puts her eye there to show me how.

It's my turn, so I put my crybaby eye to the little end and look through.

First, I see the junk from behind Headquarters, reaching like scary arms around both sides of the house, past the front porch and the dead grass field, all the way to the hedge wall that protects us from the Shit Show. Sometimes I like to look through the hole in the hedge at the busy road when the front door is open, but now I can see *over* the entire wall and across the road and right up a path made of big stones on the other side of it.

I take a big breath when I finally see what Charlie wants me to see.

At the end of the stone pathway, on top of a hill, is a fairy-tale castle right from her stories. A real one!

Now I've seen an even more most beautiful thing than I have ever seen.

"One day," Charlie whispers into my ear, "I'm going to live there. One day soon."

My eye moves away from the spyglass and looks at her even bigger than my big breath.

And then she says something even better!

"And you can live with me. I'll be your real mom if you want me to be."

And then—*poof!* Just like magic, my tears are all gone.

Which is only fair because at THE END of Charlie's best stories the bad guys get banished forever.

TEN YEARS LATER

2018

PART I

HEADQUARTERS

1

ASSES & ELBOWS

"ASSES AND ELBOWS, SUCKS! *FIELD DAY!*"

My eyes snap open at the sound of the Wolf issuing this order in his Big Voice as he stomps up and down the halls, banging on doors. It's still deliciously dark, so I savor the remnants of night for a few moments more. I love to sleep. It's the only thing in the world I'm good at. I sleep blissfully, except when I have the Charlie Dream, so I'm happy to be woken this morning, even by the Wolf. And I'm happier still when I remember I only have to wake up here at Headquarters three more times. Three. More. Times. Then, like Charlie before me, I'll be Discharged. Lately, I've been having the Charlie Dream a lot. Maybe when I'm finally out of here, it'll leave me alone.

"*ASSES! AND! ELBOWS!*"

It's early Saturday morning, so the Wolf, like clockwork, is on the warpath. Saturday morning is always Field Day, which means Cleaning Day in his stupid military lingo. Which I can't keep from getting stuck in my head. Every Saturday he wakes the Sucks up at ZERO DARK THIRTY to get Headquarters squared away for Sunday—Sucker Day. I can already hear three floors full of Sucks scrambling out of their beds to start their frantic tidying up. They'll be running around for the next few hours, shoving piles of their handmade toys—jacks and knucklebones, checkerboards and cornhusk dolls, dominoes and cup-and-ball catchers, a billion wooden blocks—under beds and into closets. Meanwhile, the Wolf will be out front from dawn to dusk, hosting his weekly junk sale.

I, and the other three Freaks, are exempt from cleaning up on Field Days, which is only fair since Sucker Days don't apply to us. The truth is the Wolf doesn't want us Freaks distracting the Sucks from trying to make this pigpen look at least slightly less condemnable. We do Kitchen Patrol after meals to pay for the privilege of sleeping in once a week. At least we don't have to prepare meals—though that's only because Sucks refuse to eat "Freak Food."

I unzip the Bag I slept in and peer up and down the empty hallway. I've become accustomed to sleeping on the warped Headquarters floors over the years. The kid I Bagged Out last night was about twelve—I stopped trying to remember their names years ago. I could sense his shock and suspicion when I unzipped him in the dark and offered to take his place for the night. He hesitated at first. No doubt he thought I was there to take revenge for the way he's treated me these past two months. But when he realized I was serious he took me up on the offer. The kids I Bag Out never turn me down. They just stand up, stretch, and slink off back to their rooms. Not one has ever thanked me.

One consequence of doing these unappreciated favors is that no one kicks Bags anymore, for fear I might be in one of them. The Sucks don't worry about hurting me, of course, they just worry that I'll stop swapping them out at night. But I don't care one bit about whether the Sucks are grateful or not. My Bagging Out routine is just a way to make up for the fact that the Wolf never Bags me, and a way to prove to myself that I, too, can take it—the stifling darkness, the muscle spasms, the cramps, the claustrophobia. I don't feel any of it anymore, so I feel like I'm doing my part to make this place just a little bit less awful.

The house shakes with pounding Suck feet as they run here and there, trying to get all their cleaning done before the Wolf pops in for an Inspection. As I make my rounds quickly through the crazy, crisscrossing halls, unBagging Sucks as I go, I'm half expecting this to be the day the decrepit old house collapses on our heads. But that will probably happen Tuesday morning, just as I'm about to be Discharged. I'll have one clog out the front door when the whole thing comes down and smashes me to powder.

Fifteen minutes later, I'm back on the third floor. There are lots of Bags today, squirming with restless Sucks. Clearly, the Wolf is on a rampage about something. But I put him out of my thoughts. I have my own Saturday business to attend to.

First, I make sure no nosy little Suck snuck into my room while I was unBagging. The younger ones sometimes spy on the Freaks for entertainment. When I see the coast is clear, I head into the closet, shut the door firmly behind me, then reach up to move the beam and loosen the rope ladder. Once I've clambered up into the attic, I pull the ladder up behind me and replace the beam.

Ah, the glorious smell of old books and new raccoon crap!

I step carefully across the floor, which is now rotted away in places, and weave my way through boxes full of valuable first-edition novels and hundred-year-old textbooks. Piles of magazines teeter in unwieldy stacks, covering every possible topic known to man, from motorcycle mechanics, to botany, to astronomy, to how to brew the best beer. These books and magazines, published from the fifties and sixties all the way through the late nineties, have taught me pretty much everything I know about the world.

I owe the magazines even more than that because I've torn probably a thousand pictures out of them, which now line every inch of the attic walls, right up to the eaves—pictures of lush forests and crystal-blue lakes, snowy mountains and raging rivers, island paradises and sunrises and sunsets and... you name it. Although they're not what I spend most of my time looking at when I'm up here.

I climb the stepped box tower to the spyglass and settle into the nest of blankets I've made for myself up here. I push aside the mess of books I'm currently re-reading—*The Wizard of Oz*, *Treasure Island*, *Frankenstein*, *Grimm's Fairy Tales*, *The Time Machine*, and a math book called *Ray's Practical Arithmetic*, which is ancient but awesome—and exhale deeply. It's such a relief to be here, away from the Wolf's glare and the Sucks' scorn, to have a moment of peace.

I must also say that every time I climb up Charlie's ladder,

I feel like I'm giving the Wolf the Left-Handed Salute. He'd go Section 8 if he knew what was up here. If there's one thing that drives the Wolf mad—besides anything electric, not including his Hotshot cattle prod, of course—it's not knowing what's going on. Of course, he *never* knows what's going on. The problems come when he knows he doesn't know. But like I said, I'm not thinking about the Wolf this morning. Trying not to, anyway.

Now that I'm comfortable, I take my helmet off and grab a hunk of wool from the wooden crate I keep up here. I stretch it thin and work it onto the leader thread I left ready on the drop spindle. After having done this so long, I can spin with my eyes closed. It's my job to provide the girls with rolls of thread so they can make our clothes, sheets, blankets, and towels. It's the only chore I'm allowed to do because it's safe and I can work alone. I'm incredibly efficient—I do far more than I have to. A lot more. Which is why I get away with making the extra blankets I'm relaxing on right now. Also, if there's an emergency and I can't get my allotment done, I have a backup supply. Not that I've ever had an emergency.

Other than my life, that is.

Anyway, the point is I can spin thread without thinking about it, so I can peer through Charlie's spyglass while I work.

And there it is, bathed in the golden light of a gorgeous sunrise—Charlie's fairy-tale castle, an enormous brick and stone mansion complete with towers and turrets, balconies and french doors, all surrounded by expansive landscaped gardens dotted with fountains. I could stare at the estate for hours—which is pretty much how I spend my Saturdays, and much of my Sundays, while I spin like the miller's daughter in *Rumpelstiltskin*. Sometimes I'll come up to the attic during the week, too, whenever the Wolf leaves Headquarters. On those days, I have to keep a close watch for his return, which makes mansion-watching and reading a little tense. But weekends are stress-free, especially Saturday, because I can see the Wolf below on the front lawn, running his junk sale all day. Saturday is also the best day to watch the mansion because the grounds are always full of activity—gardeners, groundskeepers, and window-washers swarm the place. Delivery trucks come and go; landscapers haul in giant trees with roots packed in burlap sacks; butlers open and close the main doors to admit all sorts of visitors. I'm constantly trying to get a peek inside the house, but I can never make out much. The mansion is a bustling center of industrious activity. Headquarters, of course, is the exact opposite, a crumbling dump where nothing new ever happens.

The day after Charlie showed me the attic all those years ago, she was Discharged, just as I will be in a few days. I didn't even get a chance to say goodbye. The Wolf told me she'd refused her Promotion, which are internships he arranges for Sucks when they leave. She wouldn't say where she was going and told him he'd never hear from her again. "SHE'S IN THE SHIT SHOW NOW, CHINA!" the Wolf shouted at me when I broke down in tears at the news. "DONE AND GONE! OVER AND OUT!"

I shut myself in my room for days after Charlie left, and I came out only when the Wolf told me I could move into her room—Charlie's final request, apparently.

I slept in Charlie's room for five years before I was big enough (and brave enough) at thirteen to climb into the attic. I could just reach the loose board if I stood on tiptoe then. All through those five years, I thought constantly of returning to the attic—I itched to read those books and gaze through that wondrous spyglass—but that would've required climbing on a stool to reach the secret board. A stool in my room would be NonRegulation, and what if the Wolf came in during a Surprise Inspection and saw one in my closet? I couldn't risk him discovering the attic, so I bided my time until I didn't need anything to stand on but my own two feet. That first time I climbed back into the attic, I was terrified. My heart kicked at my chest, my hands were slick with sweat, my legs trembled beneath my pads. But once I got up there and saw the books and magazines, the spyglass, and that magical mansion, my fears faded fast. I felt joy.

I must admit that I started watching the mansion because I'd deluded myself into thinking Charlie had made enough money by then to buy it. I watched and watched and watched, waiting for her to signal—perhaps a lamp flashing Morse code in a window or a red flag waved discreetly from the rooftop—that she was coming to get me. To adopt me. To be my mom. I eventually gave up on that fantasy, but I never stopped watching the house, admiring it, and wondering about the people who live there.

At some point I decided that when I was Discharged, I would find Charlie—just so I could tell her I made it out too. And to thank her for the gift of the attic and the spyglass, which have kept me sane in this lunatic asylum.

I don't blame her for never coming back.

After all these years of watching the mansion, I've learned only a few things about the people who live there—they're rich, they want their grounds to be gorgeous, and they love electric cars. Their garage houses at least four vehicles, all in mint condition. When the garage doors open, I can see the chauffeur unplug black cables that connect the car batteries to the wall. Even the old cars, with rounded hubcaps and soft leather roofs, cars that look a hundred years old, are all charged that same way. Who knew they had electric cars so long ago? I knew. Because there's a book about the history of electric cars in the attic. It's sort of funny that whoever lives there is probably an expert in electricity, while we all live here with a Hotshot-wielding lunatic who thinks it's only good for fear conditioning, which is something I read about in an old issue of *Psychology Today*.

Sometimes I see sparks of light flickering in various windows of the house. At night, spotlights wander over the outside walls, like the whole place is on a stage, or like it's a prison, I guess. Of course, I'm the one who lives in a prison.

I have a ritual that I follow every time I look at the mansion through the spyglass—a routine no less strict than the Wolf's Saturday schedule. I start by gazing at the main entrance, with its medieval-looking wooden door. The mammoth thing is studded with brass bolts and set beneath an arch made of thirty-three stones. It's a door a giant might live behind. From there, my gaze travels upward to the three balconies that overhang the rose garden, one above the other. And then I cross over to the main terraces, sweeping the spyglass over to the right and up toward the four dormers with their triangular roofs. I count three brick chimneys and take in the stunning colors reflected by the ceramic roof tiles, colors that vary depending on the weather and the time of day. Sometimes, during the week, when I cannot escape to the attic, I lie in bed, seeing all these minute architectural details in my mind's eye.

There are twenty-five windows altogether, each divided into six sections by white slats. You might think I'd have plenty of chances to see something or someone inside, but the window drapes are always drawn.

I always save the round corner tower for last. It's by far my favorite thing about the place. It really does look like part of a fairy-tale castle, especially the way it reaches well above the rest of the house with its cone-shaped roof. A single round window nestles under the roofline, but its lacy white curtains prevent me from seeing inside. Sometimes I imagine that Charlie is trapped in that tower, a damsel in distress, pining for a prince to rescue her. I imagine that I'm the prince, of course.

Pathetic, I know. Extremely, pathetically pathetic.

I settle in for a long watch of the window anyway while my hands spin furiously all on their own. But then, for the first time in the five years I've spent watching it, a light comes on in the tower room. Jolted, I drop the spindle.

A silhouette is revealed, a female one. And then, to my utter amazement, the silhouette throws the curtains open.

I press my eye into the spyglass hard enough to hurt. The word "Charlie!" involuntarily escapes my lips.

But it's not Charlie.

It's a girl with braided auburn hair wrapped around her head like a crown. I can't tell how old she is. My age? Younger maybe.

Her pale, oval face is beautiful. Her nose turns up just a bit, and she has a small cleft in her chin. But it's her eyes that grip me. They are big and blue and burning with an intensity that sends a stab of fear through me. I'm so mesmerized by those eyes that I'm jolted again when something covers them—binoculars! The girl sweeps them around, and then, before I can summon the sense to hide—she aims them right at me.

2

THE WATCHING MAN

I collapse onto my back, breathing hard, afraid she saw me, afraid that she'll tell the Wolf and I'll lose my attic. But why should I care about that three days before I turn eighteen and get the hell out of here forever? But what if she reports me for being a pervert and the Wolf won't let me leave—ever? Can he do that? Or, worse, what if I get arrested? The Wolf might consider this Treason and Bag everyone. I've had a few nightmares about him tromping after me in the dark, his Hotshot snapping, the wolf-skin hat alive, flashing its yellow eyes and thrashing its tail—while I stumble and fall over Bagged bodies that fill the hallways.

But that girl.

Charlie is the only other girl I've ever thought of as pretty. But that was so long ago, and I don't know if the Charlie of my dreams really looks like that or if she's just a patchwork of all the girls I've seen in the magazines up here. She's twenty-seven now, after all. The girls at Headquarters are just kids, and they seem to get younger every year that I get older.

Carefully, I sit up, raising my face to the spyglass again. I tell myself not to do this. Even as I'm doing it.

She's gone.

I'm incredibly relieved. And incredibly disappointed.

Did I imagine her? Did I fall asleep on my blankets and dream the whole thing?

The lace curtains are closed and the light behind them is off. I've finally lost my marbles sitting up here for so long fantasizing about something like this happening. Maybe I've conjured up a vision because I'm afraid to be Discharged. No matter how much I want out of here, the truth is I'm petrified to slide even one clog out into the Shit Show. The Wolf tells me all the time I won't last a day out there. *Not. One. Day.* He's probably right.

I still don't know what kind of internship my Promotion will be. I'm nervous about it. I'm sure it'll be boring and tedious. I don't really care, as long as it isn't spinning yarn. Or maybe I should refuse whatever it is, like Charlie did. Maybe she figured anything the Wolf arranged for her couldn't be good.

I keep my eye glued to the tower window for an hour, waiting to see if the girl might appear again. Or to make sure she doesn't. Or both. I'm shaking so hard that I worry about falling off the stack of boxes. I put my helmet back on, just in case.

The only sign of life at the mansion is the hustling landscapers, who mow and prune and trim like they have no idea anything wonderful and terrible has just happened. Eventually I decide that's because it didn't. I've probably read too many books about knights and ladies and castles. My brain's gone as soft as Don Quixote's. But just as I laugh at myself for being so dumb, the front door of the mansion bursts open, and the girl flies through it, pausing only to slam it shut before she's off, running full-tilt down the stone driveway. She's wearing a striped dress, purple tights, and spotless white sneakers. Her braid has come loose, and it's whipping out behind her like a dragon's tongue. By the time she reaches the main road, my palms are sweaty and my heart has stopped in my chest. She waits for a break in the traffic, then jogs across the street. Maybe she's going to catch a bus on this side of the road. Maybe she's running away! But no. She jogs past the bus shelter, onto our dirt road, and then I see her strolling through the hedge arch and up toward Headquarters, fixing her braid-crown as she goes.

A painful pounding is building behind my eyes with every step she takes in my direction. I look frantically around the attic, as if I'll find instructions on what to do next in a book or magazine. I look out the window again. This time without the spyglass because I don't need it.

The yard sale! I completely forgot about it.

People are milling around, browsing through the junk arranged on card tables and tarps spread on the ground. I see the

Wolf out there, flapping his hairy gums. He stops yakking when he sees the girl.

Maybe she saw the yard sale through her binoculars and came over to look through the junk? The Wolf sometimes brags about having "priceless heirlooms," although everything he sells looks like worthless crap to me. But what do I know about antiques?

But why *today* of all days? Why right *now*?

Because of me. Obviously.

The girl gives Headquarters a once-over on her way to one of the Wolf's tables. She's here to tell him he has a Peeping Tom. Why else would she have come over right after catching me staring at her?

I'm starting to hyperventilate.

But if that's the case, why not just send the police? And now that I think of it, she doesn't look mad. As far as I can tell. She looks serious, though. Deadly serious. Why would she browse a sale table if she came to accuse a deviant?

Breathe.

Oh no.

The Wolf is heading her way. He's like a moose stalking a mouse. The girl sees him now. His weird gloves. The hideous hat he wears, even though it's July and we live in Nevada. The girl is tiny, maybe five and a half feet tall. The Wolf could step on her without even noticing. I reposition my spyglass and focus it down in the yard, so I can see her up close. I notice a smattering of freckles across the bridge of her nose and the thick dark lashes that frame her unsettling blue eyes. I have to pivot the spyglass quickly to keep up with her as she strides right up to the Wolf. He says something, then takes her outstretched hand in one yellow rubber glove. He shakes it, and shakes it, and shakes it. I'm afraid he's never going to let it go, but the girl's gleaming smile never falters. Her teeth are so white, whiter than her shoes.

Doc checks our teeth twice a year, and the Wolf goes Section 8 if he detects Improper Hygiene of any sort at Headquarters— I've seen him Hotshot Sucks for not brushing their teeth long enough. No one here has teeth like hers though. When the Wolf finally releases her hand, the girl speaks again. Whatever she's saying, she's saying it without any signs of disgust or fear. She's not intimidated.

Now it seems that the girl is the one asking questions, because the Wolf appears to be listening closely.

I'm done for.

Breathe, Felix. Breathe. If she were mentioning the attic, the Wolf would already be bashing his way up here.

Breathe!

She's walking away from him now. I calm down. A little.

The Wolf, with narrowed eyes, watches the girl browse. She moves past tables full of rusty tools, then goes over to examine the pair of old gas pumps that mark the entryway into the field of junk.

A sudden movement under the hedge arch catches my eye, so I swing the spyglass in that direction. A lanky bald man with a pockmarked face is lurking behind a branch, clearly wanting to be hidden from the crowd in the yard. His expression is so dark that I have to stare at it awhile to decide whether he's wearing a mask. He's not, though black sunglasses cover his eyes. He's dressed in a black jacket, with four large zipper pockets, and black pants, which are full of zippers too. The intensity of his gaze sends shivers down my spine. What's he so interested in? But I already know.

He's watching her too.

The girl has left the pumps now and is heading back toward the hedge. I jerk the spyglass back there to see what Watching Man will do.

But he's gone.

The girl passes through the arch, crosses the street, walks up her hill, and then disappears through the front door of the mansion. A moment later Watching Man follows in her footsteps. I'm expecting him to kick in the door when he reaches it, but to my astonishment, he lets himself in with a key!

Is he her father? But how could a man so sinister be related to such a beautiful person?

I struggle to make sense of what I've seen. I can hardly believe that, after so many years of seeing neither hide nor hair of anyone who lives in the mansion, I've just seen *two*, only minutes apart. Now I'm worried not just for me but for the girl too. That man cannot be up to anything good.

All I can do is watch the windows of the mansion. And the tower.

But nothing happens.

I watch for an hour. Then another. And another.

I'm the Watching Man now.

I watch and watch and watch until my eyes just can't watch anymore.

3

THE COWARDLY MURDERER

I've spent the last hour lying flat on my back with blood pounding in my ears. I'm expecting the Wolf to burst up into the attic like a baboon gone berserk. He's going to stuff me into a Bag that doesn't unzip, then toss me out the window like trash.

The attic is still and quiet.

I'm a wreck anyway.

I go back to watching the mansion, but there's nothing to see. Even the gardeners have disappeared. The only movement is the sun as it slowly tracks across the sky, gleaming and glinting on the ceramic-tiled roof.

I take up my spindle again and start spinning.

I'm stupid to imagine that a few coincidences mean something significant is happening in my life—but I keep glancing up at the mansion, just to make sure it isn't, while wishing it is.

Pounding feet below announce the lunch-hour rush, but I'm too rattled to even think about eating. So it's back to watching and spinning.

The mailman arrives at the mansion right on schedule, shoves a stack of letters through the fancy mail slot, and goes whistling on his way. A flock of birds land on the roof. They fly away. They come back. They fly away again.

I try to read *Tom Sawyer*, but the words are a meaningless jumble.

Sighing, I settle in for a nap in a patch of afternoon light, but for the first time I can recall, I can't fall asleep when I want to.

So I watch some more. And spin some more. I watch and spin and watch and spin.

Pounding feet announce the dinner hour, and I realize I'm starving. My fellow Freaks will not be happy if I leave them to clean up two meals in a row. I feel bad about not pulling my weight, but I can't tear myself away from the mansion. They'll just have to deal with it. I'm being cautious because *if* anything happens, I'll see it coming and have time to…do something.

Yeah, right.

I'm watching for the girl, I know, trying to will the lace curtains in the tower window to part again. I watch and I will, and I watch and I will, trying to cast a spell like Merlin.

But I'm Merlin with no magic.

My concentration on the curtain is interrupted by the Wolf bellowing, "OH-TEN-HUNDRED HOURS, SUCKS! RACK-OUT TIME!" from the third-floor halls, which means it's time for Headquarters to go dark.

It suddenly occurs to me that I've been awake for most of the day. I normally get in at least twelve hours of sleep, sometimes a lot more. I'm exhausted, so after one last useless look at the mansion through the spyglass, I climb down from my box tower and move the beam, just enough to peek down into the dimness of my closet. You can't be too careful in a house where the word *privacy* has no meaning. The closet is empty, so I let the rope ladder unfurl. Once I'm down, I toss it back up and replace the beam.

In bed, I roll over to face the wall, with the blanket pulled over my head. Then I wait, working to slow my breathing to mimic a deep and restful sleep. The Wolf rarely skips Bed Check, and no one wants to show up back in their room after Curfew to find him waiting with a Bag. Sometimes he'll hide behind the door in a Suck's empty room, and the moment they come in late, he'll Hotshot them. The Sucks call that getting Hotshocked.

So I lie quietly and wait.

Soon enough, my door opens. My eyes are closed, but I know it's him—the Wolf has a particular smell, made up of many different things: rubber, dirt, oil, sweat, leather. Mostly hostility. But I smell something new tonight—caustic fumes, which I know must be alcohol.

The Wolf is a lot of things, but he's never been a drinker. "DRUGGIES AND WINOS LACK DISCIPLINE," he always

says, and "HOW CAN YOU SEE THE LIGHT IF YOUR
BRAIN IS FRIED?" I try to remain still as he approaches my
bed and lifts my blanket just enough to confirm I'm under it.
After dropping it, he stands by my bed for an impossibly
long time, breathing out toxic exhalations. Finally, he mutters to
himself, "You weren't going to make it anyway, China! To hell
with the both of you. Time to pop smoke!"

And then he leaves.

What was that? What does he mean, I wouldn't make it anyway?

Did my Promotion fall through? And who is the *both* of us?

I lie in bed, gazing up at the ceiling, trying to figure out what
the Wolf was talking about. I can hear the thud of his footsteps
as he moves about the hall, along with the occasional growl and
ZAP! of his Hotshot when he finds a Suck out of bed.

At last, all is quiet. I stew about all the unexplainable things
that happened today until I'm finally about to fall asleep.

But then I bolt upright.

Mila!

I almost forgot her! I've *never* forgotten her! Not once!

I scramble out of bed and pad over to my door to peek into
the dark and silent hall. Then I go out into it.

I know the ins and outs of Headquarters like a turtle knows
its shell, so I keep to the center of the halls to avoid tripping
over Bags along the walls, which appear as black lumps, darker
than the darkness.

I also know precisely where to step to avoid creaking boards,
and I make my quiet way to the nearest Bag Room, this one full
of old tools, and through the doorway inside its grandfather
clock. A moment later I'm making my way down the Clock
Steps behind it.

It took me years to map out all the hidden corridors at
Headquarters. The musty, narrow halls run between the walls
of rooms that look otherwise directly connected. I wouldn't
be surprised if they make up a full quarter of the house, along
with the skinny, musty stairwells that connect them crookedly
between the floors. The ones I'm descending now take me to

the first-floor Bag Room where broken sporting equipment is kept, which is only two doors away from Mila's room. If she'd let me take care of this during the day, I wouldn't have to creep around, but she insists it has to be after Rack Out.

I crack open the Bag Room door. The coast is clear, so I walk swiftly to Mila's room, step inside, then turn to lock it behind me. The four Freaks, me included, are the only ones at Headquarters who have locks on our doors, locks that can only be used until lunch time on Sucker Days, when the coast is clear of Suckers—the adults who come once in a while to adopt a Suck. The Freaks, the Wolf tells us, don't make a good impression, which is why we need to be neither seen nor heard on those mornings. ZAP ZIP if any of us is out and about on Sucker Days, or if the Wolf finds our doors locked any other time.

In the yellow light of the kerosene lamp—Mila left it burning for me—I find her lying on her belly on the bed with her face turned to the wall. Her creaky old wheelchair sits, as always, against the bed frame by her head.

"In the black of night," I whisper, tiptoeing to her bedside, "the assassin slithers into the CEO's penthouse bedroom. He's not leaving without the blueprints to her company's top-secret project: the perpetual motion machine." Beneath Mila's bed, I retrieve the old ice box and remove the syringe inside. The green medicine gleams in the light of the lamp. I depress the syringe a little until a drop glistens at the end of the needle.

"His choice of murder weapon?" Mila whispers.

"Poison, of course! The weapon of cowards."

I can't help it. I grin like an idiot every time we do this. But I can't laugh or the whole thing is ruined and Mila gets upset. She's lying quietly now with her T-shirt pulled up to reveal her lower back. Her broad shoulders are covered by her long hair.

Mila is always the boss in our scenarios. She's either a queen, a president, a mob kingpin, or a general, but I'm always the cowardly murderer who has come to do her in.

Mila has a catheter tube inserted into her spine and held in place with medical tape. Doc, who does check-ups on Freaks and Sucks alike, changes it every few weeks. She needs daily injections, and the Wolf, when Mila asked, allowed me to be the one to administer them—although I'm supposed to do it before Rack Out. The Wolf cannot be around when Doc gives injections. His face goes pale and he staggers out of the room. I think he hates needles more than he hates electricity. As far as Doc knows, the Wolf gives Mila her shots, and he's threatened to pulverize me a thousand times if I ever tell Doc otherwise.

Why Mila wanted *me* to give her these injections, I don't know. Maybe since she's fourteen and the youngest Freak, and I'm the oldest, she looks up to me. I guess all the Freaks look up to me because I know so many things they don't, and they don't understand how. Especially since I never leave Headquarters. I guess they think I'm just special somehow. Which is kind of sad. Like the Wolf says, NO ONE IS SPECIAL.

"By the time the CEO knows what's happening," I whisper, "it's too late. But she'll go out laughing at the thought of what will happen when the thief opens her safe." I insert the syringe into the tube, then squeeze the plunger.

"What will happen?" Mila can't help asking. She can never help asking.

"Deadly gas will send him straight to hell."

"Ugh. Gurgle. Die," Mila says. "And yay."

I set the empty syringe on top of the ice box, shove both back under Mila's bed, then head for the door. But before I leave, I take Mila's lamp off its nail and turn down the wick until the flame is extinguished. The room is plunged into darkness. I set the lamp on the floor and reach for the doorknob.

"Felix?" Mila says, startling me. She always stays in character until I'm gone. My palms start to sweat, and my chest tightens. One last disturbing thing to cap off a very disturbing day.

"What?" I whisper, fearfully. "Is something wrong? Did I mess—?"

"Are you really leaving us?"

"Yeah," I tell her.

"Who's going to give me my shots?"

Motionless at the door, I am furious with myself. How could I not have thought about that? "I can ask Klaus," I offer apologetically.

"He'll inject me with skin cream."

"Don't worry," I promise. "He'll do it right—I'll make sure of it. He'll even assassinate you every night."

"He can't do that part," Mila says. "But that's okay. You may be a cowardly murderer, but you're also the best storyteller I know. I hope you write a book about us someday."

"Count on it," I say, ashamed that I haven't thought once about how my leaving would affect anyone but me.

I try to leave again, but Mila says, "Felix?"

"Yeah?"

"Can I ask you something else?"

"Sure."

"You can't tell anyone I asked you, though."

"Okay."

"Promise."

"I promise."

"I was thinking…maybe when you're out there…I mean, you're so smart. I was wondering if you could maybe look into…if you had the time—?"

"What, Mila? Look into what?"

"Who my parents are."

For a moment, I cannot find any words. Her request is so unexpected, and I don't know what to tell her. If there's one Law of the Land created by the inmates at Headquarters, it's no one ever talks about who their parents might be. No one even talks about not talking about it. The rule is unwritten but set in stone. I'm doubly flummoxed, though, because I can't even remember the last time I pondered who my parents might be. I do know why this rule was established, though—because no one wants to learn why they were abandoned. It's much better to focus on finding new parents who actually want children.

"It's okay," Mila whispers. "Never mind. I just thought—"

"I'll do it," I tell her.

"You will? Are you—?"

"Sure. I'll probably be working in a library or something like that anyway."

"Thanks, Felix. Just—"

"I won't tell a soul," I say.

"Thank you so much."

And then, finally, she lets me go.

A fall down a flight of stairs when Mila was three—before she was left at Headquarters in the middle of the night—left her paralyzed from the waist down. She suffers from circulation issues in her legs, and the green medicine helps keep the blood flowing so they don't have to be amputated.

I move stealthily through the halls, worrying about Mila. How will I persuade Klaus to take over her shots? He's not much for doing, well, anything. Distracted by this new question, I walk right into a full Bag on the third floor and almost tumble head over heels. A grunt escapes the Suck inside.

After recovering from the heart attack my near-fall caused, I'm relieved. A little Bag time always helps me figure things out.

I unzip the Bag.

While it's too dark for us to see each other well, I recognize the boy inside by the silhouette of his long, corkscrewy hair. I don't know his name, of course. He knows me, though. Not only because I'm me, but because I've unBagged him at least three times since he arrived last month. Frequent Bagging upon arrival is typical of Bug Company Sucks. It always takes new recruits time to learn the ropes, and the Wolf isn't big on orientation. He just gives new Sucks the one rule that rules them all: VIOLATE THE LAWS OF THE LAND AND ITS ZAP ZIP TIME. That and don't break the China. So Sucks mostly learn the Laws of the Land the hard way, via Hotshot. Last week I saw Corkscrew cut in line at dinner. He didn't see the Wolf standing right there. ZAP! His tray went flying, and he crumpled to the ground. ZIP! Bagged on the spot. I Bagged him out after Rack Out, and that was the first and only time I've slept in the Mess.

Corkscrew stands without saying a word, then turns and

races down the hall, as if my taking his place is simply the natural order of things.

I climb into the empty Bag and zip it shut over my head. It takes only a few seconds to get comfortable. Closing my eyes, I breathe deeply, relishing the rich, sharp smell of leather. I let out a long sigh as my muscles finally relax. Inside the darkness of the Bag I am floating in a warm sea, at peace in an ever-expanding universe. I am without limits, unconstrained. I am not in a Bag. I am not at Headquarters. I am nowhere. I am everywhere.

I am free.

But just when I expect to fall asleep, I find my mind returning to the bizarre events of the day and to the girl with the hypnotic blue eyes.

I figure I'll be awake all night with the gears turning in my brain: the girl, the Watching Man, the Wolf, the Freaks, the Sucks—they're all moving round and round in some inexplicable pattern destined for a horrible end, just like those doomed figures in the Wolf's sickening coin-ops, the ones I used to call Tango Uniform machines.

But fortunately, my world-class sleeping skills finally take over and, comforted by the warm, familiar confines of the Bag, I'm out.

4.

THESE TYPES OF BONDING EXPERIENCES

Darkness. I reach out for the reassuring feel of leather. But my hands touch nothing. I open my eyes and see metal all around me. I'm standing in a tunnel, round, like a tube. To my left, I see light shining on piles of rusted junk in Headquarters' backyard.

Two figures come out of the light, racing toward me. Metal monsters with grasping mechanical claws are close at their heels. When the two approach, I can see one is the girl with the auburn braid crown...and the other is Charlie! They come to a halt when they reach me and gasp in horror at something over my shoulder. I turn to see the tunnel shrinking rapidly, and just then the slick metal surface beneath our feet begins to rise up.

We fall to our hands and knees as the tunnel tilts further, and I see a giant black hole of an eye staring at us, blinking once, twice. It's the Wolf's eye. We are in the spyglass. The three of us try to scrabble up the tunnel toward the Wolf's blinking eye, but we're slipping and sliding toward the metal monsters instead. They wait below with hooks and blades slashing the air. The tunnel has tilted too far now, and so we fall to our fates: we will be sliced to pieces, flesh and bone.

I wake from my nightmare in a sweaty clench, trembling and shaking. Morning light filters in through the space around the zipper. I've slept in longer than normal, I realize, and today is Sunday. Sucker Day. After Morning Mess, I'm supposed to be confined to quarters until lunch. Which works out nicely for me. With my door locked, and with the Law of the Land on Sunday mornings requiring Freaks not to make a peep—even if the house is on fire—the chances of the Wolf finding me in the attic are zilch.

I climb out of the Bag to find an empty hallway. Nobody else is up yet. If I hustle, I can finish unBagging, get a quick shower, and be back in my room before Freak lockdown.

I move up and down the halls, unBagging as I go. When the Bags are all empty, I return to my room to grab my towel—which has the texture of sandpaper—and a bar of Headquarters-made soap—which smells like rancid oil.

Once safely inside the third-floor bathroom, it takes me a few minutes to get my gear off: my helmet, followed by my shoulder, chest, elbow, knee, and shinpads. I drop them all in a heap and duck into the shower. The water is freezing cold, as always. The Wolf insists that ice-cold showers build DISCIPLINE WITH A CAPITAL D. And Discipline, in turn, builds character. The Sucks are always complaining about the water, but it doesn't bother me.

As I am working my hair into a soapy lather, I hear a pounding on the bathroom door. Fortunately, the bathroom doors, like the Freaks' rooms, have locks. I finish scrubbing down, rinse off, then towel myself dry. All the while, the pounder keeps pounding.

"Whoever's in there," he growls through the door, "you're Bagged!"

"Bagged and Dragged!" someone else shouts, which sends a shiver down my spine. Bagged and Dragged is bad, really bad. If the Wolf hears a Bag talking or sees one moving, even twitching, or if a kid unBags himself without permission—which is the ultimate crime of Failure to Find Discipline—they're not only reBagged but also Dragged through the halls and up and down stairs to the Brig. Nobody knows exactly where the Brig is because victims go in and come out while Bagged. Even I don't know.

Anyway, there's a rule among Sucks that the older kids get first showers. At nearly eighteen, I'm the oldest kid in the house, but this rule apparently doesn't apply to Freaks.

I get into my clothes and reassemble my pads. In my haste, my feet slide on a puddle—my heart seizes and I realize this is how I'll die, in pieces on the bathroom floor. But I catch myself on the towel railing and manage to avert disaster.

"Open up!" the door-pounder shouts, "or you'll be wearing the Old Tango Uniform when you come out of there!"

I open the door to find Corkscrew on the other side, his fist raised mid-pound. He freezes in surprise when he sees me. When our eyes meet, I can see he's processing the fact that I Bagged him out him last night. Again.

"We're first, Freak," he says, finally recovering his cocky composure. "What are you even doing out of your cage on Sucker Day?"

"Sorry, forgot it was Sunday," I mutter, moving past him into the hallway.

"You gonna apologize, Freak?" Corkscrew's sidekick shouts at my back.

I keep walking as the boys bolt after me, inserting themselves between me and the door to my room.

"I *said*," Sidekick says—he's maybe ten, with drooping ratty hair and a crooked nose—"ain't you gonna 'pologize."

"I did," I say quietly. "I said, 'Sorry, I forgot it was Sunday.'"

This seems to stump Sidekick, who looks to Corkscrew for guidance.

I guess he gets it because he, shrimp that he is, cocks his fist and throws it toward my sternum, stopping just short of my chest protector. Pads or no pads, I flinch. Hard. Which excites him. So now he's bouncing on his toes, shadowboxing me.

"Put 'em up, Fragile Freak," he says.

I'm flinching and sweating and gasping for breath until I'm hyperventilating and getting dizzy fast. To avoid fainting and falling, I sink to the floor as the boys dance around, pretending to kick me to smithereens. They laugh and shout and have the time of their lives while I curl up into a ball and tuck my face between my knees.

I try to breathe slowly through my nose, the way Doc taught me, and count my breaths.

"Look at these losers," another voice says.

I glance out between my fingers at two other boys

approaching. One I recognize by his inward-turning right eye, a condition known as *strabismus*, which I read about in an old edition of *Journal of American Medicine*. His friend is a tall dark-skinned kid whose square head is topped with a thatch of thick black hair.

I know what's coming, so I slowly edge away from the group on my behind.

"What's your problem, Blockhead?" Corkscrew says. "Or should I say *Blackhead?*"

"Say that again," Blockhead demands.

"What, Blackhead?" Corkscrew taunts.

Blockhead throws a punch, and before I know it all four boys are pummeling one another. I get to my feet, ease into my room, and lock the door. Now I can breathe again. I'm usually not much bothered by these types of bonding experiences with my orphan brothers and sisters, though I must admit I was the first time. Which was the day after my one and only attempt to leave Headquarters got that poor kid Bagged in the kitchen on the day Charlie got Discharged. He wanted revenge for that, so he started the Suck tradition of pretending to beat the holy hell out of me—which was the best he could do, considering the Wolf bans all Sucks from so much as touching me. But I guess it's satisfying enough for smaller kids to watch me, at six feet tall and 175 pounds (or so Doc tells me), cringe and quiver like a baby. Ever since then, it's become a Suck badge of honor to pretend to kick my ass.

Through the door, I can hear the Sucks fight until, suddenly, ZAP! ZAP! ZAP! ZAP! puts an end to it and four bodies hit the floor. Justice is served, I guess.

I polish off a bag of tasteless cereal I swiped from the Mess by stashing it in my chest pads. I keep the bag hidden under my mattress, so the cereal is crushed to bits, but it's better than nothing.

After eating, I pull my blanket over my head and fall asleep. Just like that. But what seems like just a moment later, I'm startled awake by the Wolf banging on doors and shouting, "MUSTER TIME, SUCKS! FALL IN FOR MANDATORY

FUN! TEN MINUTES! IF YOU'RE ON TIME, YOU'RE LATE! IF YOU'RE LATE? BAG CITY!"

Finally, I can safely snooze.

But then the Wolf adds, ominously, "FREAKS TOO!"

5.

MUSTER

There's a stampede outside my door as the third-floor Sucks sprint downstairs. I'm still sleepy and confused. Freaks are never called to Muster on Sucker Day. But I heard right, and I realize Elsa will get Bagged if I don't do something. Fast.

I open my door, expecting to find four Bags full of yesterday's brawling boys, but strangely, the hallway is empty. I don't have time to contemplate the meaning of this, so I move through the maze of Headquarters hallways as quickly as I dare. Avoiding collisions is always my top priority, but I'm anxious about Elsa. Fortunately, her room is not far from the Muster Room, where the Wolf will take attendance.

Clock Steps get me quickly to the first floor, and I find Elsa shuffling down the corridor in her long pioneer dress and clogs. She has a frantic look in her lively eyes. Elsa's eyes are, unfortunately, the only lively thing about her. She moves at the pace of a sloth with her ropy black hair covering much of her face. Her meds suck the life out of her, but Elsa maintains that living in slow motion is better than suffering from a rare form of hyperactivity disorder that prevents her from having a single coherent thought. If left untreated, she could become a vegetable. She's fifteen.

Elsa stops shuffling when I rush up to her.

"Hey…Felix," she says—she talks about as rapidly as she moves. "Where you been…slowpoke?" She's making an effort to sound cool and casual, but the expression in her eyes shows how terrified she is of getting Bagged.

"If you're planning to sweep me…off my…feet," Elsa says, "I'll definitely break…your heart. Get it? Break your…heart?"

She laughs, a slow chortle, before asking, "Where's Mila? Standing up to…the Wolf? Get it? Standing…up?"

"This is no time for joking, Elsa!" I tell her. "We need to get you to Muster." Usually, Elsa sits on Mila's lap in the wheelchair and I push them both. "Damn!" I shout. I should have picked Mila up first. I'm losing my mind!

"Bag and Drag?" Elsa suggests. "Cut out…the…middle man?"

"Yeah, right," I say, frantically running through options in my mind.

"Roller…skates?"

"Come on, Elsa," I sigh. But her joke gives me an idea. "Hold on!" I tell her, then hurry down the hall to the Bag Room with sporting equipment. Behind me, I hear Elsa gasp when I duck inside. I'm shocked by my recklessness too. I've never entered a Bag Room in front of anyone else. I use them only at night, and only after I've made sure and double-sure nobody else is around.

All I know is that Elsa is not getting Bagged this morning.

"TWO MINUTES!" the Wolf roars from one hall over. "DOUBLE TIME, DIRTBALLS!"

Inside the Bag Room, I find mitts and hockey sticks, uniforms and trophies, pennants and whistles, all piled up on a ping-pong table. Broken exercise equipment is scattered here and there. I even spot an old canoe. In the corner I see a coin-op machine I've never noticed before. It's not an execution scene, which surprises me. Instead, it has a miniature baseball field inside, although the players are missing. The front glass panel is gone too, and the guts of the machine are spilled out onto an open front panel.

What am I doing?

I wheel around to look again for what I came for. On a bookshelf standing in the back of the room, I find it—an old wooden skateboard. I return to Elsa with it under my arm.

"But… Felix?" she says, staring at the skateboard with simultaneous delight and distress. I know she's asking, *How the hell are we going to do this without me grabbing and holding on to you?*

"Damn!" I cry. "Hold on!" I'm already rushing the skate-board back to the Bag Room.

"Hurry!" Elsa calls.

"ONE MINUTE!"

I see a better option the moment I'm back in the Bag Room. I grab the handle of a large red wagon and wheel it back out to Elsa, who slowly, agonizingly slowly, lowers herself to a seated position inside.

But at least we're moving now. Elsa's riding fine, and my plan is working!

"THIRTY SECONDS!" the Wolf brays, his voice louder as we approach the Muster Room. I'm going as quickly as I can, but I don't want to run into him in the hallway. Showing up with a wagon stolen from a Bag Room on time would be far worse than showing up late on foot. Or even not showing up at all. Fortunately, the Muster Room is only three turns away, and the Wolf is nowhere in sight.

We find Klaus and Mila waiting for us in front of the room, both looking very concerned. Klaus is, as always, rubbing mint-scented cream on his pink skin. He's standing with one leg wound around the other because he does bizarre things when he's nervous. But he relaxes at the sight of us, as does Mila. They smile and sigh with relief, but only until they register the presence of the wagon. Then their eyes goggle. Elsa gets to her feet, and I shove the wagon down a neighboring hall with my foot. I'll stash it back in the Bag Room after Muster.

"WHERE THE HELL ARE THE FREEE—!" the Wolf screams from inside the Muster Room. The door flies open and he sees us standing here. "Oh," he says. "Get the hell inside already."

While this feels like a real victory, I'm uneasy as we follow him into the room. Something is very wrong, although I don't know what exactly. The Wolf has a Bag over his shoulder, its strap crossing his white wool shirt and suspenders. A strange scarf has been added to his attire this morning, an old-timey red tie like the kind I've seen in magazines from the seventies. He doesn't appear drunk, which is a relief. In fact, he seems rather sober. More than sober. He looks excited. Did he comb his hair?

Whatever the case, the timing of our arrival is too enticing for the twenty or so Sucks who stand in obedient formation. "Freaks! Freaks! Freaks!" they chant as we find our places against the wall just inside the door. "Freeeeee—!"

"SHUT YOUR PIE HOLES, SUCKS!" the Wolf commands.

They shut their pie holes.

"BLACK, BLUE, PURPLE, OR RED, WHAT ARE EVERY LAST ONE OF YOU?"

"Ten pounds of shit in five-pound bags!" shout the Sucks.

"YOU'RE GODDAMN RIGHT! WHAT'S TODAY?"

"Sucker Day!"

Next to me, Elsa sighs deeply. I see Corkscrew lined up with the other three who got Hotshotted for fighting outside my door. Why weren't they Bagged?

"WHAT DOES SUCKER DAY MEAN?" the Wolf shouts.

"Ship-shape!" the Sucks shout back.

"WHERE WILL YOU BE FIFTEEN SECONDS AFTER YOU'RE DISMISSED?"

"Rooms!"

"DOING WHAT?"

"Bibles!"

"HOW WILL YOU ADDRESS ANY SUCKER WHO SPEAKS TO YOU?"

"Sir or ma'am!"

"WHAT WILL HAPPEN IF YOU SAY ONE SINGLE NEGATIVE THING ABOUT LIVING HERE AT WOLFGANG LAW'S GREAT HOME FOR GOOD GIRLS AND BOYS?"

"You will show us the Light!"

"WRONG! ANYONE WHO STEPS OUT OF LINE TODAY WINS THE BIG CHICKEN DINNER!"

My mouth drops open and a gasp sounds from the Sucks. The Big Chicken Dinner is even worse than being Bagged and Dragged. It's the worst thing. It means a Dishonorable Discharge from Headquarters—which means getting booted out into the Shit Show unprepared. I don't understand why the Wolf would use his ultimate threat for Sucker Day. Sucks are highly motivated to perform well on these days. After all, they want new parents.

The Wolf isn't done.

"WHAT WILL YOU SAY IF THEY ASK ABOUT SCHOOLING?"

"Home school!"

"YOU! CORNFLAKE!" the Wolf roars, pointing at a Suck front and center. "LINE UP! *NOW!* MANDATORY FUN!"

A twiggy little girl of nine or so steps reluctantly forward, trembling violently. She looks confused, like she has no idea what's going on. Classic Bug Company Suck material. We all know what's coming. She hadn't been doing anything wrong in line, but I could see she didn't know the correct responses to the Wolf's questions. She's just green, but the Wolf doesn't care. He wants to make a point today.

What the hell is going on with him?

"IS MUSTER BORING YOU?" the Wolf barks. The little girl shakes her head and manages to mouth the word *no*. The Wolf whips out his Hotshot anyway and jabs her in the chest. ZAP! She's on the ground and spasming like she's having a seizure. The Wolf drops the Bag from his shoulder and rolls her inside with a clown-sized clog. Then, in a swift and smooth motion, he zips the Bag up, throws the strap over a rafter, and hoists it into air. Once the strap is latched, the Bag swings from the rafter, and while the Bagged little girl manages to control her crying, it's clear she can't control much else. A thin stream of urine leaks through the zipper and pools on the floor.

I desperately wish I could unBag her here and now. What the hell is going on? First, the Wolf Hotshots boys for fighting, but doesn't Bag them. And now he Bags a little Bug Company Suck on her first Muster? This was harsh, even for him. And from the wide eyes of all the Sucks staring at the swinging, leaking

Bag, I can tell they think so too. The temperature in the room drops as everyone realizes something unpredictable, something terrible, is happening.

"WHAT MIGHT HAPPEN TODAY, SUCKS?" the Wolf wants to know, "IF YOU DISPLAY EXEMPLARY DISCIPLINE?"

"Parents!" everyone shouts.

"BECAUSE WHAT DOES EVERY SUCKER WANT MORE THAN ANYTHING IN THE WORLD?"

"A really good Suck!"

"WHAT HAPPENS IF YOU DISPARAGE WOLFGANG LAW'S GREAT HOME FOR GOOD GIRLS AND BOYS IN ANY WAY SHAPE OR FORM AFTER YOU GET ADOPTED?"

"You bring us the Old Tango Uniform at Zero Dark Thirty!"

"THEN POP SMOKE, SHITBAGS!"

The Sucks make a mad rush for the door. Elsa, Mila, Klaus, and I attempt to follow the mob out, but the Wolf shouts, "FREEZE, FREAKS! YOU ARE NOT DISMISSED!"

When the room is clear, the Wolf says, "WHAT'S YOUR JOB THIS MORNING, FREAKS?"

I can't help watching the Bag swing out of the corner of my eye. The dripping has stopped. I want to go over and whisper that everything will be all right. Which is probably not true.

"To lock ourselves in our rooms until you give the All Clear," I answer before the Wolf decides to stuff us all into the Bag with the little girl.

"WRONG."

We Freaks exchange confused glances. Klaus starts bouncing on his toes as if he's warming up for a race—and frantically rubbing his cream into his arms. Locking ourselves in our rooms is *always* our job on Sucker Day, because the Wolf thinks the sight of us makes potential adoptive parents think about all the things that can go wrong with a kid. Which is probably true.

"TODAY YOU LEAVE YOUR DOORS UNLOCKED. AND OPEN."

We have no idea why he wants this, but none of us has the guts to say so.

"AND I'LL TELL YOU WHY," the Wolf says, saving us the trouble. He drops his usual roar into a half-whisper, like he's sharing a secret. "Got a call this morning from a very unusual Sucker," he explains. "A rich one. An incredibly filthy, stinking rich one. She's thinking about financing"—and he says this next part with a mocking air of fanciness—"*a refurbishment of the premises*. A MAJOR FUCKING REFURBISHMENT. She was very specific about wanting to meet every kid in the place before deciding whether to hand over the dough. Even the freaks. DO YOU COPY?"

None of us copy.

The Wolf draws in an annoyed breath and says, "The filthy rich Sucker is *moved* by the mission of Wolfgang Law's Great Home for Good Girls and Boys. She is especially *touched* by the compassion we have here for disadvantaged children. Sucks warm her heart. Freaks will probably melt it. DO YOU COPY NOW?"

"We copy," the four of us say.

"WHAT ARE YOU GOING TO TELL HER WHEN SHE ASKS YOU HOW YOU LIKE IT HERE?"

I can tell no one else is going to answer, so I do it for all of us: "That we are eternally grateful to you for giving us the chance to live normal lives in a world that has no love for unfortunate children like us."

The Wolf blinks at this for a moment. "Damn straight," he says when my words sink in. "NOW SHOVE OFF, SNOT SPOONS!"

6.

BULLSHIT BOMBS

We shove off.

Elsa lowers herself slowly, so slowly, onto Mila's lap, and I push them into the hallway. The wheelchair is an ancient wobbly contraption made of wood with two big wheels on the sides and a little one in the back. The fraying wicker seat doesn't look strong enough to hold double-weight, but it's all we have. Klaus, walking beside us, wipes so much cream on his neck and ears that it drips in steady blobs down the back of his neck. As far as I can tell, he's spent every moment of his seventeen years smearing cream onto himself. He has a skin condition so severe that, without the constant application of medicinal lotion, he'll turn red as a beet and feel like he's on fire. Klaus doesn't remember anything of his life before arriving at Headquarters, but the Wolf told him he'd been left in a basket on the doorstep, half-drowned in that minty goo. The cream works pretty well, but he'd still prefer that no one look at him. We try to play along. Even when we're talking to him.

"LIVE FIRE IN THIRTY-TWO MINUTES, FREAKS!" the Wolf bellows, following us out of the Muster Room. He's got the Bag over his shoulder with the little girl still in it. I'm afraid he's going to haul her off to the Brig—or worse. But instead he sets the bag down, unzips it, and tells the girl to "HAUL ASS." Which she does, like a mouse scurrying for a hole in the wall. The Wolf looks at the wet Bag with disdain and clogs off with it, muttering under his breath.

I've never seen him let someone out of a Bag so soon after Bagging. Never. Not once. *I'm* the UnBagger.

"Is it just me," I ask my fellow Freaks, "or is the Wolf losing it lately?"

"He smells…money," Elsa says.

"You're probably right," I say. Because she probably is. "I bet he's planning to trick this filthy rich Sucker into marrying him by making her read something in another language in some crusty old book that's a legally binding wedding vow. Then he's going to Bag and Bury her to inherit her dough."

"Oooh," Mila says. "That's your best one ever, Felix!"

"Bag and...*bury*?" Elsa says. "Wow."

"Definitely happening," is all Klaus has to say. He uses as few words as possible to communicate.

But I'm in no mood to appreciate the Freaks' appreciation. Who is this filthy rich Sucker? I wonder. Does she have anything to do with the rich girl from the mansion across the street? It can't be a coincidence that *two* rich people have gotten involved with Headquarters in less than twenty-four hours.

Can it?

"Speaking of...losing it," Elsa says. "Felix got that...wagon from a...Bag Room."

The others look at me, amazed, waiting for an explanation. I shrug. "Going out with a bang," I tell them.

"I...get it!" Elsa says. "You and the Wolf are...popping smoke together. He's...adopting you!"

Which brings me to a sudden halt. The Wolf's drunken Bed Check rambling comes to mind again. He said it was time to pop smoke, but I assumed he was talking about *me*. Maybe he *is* planning to ditch Headquarters? I start pushing again.

"But seriously, Felix," Mila says. "Two days. You ready for the Shit Show? Tell the world about us after we're all Bagged and Buried. Make a movie called *Adventures of the Headquarters Freaks*."

We've made it to Mila's room. For some reason, Klaus is still with us, still smearing himself silly. But none of us says anything else. Despite our earlier banter, there's a wretchedness in the air—worse than the normal version we usually live and breathe. Something really bad is happening, but nobody wants to talk about it anymore. Mila gets to her feet and shuffles, snail-like, into her room. Without a word, Elsa wheels herself off, leaving me and Klaus alone in the hall.

"Klaus," I say, looking at the floor, "I need you to take over Mila's shots."

No reply. He doesn't want to do it, I know. I look up at him, and he squirms sideways to avoid my gaze, rubbing cream into his legs in a distracted, robotic fashion.

"Who else is going to do it?" I ask him.

"Are you really leaving?" he asks.

"Yes, I'm leaving," I tell him. "And you will be too in a year. You only need to do the job until then." *Who's going to do it when Klaus is gone?*

"What's your Promotion?" he asks.

"Research librarian," I tell him, since that's what I guess I'm hoping for. "Or maybe accountant. Which is the safest job in the world."

"I want to be a mascot."

"A mascot? Like, for a sports team?"

No answer. Because the answer is obviously yes. I don't have the mental power to dig into this weirdness right now. "Not the easiest gig to get," he says.

Now I see what he's hinting at. He thinks I can pull some strings for him in the Shit Show. "If I help find you a mascot job when I'm out," I say, "will you do the shots?"

"I want something else," Klaus says.

"What?"

"You have to swear not to tell anyone."

"I swear," I say. Because I know what's coming.

"If you can find my parents—"

"Deal."

Klaus nods, clearly surprised I agreed so readily. I feel like we should shake on the deal, but I know the moment we do, the Wolf will appear out of thin air to Hotshot Klaus for touching me.

Klaus heads down the hallway, spreading cream inside his shirt through an open button as he goes. "Ha," he says without looking back. "Would've done it anyway."

I sigh. Something finally went right. I head for the stairs.

Through open doorways, I see kids wiping their faces with

dampened blankets, combing their hair with fingers, or practicing their reading positions on their beds. Some are furiously searching for their mislaid Bibles.

Before I reach the stairs, I hear insults being thrown back and forth around a corner, and since it sounds like the insulters are heading my way, I step into the Infirmary Closet. Which is full of peroxide bottles and pretty much nothing else. The Wolf is big on hydrogen peroxide. If you go to him with any kind of injury—scrape, cut, broken bone, or even a sore throat—he dumps it on you.

But there's more than peroxide in here today. There's also two Sucks with their tongues down each other's throats. Two girls, who look about fourteen. They don't bother stopping when they see me, either. Because this happens fairly often since I'm always hiding in closets to avoid people. I just stand in there like an idiot while they go at each other.

But then the door swings open and a yellow glove reaches in to grab a bottle of peroxide. It freezes when the Wolf sees what's going on.

"CHRIST ON A CRUTCH, CHINA!" he yells. "YOU SOME KIND OF PERVERT?"

"I—I—I," is all I can manage. Because I'm instantly hyperventilating.

"MAN YOUR STATIONS!" he yells at the three of us. "MOVE!"

We move.

Sweating through my shirt and breathing like a maniac, I hurry up the steps to the third floor. Leaving my door open, I stumble to my bed, dizzy with anxiety.

Of course, I can't sleep. If they come and accuse me of being a pervert, the Wolf will believe it now! Why did this happen today? It's like the world is plotting against me! I feel a rising nausea in the pit of my belly. Somehow this is all going to affect my Promotion, my way out, my only hope these past seven years. My thoughts are like cats trapped in a bag, spitting and hissing and scratching.

First, a rich girl and now a rich lady. Could it be her mother?

Maybe the Watching Man is her father. Maybe he told her mother about their daughter's little trip through the hedge, and the girl was in trouble for it. What if, then, the girl told them about the Peeping Tom in the tower? And now her mother is coming over to see if it's true!

I'm doomed.

But why would she bother pretending she was interested in helping the orphans? Maybe she just wants to find out what's going on before making a scene. Or…maybe she wants to get to me without the Wolf catching on—to blackmail me! But…I have literally nothing to give her. Except the spyglass, which maybe the girl also told her about. Maybe it's an incredibly valuable antique and the parents want to get their hands on it!

I can't sleep.

What the hell is going on?

My breath comes quick in my throat, and my heart pounds so hard that it's certain to crack my ribs. This strikes me as a real possibility, which makes me even more anxious.

Breathe, Felix. Breathe.

I hear footsteps and muffled voices in the hall, so I lie face down, turned toward the wall, counting my breaths.

"That one lacks Discipline—trust me," I hear the Wolf say as he passes my door. My eyelids feel heavy, and finally I drift into a shallow sleep, only to be awakened sometime later by a yelp of joy from a Suck. "Roger that!" the Wolf says. "Let's go put some red tape to the sword."

After that, finally, I drift into a deep, deep sleep.

In a Bag Room cluttered with the dusty remnants of broken toys, I lie on a table piled with dolls. I, too, am limp and lifeless. I become aware of the Wolf, accompanied by the rich lady—Charlie—who is looking over the merchandise. She gestures toward me and says, "This one looks fragile." The Wolf tells her I'm incredibly rare, the genuine article from pioneer times. Very expensive. "I don't like the way it's looking at me," she says, yanking on my arm to force me into a sitting position. "So needy." My arm—a cornhusk—comes apart. "You break it you bought it," *the Wolf says.* "Hardly," *Charlie replies, tossing my arm aside.* "Got anything sturdier?" *The Wolf says,* "How 'bout this beauty?" *He hands her a pristine-looking doll with an auburn braid crown and brilliant blue eyes.* "Perfect. I'll take this one," *Charlie says. The girl-doll smiles bright white teeth at me as she's carried away.*

A cry wakes me up, and it takes me a moment to realize the cry was my own. My heart is still racing, and a light sweat has left my clothes damp.

"He doesn't sound asleep," a lady says from the hallway outside my room.

"Nightmares, ma'am," the Wolf says. "Keeps everyone on the floor awake to all hours almost every night."

The word *ma'am* shakes me fully awake. I rarely hear the Wolf speaking to important people, but sometimes inspectors and reporters visit Headquarters. Once a journalist came to do a story about Wolfgang Law's Great Home for Good Girls and Boys. He was writing an exposé on group homes with "old-school values," and we all had to convince him how we thrived without electricity, and how self-sufficiency encouraged Discipline with a capital *D*—which, in turn, built character. These extra benefits, the Wolf told him, make his poor orphans contributing members of society when they grow up. The Wolf called him *sir* the whole time.

"As I said," the lady says, "I'd like to talk with *every* child in the house."

"All right, all right," the Wolf mutters. "If you say so, ma'am. Can't say no to a pretty piece of…thing like you." He slams my door all the way open and shouts, "GET UP, CHI—!" before catching himself. "I mean, *Felix,*" he says, trying for a polite, civilized tone. "There's a lady here who desires to conversate with you."

I roll over and sit up against the wall. The lady, standing in the doorway, has long black hair and wears large, tinted sunglasses. She's dressed in a business suit—a tightly fastened blue jacket with silver buttons and pants to match. High heels and red lipstick complete the outfit.

"Hello?" she says. "I'm sorry to bother you, Felix, but I'd like to ask you a few questions. Would that be all right?"

"AT ATTENTION," the Wolf shouts when I don't promptly respond. "NOW!"

"That's not necessary," the lady says, frowning.

"Lima Charlie," the Wolf tells her, backing down.

"What's that?"

"Loud and clear, ma'am."

"Sounds like army talk, Mr. Law. Were you in the military?"

"Damn straight," the Wolf says. "Purple Heart. Medal of Honor. Distinguished Service Cross. Took six bullets dragging half my platoon to safety after an ambush in South America. Where do you think these scars came from? Girl Scout camp? It was TARFU, in the extreme. But you don't want to hear about nasty stuff like that, I'm sure."

The Wolf has just dropped what he'd call a Bullshit Bomb. He only talks about his "service" when he's trying to impress or intimidate someone, and I've noticed that his glorious record becomes ever more glorious when he's talking to women. None of us believes he was ever in the military. But who knows? I overheard him tell a Suck who asked to see his medals that he sold them to open Headquarters, all so he could take care of snot-nosed little ingrates like him. He Hotshocked the kid twice and Bagged him on the spot.

"Did you injure your hands?" the lady asks him. "Is that why you wear the rubber gloves?"

"Fourth-degree burns, ma'am. You'd puke if you saw them."

That's a line I'd never heard him use before. I've seen his hands. They're hairy but normal.

"Well, thank you for your service, Mr. Law."

"Please, ma'am, call me Wolf," he replies with his gross gap-toothed grin. "It was my honor to serve this great country. Now, Felix," he adds, just slightly hostile now, "talk to this fine lady. She is interested in helping our fine institution."

"What's with all these pads you wear?" she asks me. "Do you play baseball? Are you a catcher? You must love the game to sleep in your gear!"

"I have *Osteogenesis imperfecta*," I tell her. "Brittle bone disease. You breathe on me too hard, I pretty much break."

"The kid's not even allowed to fart too hard," the Wolf says, shooting me a suspicious look. He's wondering how I learned the real name for my disease. I'm usually more careful about hiding what I've learned in the attic, but right now I can barely think straight. I'll tell him Doc told me if he demands to know later. "He wasn't supposed to live past ten," the Wolf continues, "but we know how to take care of Frea—special needs around here. Seen enough?"

"Definitely not," the lady replies, removing her glasses and turning to look directly at me.

My heart seizes. The lady is not a lady at all. She's the girl with the burning blue eyes.

7.

SOUP SANDWICHES

The girl's gaze pierces me. I feel like a butterfly on a board. How could someone so young have the guts to do what she's doing? What *is* she doing? She's wearing a wig, but the Wolf seems as fooled as I was.

The girl puts her glasses back on and says, "So you have to wear a helmet and pads all the time? Even in bed?"

"Yes…ma'am," I croak. "Pretty much 24-7."

"Have you ever gotten hurt here? Broken any bones?" Her eyes bore into mine with an intensity that almost hurts. Her expression says something different than her words. But I don't know what it means.

I don't think she's here to accuse me of anything, and that is a huge relief.

"No, ma'am," I say, trying to catch my breath. "Not since I was little. I guess I broke bones pretty much all the time back then, but I don't remember."

"Regular swab, this one used to be," the Wolf pipes in. "Before we got him broke in." He snorts like this is funny.

"Do you like living here?" the girl asks me, ignoring the Wolf. "This place seems incredibly dangerous for someone with your condition, what with all the crazy halls and uneven floors. And I'm sure, with all the children living here, there's a lot of roughhousing."

"Oh, the kids here are very well-behaved," I say, forgetting for a moment that she's not a rich grown-up. "And I've been here so long, I could get around with my eyes closed if I had to."

"I know there are a few other children here with…struggles. How do the other kids treat you—?"

In unison, the Wolf and I say, "Everyone gets along at Wolfgang Law's Great Home for Good Girls and Boys."

The Wolf and I exchange glances. I'm not sure if he's pleased or pissed.

"Do you not have chairs in your rooms?" the girl asks, apparently not interested in our double Bullshit Bomb. Her heels click loudly on the wooden floor as she approaches the bed and perches on the mattress beside me. "I'd like to talk to this young man privately," she tells the Wolf. "I want to hear more about his challenges."

I hold my breath, hoping the Wolf will leave her alone with me. But also hoping he won't.

"No can do, ma'am," the Wolf says, shaking his head. "State regs." He straightens his old-fashioned tie, as if calling attention to it makes what he's saying true. "Can't leave a kid alone with a stranger. But if we can reach some sort of financial agreement along the lines of what you suggested earlier, in terms of a home improvement fund, I'm sure we can arrange for all the visits you like. You'd be part of the family at said time, is what I'm thinking. Legally speaking."

The girl's eyes tell me she knows the Wolf is full of it. But instead of replying to him, she says, pointing into the closet, "I think we have company."

Her words send a stabbing shard of ice into my chest. The closet door, I see, is partway open.

"What?" the Wolf cries, flinging the closet door wide open.

The Wolf has never gone into my closet before—not that I know of anyway, and suddenly I'm certain I've left the beam askew and the ladder down. My heart pounds, and perspiration breaks out on my brow.

The Wolf drags a little girl of five or so out by the wrist. Furious, he reaches for the Hotshot at his hip, only to realize he's hidden it away for this fundraising opportunity. Seeing the appalled expression on his visitor's face, he awkwardly pats the little girl's head and forces a smile.

"Scram, Susie," the Wolf says, shooing her out of the room. "Spying is a Violation of—it's not nice!"

"I'm Franny," the little girl calls from the hallway.

She's going to get it later.

"Apologies, ma'am," the Wolf says. "We usually have better manners around here."

"Anyway," our visitor says, rising to her feet. "I'm afraid I don't quite have time to talk further with Felix at the moment anyway. I have an important business appointment in an hour, but I will return tomorrow to discuss a very large donation." I cringe inwardly—now she sounds as ridiculous and phony as the Wolf, but he's apparently buying it, hook, line, and sinker. "I will come tomorrow at ten o'clock," the girl adds, looking at me pointedly over the rim of her glasses.

"Roger that, ma'am. I would just like to say again how on target your timing is in regards to the home improvement situation. We are in desperate need at this time. Financials are a real soup sandwich. Can't even imagine what would happen to the Frea—to the special ones—if we go tits up."

The girl nods, still looking at me over her glasses. "It was very nice to meet you, Felix," she says.

"I'll show you out," the Wolf says, and after a quick glare in my direction, he strides out the door.

The girl, alone in the room with me now, makes quick circles with each of her hands and places them over her eyes. She peers at me through them.

Binoculars.

My hands make circles too, and I stack them together over one eye.

A spyglass.

We look at each other through our fingers for a few moments.

She's sure we recognize each other now, so she turns and leaves the room.

What just happened?

I lie down on my bed and turn onto my side. The faint scent of flowers lingers in the sheets—her perfume—so I pull the covers over me to trap the smell.

And just like that, I'm asleep.

In the junkyard behind Headquarters, a flash of red catches my eye. Passing a colossal heap of military medals, I see a girl with a braided auburn crown wearing a red hooded cape and swinging a basket full of money. She skips along, turns a corner, and makes for a little gingerbread house nestled in the forest of junk.

STOP! I call, but she doesn't seem to hear me. She disappears into the gingerbread house, and I rush to the door to yank on the handle. The door is locked, but through the window, I see the girl bent over a figure reclining in the bed. It's the Wolf, I realize, dressed up like a grandma, grinning and slobbering. I bang furiously on the window, and the Wolf's black eyes meet mine. He grabs the girl, pulls her into his sheets, which are, in fact, a large leather Bag. The girl's basket, which has fallen to the floor, spills money and the severed bald head of the Watching Man. The head is alive, and its glaring eyes watch the girl thrash inside the Wolf's Bag. I bang on the window, but nobody pays me any mind. The girl is quiet now, the Bag still. I can hear the growl of the Wolf, a low, satisfied sound, almost a purring. I can't stand to hear it, so I raise my hands to cover my ears.

Awake now, I find myself groping under my pillow, where something is purring or buzzing. I find a slim metal device with a screen, and I realize what it is.

A cell phone. I've seen pictures of these devices in several of the attic's newer technology magazines. This cell phone, however, is much, much fancier. It looks like a small computer. The screen, I see, is lit up, and a name appears at the top: Willy Adelstein. A small image of a clock at the top of the screen tells me it's two minutes past five. How strange it is to know exactly what time it is.

Clearly, the girl slipped the phone under my pillow when the Wolf ran into my closet. But why? And who the heck is Willy Adelstein?

I shove the phone back under the pillow and slide back down into my sheets. My heart is throbbing, so I try to take long slow breaths to calm myself. *One. Two. Three.*

What if the phone is some kind of integrity test? Maybe she left something valuable in every room to see if there's an honest kid in the house, a kid who would dutifully return the phone. Maybe that kid would get adopted by her parents and live happily ever after as her brother or sister.

Stupid, I know.

Maybe she left the phone under my pillow so she could accuse me of stealing it. That way she'd have her revenge for my peeping at her without having to explain why she was peeping at me. Maybe the phone is blackmail material, and she's going to use it as leverage to force me to hand over the priceless spyglass from pirate times!

Maybe I'm an idiot.

I roll over and retrieve the phone, tapping the screen to bring it to life.

A series of little boxes of text appear, all saying the same thing:

Hello?

Hello?

Hello?

My brain says, *Do. Not. Get. Involved. You'll wind up broken into a million pieces.*

Little dots appear on the screen, and then a new message appears:

I'm a Freak too, Felix!

I desperately want to put the phone down, but my hand won't obey my brain. Dots appear again, and then a longer message:

…I know you don't know me but I really really need your help. My name is Annika Adelstein. You're holding one of my father's old phones. I was in my tower searching for a miracle when I saw you. Is it possible you were searching for one too?

I guess I was. I guess I always have been. How long have I imagined rescuing her, the imaginary her, prisoner in the tower, from the clutches of some evil overlord?

But how could she possibly think I could help her after meeting me?

…My father owns your Headquarters. It gets special "allowances" paid for by my dad from the legislature to experiment with "traditional" ways of raising orphaned children. I was adopted from that place myself when I was a few months old. My parents died in a car crash

"What?" I exclaim. Annika went from this dungeon to that castle?

...Anyway, I need your help *please* I need you to find and take pictures of that sleazebag Wolf's financial records. There's some shady business going on over there I'm certain of it. Use the cell

No. Hell no. Absolutely not. Why should I care about this girl's problems? Her entire life is the miracle I've always hoped for!

...My father is Willy Adelstein. He owns a chain of pawnshops all over Nevada called Battle Born Pawn. He's a doctor and he's obsessed with collecting antiques especially electrotherapy devices those goofy machines that supposedly cured medical problems with electricity way back when

Electrotherapy devices? I suddenly recall seeing something about those in an old copy of *Harper's Magazine* from the fifties—there were pictures of large box-like contraptions with generators and cranks that customers could use to shock themselves out of Nervous Diseases.

I feel like I could use one now, because I'm starting to shake.

...My father's so obsessed with electricity that he moved from Reno to Sparks because of its name! He doesn't care about anything else, including me. Here's what else I know about him—he's old, even though he doesn't look it. His entire family was murdered in the Holocaust, all but his teenage mother, who escaped from Germany pregnant with him after being raped by a Nazi soldier. She died giving birth to him and he was raised in an orphanage where they tortured him every day for being Jewish. He told me he started that place to give kids like him a better shot in life. But as far as I can tell, he has no involvement with it. And if he cares about orphans, if he cares about anyone but himself, I'm Charles Dickens

I know Charles Dickens. I've read *Oliver Twist* six times. And I read about the Holocaust in *Time* magazine. The photos inside made me physically sick, and for the first and only time in my life I was grateful to live at Headquarters. But Annika lives in a mansion, not a concentration camp. Sure, it's strange that her dad loves electricity as much as the Wolf hates it, but so what? And maybe he had to adopt a child because he was too old to have one naturally—that was hardly a crime.

I don't feel like writing anything back.

I'm not writing back.

But for some reason, I find myself watching for the little dots again.

…My father says the world is full of vermin and I need to be protected from it until I'm an adult able to protect myself. But that's no excuse for treating me like a prisoner! It's 2018! I'm literally trapped here Felix. I'm "protected" every waking hour by my psycho "manny" Adolf (fine his real name is Axel). He does nothing all day but make sure I cooperate with my teachers and coaches who come here—and make sure I don't try to break into my father's sacred workshop or jump out a window. I can't stand it anymore. My teachers get fired if they discuss anything but their lessons with me but last year my history professor was telling me about the emancipation of the slaves. I told him I was a slave and he joked about the fact there's something called minor emancipation nowadays. Sixteen-year-olds can petition the court for it. I WILL BE SIXTEEN NEXT WEEK!

She's not even sixteen? A fifteen-year-old princess with the guts to fight dragons. But what dragons? A strict daddy? Too many private tutors? How dare she call herself a Freak! I'm tempted to suggest we trade lives.

But I don't.

Because I'm not writing back.

Because I'm not getting involved. Period.

…If I prove that I can provide for myself I can be declared an adult and leave here forever. But my father has lots of lawyers and will never let it happen unless I have something over him. I've spent the last year searching this house for anything I could use against him but I found nothing. I only thought of your orphanage the other day when my father threatened to send me BACK ACROSS THE ROAD for being a bitch to him. He used to threaten me with that all the time when I was little. It scared the hell out of me since I knew about his orphanage days. But that got me wondering so I did some research and found out a girl died at Headquarters in 2008 so I decided to investigate that. But it was too long ago and there just isn't much info out there about it

Wait. *2008?* Oh god.

What girl? I type, feeling nauseous.

…I think her name was Charlotte?

Now my finger won't move. It's made of stone. *I'm* made of

stone because I've looked right into Medusa's eyes. I stare at the words, which no longer look like English.

Dots appear while my mind attempts to shut itself down. Then a message.

...Just double-checked. Charlotte "Charlie" Law. She died of a heroin overdose. There was an investigation and the home almost got shut down. Did you know her? You would have been pretty young...

Charlie is dead? Dead all these years? From heroin? It's not true.

...When I saw you through my binoculars I knew right away I'd found an ally. So I snuck over. As soon as I met that Wolf guy I knew something wasn't right. That's why I need records! They're my ticket to freedom! Will you help?

I will not help. I dreamed of fighting dragons, but my fantasy has turned out to be even more brittle than my bones.

Charlie is dead! I was going to find her when I got out of here! We were going to live together! All at once, my life feels pointless. Like an empty bag.

I think about my promise to find Mila's and Klaus's parents, and I realize suddenly that the reason why I've never much thought about finding my own *isn't* because I preferred to focus on finding new parents. I've never expected to be adopted. It's because I've always had Charlie. I knew she was out there somewhere, waiting for me. A wave of longing and loneliness swamps me, and for the first time in my life, I want to know who my mother and father are.

Have I been asleep my entire life?

Without thinking, I type: *Is Axel/Adolf tall and bald with a face full of craters?*

...OMG HOW DO YOU KNOW THAT?!

...He followed you here. To the yard sale

...OMG. OMG. OMG. And he hasn't told my father yet because he's out of town searching for his "holy grail" in Europe somewhere. But my father's due back tomorrow! I have even less time now! You've GOT to help me!

I'm trying to care. But I don't care. All my life I've dreamed of helping a princess, but it never occurred to me that they

might be spoiled little girls who get tired of their privileges. She
has no idea how lucky her life is. At least she *has* a father!

I. Am. Not. Getting. Involved. Charlie is dead!

I toss the phone down and stare at the wall. Then I pick the
phone back up.

*…Wolf told me that kids who leave Headquarters get internships. I
could ask any of my teachers to help find you something. They're all top
of their fields*

She's trying to bribe me.

I'm sorry, I type. *I can't. I'll be leaving here forever in a matter of days*

*…I can give you money. My father keeps it all over the house in secret
stashes in case another Holocaust happens and he has to run for it. I've
been skimming from them for years so I can give you enough money to get
you started anywhere you want*

Anywhere. Nowhere. What's the difference to me now?
But…maybe money could help me find my parents. But, no…

If I get caught stealing, I type. *If the Wolf finds out. You have no idea
what he's like*

*…I can report that loser. Once I get the information I need I'll get the
whole place shut down. Literally everything he told me was an obvious lie*

I'm sorry

*… Shit. I really better go. Don't worry. I promise it'll be okay. I'll see
you tomorrow to get the phone. I wouldn't want you to get in trouble for
having it. Or for being in the attic if that's off-limits. I wouldn't want to
cause any delays in your getting out of there*

None of that will happen unless she makes it happen. She's
threatening me!

I swallow something sharp and sour. My future is at risk if I
help her, but now it seems at risk if I don't.

I'm sorry, I type one more time.

But there's no reply.

And I am sorry—sorry I tried to see the junkyard when I
was eight; sorry Charlie took me up to the attic and showed
me the spyglass; sorry I ever saw that stupid mansion; sorry
she made the Wolf give me her room. I'm sorry I've watched
that place all these years, and I'm even sorrier that I happened
to look at that tower when that girl was looking out. I'm sorry

I watched Rags-to-Riches Princess Annika Adelstein flounce from her fairy-tale castle over to the lowly Headquarters. Where she didn't have to spend her childhood. I'm sorry that little girl got into my closet. And I'm sorriest of all that I looked at this goddamn phone.

My heart is beating out of control. The room is blurring. I think my skull is going to implode.

I count twenty breaths, then get up and peek into the hall. The coast is clear, so I head quickly down to the second-floor Bag Room that's full of tools. I find the table-mounted vise and set the phone into its jaws, then slowly twist the handle until the phone is crushed to splinters. Better it than me. I scatter the pieces in various boxes around the room. The evidence is gone. The princess can rat me out about the attic if she wants, but the Wolf can't keep me here once I turn eighteen.

Emancipation.

Ten minutes later, I'm back in bed. There's nothing more to do.

Except the one thing I'm good at.

So I pull my sheets up over my head and do it.

8.

UP HIGH/DOWN LOW

The stack of boxes reaches clear up to the sky, and from the ground I can see all the way up to the top with my spyglass. The diamond-shaped box at the very top is a cardboard throne for a girl with a braided crown of auburn hair. A wild gust of wind loosens her braid, causing it to unfurl all the way to the ground.

I step backward when it lands at my feet, but the braid winds like a snake around my ankle, then yanks me into the air. It lifts me higher and higher, all the way up to the top of the tower, where I see that the girl is dead, a needle in her arm. Her face is nothing but a skull with a long, thick ponytail. Charlie's ponytail.

"Your parents despise you," she says. "I told you I'd come back for you. I'm the only one who loved you!" She snatches the spyglass out of my hand, adding, "But you don't deserve to be loved."

Her braid releases me, and I fall into the depths below.

I wake with a start in a full-body sweat. The morning light is filtering through my window, and my first thought is Annika is coming…and I will get to see her again! But my second thought is that I *never* want to see her again. The Wolf may have ruined my past, but Annika Adelstein is going to ruin my future, just because she can't wait two measly years to be on her own. I've done my time, why can't she do hers? I only have to wake up one more time at Headquarters. One. More. Time. If I don't blow it. Annika can't hurt me. She's told me too much. She's bluffing. She can find someone else to do her dirty work. Any Suck will do.

But I do want to see her face again. Her radioactive eyes.

Idiot!

How could I not have known about Charlie's death? How could I have spent years of my life waiting for a dead person to rescue me? Deep down, in my guts and bones, I know Charlie would never have taken drugs. But...what did I really know about her? I didn't know anything about anyone then. Just like I don't know anything about anyone now.

Oh, no. I forgot to Bag someone out last night! And I'm late for UnBagging!

I leap out of my bed—not smart—and rush into the quiet halls. The Sucks must be at breakfast, which means they'll all be storming upstairs soon. Luckily, there are no Bags in the hallway, which is strange—there are *always* Bags.

No Bags on the second floor either.

Very strange.

When Headquarters starts to shake from the pounding feet of Sucks returning to their rooms, I slip into a Bag Room and head down the Clock Steps to the first floor. Which is empty by the time I get there.

Not a Bag in sight.

Unprecedented.

The Wolf's mood seems to have swung from violent irritability to...what? *Benevolence?*

It must be Annika.

The Mess is quiet, too, by the time I get there. *Mess* is an appropriate name for the room, though Complete Disaster would be even better. The Sucks, as usual, left it that way. There are cracked plates piled on the tables, caked with food, and orange peels and eggshells are strewn across the floor, where powdered milk congeals in puddles. The Sucks are natural slobs, but they overdo it on purpose at Chow Time because they know we have to clean up after them. They literally throw food at the walls.

Klaus and Elsa are eating peacefully at a table in the middle of it all. I feel a profound relief to see something normal in what has been the craziest twenty-four hours of my life.

"Speak of the...devil," Elsa says when I approach the table. "We thought...you got your...Promotion...early. To the... Brig. Brigadier...general."

"No such luck," I tell her. "Sorry I missed a couple meals."

As usual, there's nothing to eat but what's been left on the plates. I find one with minimal ketchup smear and create a breakfast of half-smashed egg yolks and bread crusts slathered with peanut butter. Then I start stuffing my face.

"What's...wrong?" Elsa asks when I sit down beside her.

"Just hungry," I tell her.

"Oh...I see," she says, sarcastically. She's not very patient for someone everyone else has to wait for. "Let me ask you this... then. *What's...wrong?*"

"He's sad about leaving us," Klaus says, putting an apple slice into his mouth with one hand while spreading cream on his knee with the other. "Eating his sorrows," he adds.

I bite down on my lip to prevent it from trembling. I might be falling apart.

"What's...really...wrong, Felix?" Elsa demands.

"Nothing," I lie. "I've just been thinking about this whole Promotion thing. I don't mind telling you that I'm nervous about it."

"Felix..." Elsa says, amazed. "You can do...anything. You're...like...the smartest person in the...world."

"But I don't know what kind of job they'll give me. What if I'm no good at it?"

"My money's on...crash test...dummy."

What I'm really thinking about is confronting the Wolf about Charlie's death. And how I don't have the guts to do it.

"Where do you want to get placed?" I ask Elsa to get her off my back.

"Olympics," she replies. "Hundred yard...dash."

"Klaus wants to be a mascot," I say before she starts prying again. "How goofy is that?"

Elsa looks at me with a painfully slow turn of her head. "For the...smartest person in the...world," she says, "you're...a real...idiot, Felix. It's so...no one can see...his...skin."

"What do you think Mila would—?" I start to say. But then the real depths of my stupidity hits me. "Mila!" I cry, leaping to my feet.

"What?" Klaus and Elsa yelp.

But I'm already running for the door, full-on running, which

is difficult in these stupid clogs and all these pads. And dangerous.

I forgot Mila's shot last night!

I can't believe it! I've totally lost my mind!

I rush around corners and down halls, praying she's okay. If
she's forced to have her legs amputated because of me, I will
never, ever forgive myself. I will grab a baseball bat from the
Bag Room and smash my own legs to bits.

I take the last turn around the last corner, and then—I trip.
Or almost trip. I stumble, staggering forward, windmilling my
arms until I'm steady enough to stop on my feet.

I stand for a frightening moment, panting. Falling on the
floor for me is like falling off a six-story building for normal
people. Even a sudden stop can break a bone in my feet or
shins. I check that I'm still in one piece. The stress makes my
head throb.

I don't have time for this!

I walk quickly to Mila's room. Even before I get there, I can
hear her crying. My heart drops like a brick into my stomach. I
whip her door open and rush inside.

Mila lies face down on her bed, her body trembling as if
she were being electrocuted. Doc told me this would happen
if she ever missed a shot—random, out-of-control nerve firing
that hurts like hell. "I'm so sorry, Mila!" I sob. "I'm so, so, so
sorry!" Then, praying our usual routine might distract her from
the pain, I say, "The torturer watches his victim, waiting for the
unbearable pain to begin."

Mila, her voice shaking with her body, whispers, "But she
will never break."

"Hold on," I urge her, overwhelmed with relief that I might
not be too late. I grab the syringe from the ice box, draw her
shirt up, and inject the medicine into her tube. Immediately,
Mila's body begins to settle, and then it stops trembling and she
lies quietly, breathing hard.

"I am so, so sorry I'm late," I say again. "Klaus promised to
give you your shots after I'm Discharged."

"Felix?" Mila says, turning to face me. I'm amazed by her

quick recovery but afraid of what she's going to say. "You won't forget us, will you?"

"No way," I promise. "When I'm filthy rich, I'm going to buy this place and burn it to the ground. Then I'm going to buy a grand mansion with butlers and groundskeepers and chauffeurs, and you and me and Klaus and Elsa can live there forever."

"And my parents."

"Right! And your parents."

"Our own castle!"

"Exactly. The Sucks will be our servants. The Wolf will be the dog that guards the gates."

"You better," Mila says, turning back to the wall.

Heading back to the Bag Room, I realize that I've never considered the possibility that my fellow Freaks would miss me when I'm gone. And it suddenly occurs to me that I should give them the attic. Charlie gave it to me, and now it's my time to pass it on. I'll just have to figure out how to get the Wolf to let Klaus have my room. Klaus can tell the girls about the attic. I'll tell him to smuggle books down for them.

Along the way, I decide that I *am* going to get rich and buy that mansion. And I *am* going to find our parents. They'll all have heartbreaking stories about how they had no choice but to give us away. And they'll weep with joy at getting a second chance to know us. Of course, all the Freaks will have been Discharged by the time I'm raking in the dough, but they— My thoughts are interrupted by laughing voices around the corner. I stop short, turn to take another route to the stairs, but then stop again. The voices are gleeful, spiteful, taunting—the tone Sucks use when torturing a Freak.

"Up high!" a girl snickers.

"Down low!" a boy laughs.

"Leave…me…alone," a third voice insists. Each word doled out like it's made of molasses—Elsa! She didn't make it back to her room from the Mess. Two Sucks, both around twelve, are having fun with her. Although it takes a moment for me to see how. The girl is on her knees, and she's got her hands up under Elsa's dress. "Down low!" she cries, then yanks Elsa's underpants down to her ankles.

The boy, leaning against the wall, laughs so hard that snot spews from his nose. "Up high!" he cackles as the girl yanks Elsa's underpants back up. Elsa tries to push the girl's hands away, but she can't manage it. "Down low! Up high! Down low!" the boy chirps, and the girl swipes the underpants up and down Elsa's legs.

A rage wells up inside me. I clench my fists and grind my teeth—both of which Doc says I should never do. But just as I'm about to charge from my hiding place, broken bones be damned, a roar stops me in my tracks.

"WHAT KIND OF FUBAR BULL*SHITE* IS THIS?"

The Wolf.

His voice reverberates through the halls, so it's hard to tell exactly where it's coming from—one of the major challenges of living at Headquarters. The Wolf has a knack for appearing out of nowhere—often just in time to hit you with a Hotshock you never saw coming. Of course, he manages these miraculous materializations the same way I do, by taking advantage of the Clock Steps and hidden hallways. The Sucks believe he has dark powers, particularly because our clogs make it pretty much impossible for anyone to sneak up on anyone else, which is maybe the point of making us all wear them. That never occurred to me before.

The boy and girl take off down the hallway, and, glancing around the corner again, I see that they've barreled right into the Wolf. I feel a flash of satisfaction, thinking they'll get what they deserve. But the Wolf, I soon see, isn't raging about the Sucks torturing Elsa. His strange good mood has evaporated. He's pulling the wagon, which is loaded down with a full Bag.

"WHO IS RESPONSIBLE," he thunders, "FOR THIS UNAUTHORIZED ACQUISITION?"

The Sucks, bug-eyed and backed against the wall, cringe.

"Don't...don't know," the boy splutters.

The Wolf brandishes his Hotshot, like a cop with a baton, and just when I think he's going to ZAP the boy, he lowers it to his side.

"POP SMOKE, SHIT PUMPS!" he roars.

They pop smoke.

"WHAT THE EVERLOVING FUCK ARE *YOU* DOING?" The Wolf has finally noticed Elsa standing there, struggling to drag her underpants up her legs. "SWEET JESUS, ANOTHER PERV?" he rages at her. "FREAK, YOU KNOW WE'RE BEING INSPECTED TODAY!" Then he jabs her in the sternum with the Hotshot. Elsa shudders, then hits the floor like a marionette whose strings were cut. It's the fastest I've ever seen her move. But now she lies there trembling in an awful sort of slow motion.

"GOT SOMETHING TO SAY?" the Wolf roars when he spies me peering around the corner. "THAT'S WHAT I THOUGHT," he snaps when I don't reply. Then, hauling the wagon behind him, he heads off down the hallway.

"Charlie didn't kill herself!"

That was me. I said that. Shouted it.

And now I'm about to hyperventilate.

The Wolf stops cold, turns slowly around, then says, in a voice that's way too quiet for him, so quiet it makes my legs feel like jelly, "What did you just say?" When I don't answer again, he marches right up to me. "Who told you that?" he asks with his face so close to mine that I can smell his awful breath and feel the coarse hairs of his unkempt beard. The snout of his asinine wolf hat pushes on my helmet. His pupils, so close to mine, look like twin black holes.

"I just know," I say, then hold my breath.

The Wolf smiles. "It's true she popped her clogs," he says. "But I told you she got Discharged. And you don't get any more Discharged than dead. Am I right? I guess you could say she Discharged herself. First breeze comes your way out there in the Shit Show, and you'll cark it too, China. But I won't say I told you so."

"I want Klaus to have my bedroom," I blurt. It's a terrible

time for this, but I don't know when I'll get another chance. My request seems to jar the Wolf for a moment. His black eyes narrow suspiciously, and I'm sure he's remembering Charlie extracting the same promise. "WHY?" he snaps.

I need a good answer. I need it now. My brain works furiously, but my tongue remains mute.

"WHY?" the Wolf demands.

"I was Charlie's best friend and she gave it to me," I say. "Klaus is my best friend, so I want to give it to him. It's a Headquarters tradition."

The Wolf stares at me while he processes this.

"I'll think about it," he finally says. "But something stinks to high hell around here."

Suddenly, I smell something, too—something besides the Wolf's nasty breath.

Mint!

"Is that Klaus in there?" I cry, pointing at the Bag in the wagon.

"WHAT IF IT IS?" the Wolf roars. "WHAT ARE YOU GOING TO DO ABOUT IT?" When he sees I'm going to do absolutely nothing about it, he picks up the wagon's handle. "YOU FREAKS WILL NOT MESS THIS UP FOR ME!" he roars, pulling it down the hall. "OVER MY DEAD BODY!"

"You'll be okay, Klaus!" I shout as the Wolf and the wagon turn the corner.

"Felix?"

I turn and see Elsa now. She's on her feet. Her face is ghostly pale—the way everyone's is after getting a Hotshot. But her underpants are up. Her eyes are red and swollen.

"Do you need help getting back to your room?" I ask gently, hoping she thinks I didn't see what happened to her.

"Who's...Charlie?" she asks.

"Oh," I say. "Just a—a girl who lived here a long time ago."

"And she killed...herself...when she was...Discharged?"

"I don't know. Just something I heard around."

"You're not...going to kill yourself, are...you?"

"Of course not!"

Elsa looks relieved, but then consternation flickers across her face. "I didn't know...Klaus was your best...friend," she says.

Now this?

"You're *all* my best friends," I say.

"But you want...him...to have your...room?"

"It's a surprise. For all three of you. It's just—he'll be the oldest when I leave. He has seniority."

"Will you come...back to visit us?" Elsa asks, apparently satisfied with this answer.

Thank god.

"You'll get sick of me, I'll be here so much," I tell her. "But only until I buy us all a chocolate factory. The Sucks will make the candy and the Wolf will be our rug."

"That would be...good," Elsa says. "Felix. I was...wondering..."

"I will definitely find your parents when I'm out."

Elsa regards me with awe. "How did...you...?"

"And they can live with us in the factory."

With tears welling up again, Elsa says, "You're a good... person...Felix," before turning to shuffle away.

I am not a good person, I think, slithering back to my room. *I am a useless person. Completely and totally useless!*

9.

UNBREAKABLY LEGALLY BINDING

I've decided to stay up in the attic until tomorrow, when I can finally leave this godforsaken place. Once up there, I climb to the top of my box-tower stack and settle into my blankets. I'm restless, though, and soon enough, I find myself looking through the spyglass at the mansion.

Immediately I see that the curtains are open in the tower window, and Annika is there with her binoculars. She's looking right at me!

Tension seizes my limbs and I almost drop the spyglass. The only thing I can hear is blood rushing in my ears.

Seeing me seeing her, Annika lowers her binoculars, then slams something white against the window—a piece of paper with a message on it. I focus my spyglass and read: HELP!

Someone grabs her shoulder from behind. Adolf! Something glints in his upraised hand. A syringe! He's trying to inject her with something!

"No!" I yell—because this is my form of helping, and what else can I do? "Leave her alone!" I cry with my eye pressed painfully to the spyglass. But then Annika knees Adolf right between the legs! He hunches over, and now she punches him right in the face! His hands go up to his nose, and—*holy!*—she *kicks* him between the legs!

Adolf falls to the floor, out of view.

Annika rushes to the window, scrawls something else on the paper, and slams it to the glass. It says, I'M COMING.

And then she's gone.

She got away.

No thanks to me.

What did I just see? Was Adolf trying to *kill* her? Whatever he was doing, it wasn't about a spoiled brat wanting more freedom. This was straight out of the murder mystery stories I make up for Mila every night. But it was real! And Annika—she was like some kind of superhero!

I look through the spyglass again, watching for Annika to emerge, sprinting through the front door. Instead, the garage door rises, sending my heart up into my throat, and one of the antique electric cars zooms out. It looks like an old phone booth on wheels. The windows are tinted, but I know who's driving it. Of course she can drive.

She's coming here right now! And once Adolf recovers, he'll be right behind her!

I have to help.

Trembling violently, I climb down the boxes, then scramble down the rope ladder into my closet. I have to get into the Wolf's office somehow. But while I've memorized the intricacies of the Clock Steps and the hidden hallways, and while I know every Bag Room inside and out, I've never been inside the Wolf's office. What interest did I ever have in the workings of this godawful place? Maybe I should have harbored some suspicions during all these years. I probably should have. I definitely should have!

Why didn't I?

Another trick I've learned living at Headquarters is that I can get places quickly by following in the Wolf's wake. Hallways always clear out when he's coming, and they take a while to refill. As I work my way closer to his office, I hear him prowling around on the second floor, shouting at Sucks to "SMARTEN UP PRONTO OR PREPARE TO SEE THE LIGHT!" So I'm home free all the way down to the first floor.

Looking through the glass panels in the Wolf's office door, I can see that this is the only room in the entire Headquarters that's not a disaster area. A large desk, clean of clutter, dominates the center of the room. Shelves, filled with boxes, line the walls, and a colorful round carpet covers the floor in front of the desk. A door in the back leads, I assume, to a closet or a bathroom.

There is no greater Violation of the Law of the Land than

entering the Wolf's Lair. It's Treason of the worst kind, the kind that wins you the Big Chicken Dinner. I try the knob with a sweaty hand, but it's locked.

I have no idea what I'm going to do now.

But then, through the window in the Wolf's office, I see Annika in the front yard, approaching Headquarters. She's wearing her black wig and sunglasses again, this time with a long, fancy billowing dress with flowers all over it. The disguise seems even more transparent than it was the first time, but I know the Wolf won't see through it. Annika, turning her head, sees me through the window, and her eyes widen questioningly. She's asking if I got the records.

I shake my head and gesture toward the door in front of me. *It's locked*, I mouth.

Hide, she mouths in return.

Then she just walks calmly on, as if she hadn't just kicked the crap out of a man twice her size who was trying to kill her. Like she doesn't have a care in the world.

I'm in awe.

I move down the hall and around the corner, and then… wait. Wait, I admit to myself, for her to do everything herself. She was foolish to think I could help, and I'm a moron for trying. But I'm here now, outside the Wolf's office, about to win the Big Chicken Dinner, and there's no going back…

Oh god. *What am I doing?*

I hear a knock on the front door, followed by footsteps, then the Wolf's voice. "Right on time, right on time," he growls. "Oh-ten-hundred hours. Antique electric vehicle, eh? I know someone who'd love to get his greedy hands on that."

"It's a 1919 Rauch and Lang," Annika says. "I hope you don't mind that I drove it here. I know you don't care for electricity."

"A man can change," the Wolf mutters, sounding very pleasantly un-Wolfish. "If you want turn this place into the Vegas Strip, darling, be my guest."

What?

There's no way the Wolf would allow electricity here. He *is* planning to take off with her money. I shudder at the thought

of what's going to happen when he finds out there is none—
none for him, anyway.

"Shall we discuss the proposal?" Annika asks. "In your office perhaps?"

"Ten-four, right this way."

The floors creak as they pass me by, and then I hear the
rattle of keys and the office door open. "After you, my dear,"
the Wolf says, but then he wails, "WHAT IN HELL?" And
then he's running back down the hall and out into the front
yard, slamming the door behind him.

"It's just a little donation celebration I arranged for the
kids!" Annika calls after him. She's in the hall again. When I
peek around the corner, she waves me into the office behind
her. "Quickly!" she whispers as I scurry past. "I'll stall as much
as I can." Then she goes after the Wolf, leaving me in the Lair.
Alone.

Curious, I glance through the window to see what all the
hubbub is outside. Three trucks, parked out front, each pull a
trailer with a gigantic blow-up bounce toy—a castle, a witch's
cauldron, and an ocean of sharks. Dozens of Sucks are already
scrambling up the sides and leaping gleefully about on top of
them. I can see the Wolf yelling and shouting and waving his
arms around like a scarecrow in the wind.

A diversion! Annika arranged all this to distract the Wolf!
Genius!

But I don't have time to waste. I have to find those records.
The desk seems like the obvious place to keep important doc-
uments, but rifling through the drawers, I don't see anything
other than a bottle of foul-smelling liquor, an extra pair of
yellow rubber gloves, and an old stained book called *The History
of Military Etiquette*. I abandon the desk and scan the room.
Against the wall, under tattered blankets, I see something that
gives me pause—four old coin-op machines that the Wolf has
clearly been tinkering with. Loose gears, wrenches, and bits of
wire lie atop one. I go over to have a closer look.

One consists of a river scene, with a miniature Bag floating
in the water near a little figure in an inner tube; the second

machine displays only a tiny figure lying on a metal bed frame; and the third contains a number of small consoles with dials and gauges, a long metal table, and a miniature video camera positioned to film the scene. The fourth machine is the most elaborate, designed to resemble a 1950s living room. A small figure, wrapped in an olive-green blanket, with one arm extending, reclines on the floor.

There's a penny in the coin-return slot of this one so I slide it in and pull the lever. The machine's gears start to grind, and the wrapped figure is hoisted into the air on a wire. A window opens in the back panel to reveal two disembodied doll hands mounted against a square of bright yellow light waiting to catch it.

A noise from the hallway brings me to my senses—the front door slamming! The Wolf is coming back! What the hell was I doing? I've wasted the precious time Annika bought me! I hear her trying to slow the Wolf down, but he's having none of it. He wants his money, and he wants it now.

I hurry to the other door in the office and open it to discover a closet full of Bags hanging on the walls. I shut the door carefully and maneuver behind a row of them, deeply inhaling their scent to slow my racing pulse. It works, until I realize there's another familiar smell in here.

Mint!

I frantically feel the Bags, but they're all empty. At the back wall, behind a rack of musty-smelling coats, I find another door, which opens into a narrow staircase hidden in the walls—Clock Steps without the clock. "Klaus?" I whisper. But there's no sign of him.

I hear a muffled whimper coming from...where? Looking down, I see the dim outlines of...a trapdoor with a small hole in one corner. Without thinking about breaking my finger, I reach into the hole with one and pull. My bones do not break. The door lifts.

Underneath is a dark hole, but I see the shadow of stairs. It's a bunker. I leave the door leaning against the closet wall and descend carefully into the dark. At the bottom of the steps

I find, faintly illuminated by the light filtering down from the closet above, a full Bag.

This is the Brig!

Unzipping the Bag, I discover Klaus. He's twisted into a pretzel, shaking and crying. Globs of mint-scented cream are clumped in his hair and smeared across his cheeks. His eyes widen when he sees me.

"He saw me without my cream," Klaus whimpers when I help him out of the Bag. As if he needs to explain this situation. "But I had more in my sock!"

I help Klaus up the steps and through the door behind the coats.

"We're in the Wolf's office," I tell him. "There are hidden stairs all throughout the house. These will take you up into a Bag Room, and from there you'll wind up in a regular hallway. Make sure no one is around before you go out into it."

His eyes are saucers.

"It's okay, Klaus. I'll handle the Wolf when he finds out. Just hurry!"

"You're a good person," Klaus whispers. "I heard what you told the Wolf when I was in the wagon," he adds. "You're my best friend too." And then he's gone.

I climb down into the bunker and lower the trapdoor most of the way down over my head. I can hear Annika's and the Wolf's muffled voices in the office through the closet door, which I left slightly ajar. I pray the Wolf won't notice that.

"Oh, it's just for a few hours," Annika is saying, "and they're having such fun. It's not *regulation*, I know, but I do so enjoy improving the lives of the less fortunate."

"This *is* against regs," the Wolf grumbles. "But since you are so…eager to help improve life here, we'll make an exception for today. We're here to do business, right?"

"Absolutely," Annika assures him. "I am truly touched by what you do here, Mr. Law. You are doing the world a great service, and I would very much like to help you. How much do you think it would take to give this place a complete makeover?"

"I think probably a hundred grand," the Wolf says,

"conservatively speaking. Especially since you want the place wired. We'll do the whole deal, top to bottom."

"Why don't we make it one fifty, to cover unforeseen overruns?"

"Maybe two, since you mention it. Just to be safe."

"I imagine you'll take a check?"

"Oh. Ah. No can do. Sorry. We're a cash-only operation. You know how the brass operates. Who knows why they want what they want? These things are above my pay grade."

"I'm not in the habit of carrying around two hundred thousand dollars in cash, Mr. Law."

"Cash only, if you really want to help the little—kids."

"I really do," Annika promises. "I'll have to come back later this afternoon."

"But we have a deal?"

"We have a deal."

"I'll need you to sign a donation pledge. Unbreakably legally binding."

"Whatever you like."

The Wolf turns toward the closet, and I try not to tense so hard that I hurt myself. He flings open the closet door, and I hear him rustling around amongst the Bags and coats. I can see his boots and trousers. He's turned away from me, so with a trembling hand, I lift the trapdoor a bit further to see what he's doing. Behind a rack of extra Bags, I see a large black safe with a shiny chrome combination lock. The Wolf, crouching down in front of it, mutters, "Forty-two, twenty-seven, eleven." Then he spins the lock three times and pulls the handle. The safe opens.

Inside I can see a bundle of notebooks. The Wolf takes one out, closes the safe, then returns to the office. "Write two hundred grand here," he tells Annika, "and then sign here."

I hear the scratch of pen on paper. "It's official," she says. "I'll be back with two hundred thousand dollars in cash this after—"

"Christ on a crutch!" the Wolf suddenly shouts. "What's *he* doing here today?"

"I'm afraid I must go," Annika says, sounding equally alarmed. "I have a full schedule this afternoon and I'm already late for an appointment. I shall see you later, Mr. Law."

I hear her heels on the wooden floor and the office door open and close.

"Small bills!" the Wolf calls after her. Then he shouts, to himself I guess, "AFI!" Which I know means 'another fucking inconvenience' because he says it every time he agrees to do something for someone. Which isn't all that often. Then I hear the office door slamming behind him.

I climb out of the Brig and push the empty Bags away from the safe. I squat down, take a deep breath, then spin the dial.

Forty-two. Twenty-seven. Eleven.

The door opens. Inside the safe are rows of thick note-books, their spines labeled with a year written in black ink. Years of business operations, I assume. But I have no idea what to take! Then I decide that, if Annika is about to turn sixteen, she would've been born in 2002. I grab the notebook with 2002 on it.

I hear footsteps, and the office door opens again. I grab the notebook labeled 2000—the year I was left at Headquarters. Then I whip open the door at the back of the closet and head through with both notebooks hugged tightly to my chest. I close the door as quietly as I can, then hurry up the steps.

I'm barely halfway up when I hear the Wolf scream, "TREEEEEEEASON!"

I forgot to close the safe.

10.

THE BIG BAD WOLF

I've done it now. There's only one place to go, so I hurry up to the third floor as quickly as I can. Luckily, the hallways are empty, the rooms quiet—there's not a Suck in sight. Passing a window, I see why. They're all outside bouncing like maniacs on the blow-up bounce toys.

Where is Annika?

I find her in my room, looking shaken for the first time. This, as much as anything, unnerves me.

"My father's back, Felix," she says, "and Adolf tried to kill me!" She sinks to the edge of my bed, fingers clenched on the mattress edge. "I—I have no idea what I've started," she says, her voice trembling slightly. But then she sees the notebooks in my hands and leaps to her feet, crying, "You got the records!" After a deep breath, she says, "Time to get busy, Felix. How do we get up to the attic?"

In the closet I reach for the board and push it aside, letting the rope ladder fall. Without hesitation, Annika scrambles up into the attic. When I get up there, I find her, eyes wide, turning a slow circle to take in the hundreds and hundreds of magazine pages that plaster the walls. Finally, she turns and looks at me with both sadness and wonder.

"I admit that interior decorating might not be in my future," I say. Because I'm embarrassed. Ashamed, really, of my home.

Annika looks like she has something to say but instead shakes off her thoughts about my pathetic life and, back to business, says, "Let's have a look at those notebooks." She swipes the dust off a pair of large boxes and motions for me to sit next to her.

I do so, and together we begin flipping through the 2002 notebook.

Suddenly, we hear a roar downstairs—the entire house seems to rattle and shudder with the force of it. "The Wolf knows these are missing," I whisper. "I forgot to close the safe. He's calling for an Inspection—"

But Annika seems heedless of my fears. She flips through the notebook, rapidly scanning the pages. "There I am!" she cries. "10-12-2002. Baby A. Age: approximately six months. Adopted by W. Adelstein. Adoption fee—forty thousand dollars. And my father's signature is right here!"

"It costs forty thousand dollars to adopt a child?" I ask, stunned.

"Actually, it does. Or close to that. I looked into it."

Annika scrutinizes the page with a sour expression, as if she were sucking on a lemon. "What the hell?" she says. "The adoptions here are listed along with antique deals, as if kids were just pieces of junk that creep sells. There are lots of adoptions, though—look—they all cost forty thousand dollars."

We hear a shout and a series of crashes below. The Wolf has reached the third floor and is surely searching for me. It sounds like he's tearing the house apart.

"He doesn't know about this attic, right?" Annika whispers.

"No," I reply, "but he knows I don't leave the house. So he won't stop looking until he finds me."

"Maybe he'll think you finally did leave. There's a first time for everything, right?"

I don't answer this question because, again, I'm ashamed.

Annika doesn't seem to notice. "Is that the year you arrived at Headquarters?" she asks, pointing at the 2000 notebook in my hand.

I nod and start flipping through it. And there I am, just a few pages from the start—Baby X (Felix). Housing fee: $40,000.

"What does *housing fee* mean?" I ask, showing her the entry.

"Hmm," she says, knitting her brow. "Maybe someone paid, not to adopt you, but to keep you here? To house you. Maybe it's the same for the other—"

Seeing the expression on my face, Annika decides not to

finish the thought. But I know she means Freaks. "I'm sorry," she says, "but that can't be legal, can it?"

I say nothing. Someone paid to adopt her, to remove her from Headquarters. Someone else paid to leave me here. Me and the other Freaks, no doubt. Shame squeezes me like the cell phone in the vise. And the results are probably going to be pretty much the same.

Who are my parents, and why did they do this to me?

I'm going to find out.

Crashing noises, now right beneath our feet.

"He's in my room!" I whisper.

Annika's eyes widen, but instead of panicking, like I'm doing, she lies down, putting her ear to the floorboards. I sit down beside her. But only because I'm starting to breathe hard.

"He's in the closet," Annika whispers.

"That fragile fuck is here somewhere," we hear the Wolf say. "He's the only one unaccounted for, so it has to be him. He somehow heard about Charlotte, so he's probably going Section 8 about getting Discharged. I'm telling you, that kid's brain is as breakable as his bones. And he wants me to give this room to one of the other Freaks for some reason. He's up to something, I know it."

I'm about to lose all control of my breathing and the attic is going dark in my peripheral vision. But then it occurs to me— the Wolf sounds different. This is not his Bullshit Bombing voice, or his weasely suck-up voice—not his normal one anyway. He sounds…nervous!

I press my ear to the floorboards beside Annika and listen closer.

"You are, and always have been, a weakling and coward, Wolfram," a man says, his voice low and commanding, yet somehow familiar. "It's you who is up to something. Have you been drinking again?"

"No! I swear—"

"We need to find him, Wolfram, you sniveling troglodyte. We need to find and Discharge him *immediately*. I've got bigger problems at home right now with my prima donna of a daughter."

Annika and I look at each other. She looks distressed, but more than that, baffled. I'm baffled too. But then it finally hits me whose voice we're hearing.

"It's Doc!" I whisper. "Our doctor. He has to give me my shot before I'm officially—"

"It's not your doctor," Annika hisses. "It's my dad!"

"What?"

"What kind of problems are you having with Annika?" the Wolf asks.

"She's here somewhere too, you idiot! They're probably together!"

"WHAT?"

"It's obvious you've lost control here, Wolfram. I am profoundly disappointed."

"I'm telling you, Willy, she's not here. No one is here that I don't—!"

"Then why the hell is my Rauch and Lang parked outside?"

"OH, SHIT! But Willy, I think someone must've stolen it."

"Never should have given her driving lessons!" Doc—or Willy Adelstein, or whoever he is—says. "And it serves me right for letting her learn martial arts. I just sent Axel to the hospital with a broken nose and god knows what else—the guy was puking up blood! But I have to keep her busy with useless lessons every minute of the goddamn day or she sticks her nose into everything! The little bitch is scheming. She's *always* scheming. While I was gone, she came here."

"Willy—I—I—"

"Is that all you can say about your monumental incompetence, Wolfram? She was up in the tower watching this place with a pair of binoculars. I'm telling you, we have to get this under control. I have sorely underestimated her capacity to destroy everything I've been working for."

Annika's face is an ice-cold mask, but the heat in her eyes could melt metal.

"Her binoculars left marks on the windowpane in the tower

room," Doc adds. "It appeared she was watching a window near the top of this house, under the eaves. Is there access to the attic in this shithole?"

"*SON OF A BITCH!*" the Wolf howls. "THAT'S WHAT THIS ROOM IS FOR!"

"Don't tell me you've never—"

The boards we're lying on suddenly shudder. Annika and I scramble to our feet. The Wolf is pounding on my closet ceiling. Annika races to the box stack, and with a few deft moves, she's at the top by the diamond-shaped window.

"What are you do—?" I start to ask. But then the loose board literally flies out of place into the attic, clattering on the floorboards as the rope ladder tumbles into my closet.

"WHISKY! TANGO! FOXTROT!" the Wolf roars.

Before I can process the full extent of this catastrophe, I hear glass breaking. Annika is smashing out the diamond-shaped window with my spyglass. "Come on!" she cries, turning back to look at me for a moment.

I rush toward the boxes and start climbing. My heart is pounding and my temples throb. What does she think she's doing?

"THIS IS AWOL!" the Wolf screams as he clambers into the attic. "THIS IS TREASON!" Spittle flies from his mouth as he looks around in utter disbelief at the overflowing boxes of books and magazines and the pictures on the walls. Then he looks up at us on the top of the stack and wails, "THIS IS THE BIG CHICKEN DINNER!"

I knew it would come to this. The moment I got involved with this girl. I knew it would come to this.

Doc, in his perfectly pressed black suit, emerges next to the Wolf. He's tall and rail-thin, with very white skin and very black sideburns. He glares at us through his monocle, holding both his black doctor's bag and walking stick in his right hand. He looks like one of the old-fashioned doctors from my out-of-date books.

"Annika!" Doc snaps. "Take off that ridiculous wig and stop this nonsense at once!"

"That's…Annika?" the Wolf cries. "But—how could I have known what she looked like?" he whines. I can't believe the Wolf is whining.

"You could have visited our home any time in the last sixteen years, Wolfram."

"But you know I can't go in there!"

"That's your problem, not mine. It has nothing to do with me."

"How could you possibly say—!"

But Doc has clearly tired of this conversation and turns to his daughter. "You have no idea what you're meddling in," he tells her. "And you are putting that boy's life in jeopardy."

She is. She absolutely is.

Breathe.

Ignoring him, Annika sticks her head out through the window frame.

"Felix," Doc says to me, in his reassuring doctor voice. "Annika has severe psychological issues and is prone to hallucinations. You must believe me when I tell you that she is a mortal danger to you right now."

"I saw that man Adolf try to kill her!" I shout.

"What you saw," Doc says calmly, "was her nurse, Axel, attempting to give her a sedative. Annika has been acting out paranoid fantasies about being a prisoner in her own home for the past few weeks. She needs help."

Could this be true?

Annika pulls her head back into the attic. "Look out there," she tells me. When I only stare at her stupidly, she says, "Just look! You'll see!"

"Annika!" Doc yells. "You are in one of your states! You need your medication."

Annika looks at her father, stares him dead in the eye, and says, "Medicate this!" And she gives him the Left-Handed Salute.

"You will hurt that boy!" Doc says, ignoring the gesture. "He needs a full battery of tests before he can leave this home. Do you want to be responsible for his death?"

Now Annika turns her electric blue eyes on me. "Do you trust me?" she asks. "Or him?"

I don't know her! I know Doc! He's taken care of me my whole life!

"Get them, Wolfram," Doc orders the Wolf. "Or you will rot in prison for the rest of your life."

"Don't threaten me, Willy," the Wolf claps back. The whine is gone—he sounds like himself again. "This soup sandwich is yours to eat," he adds. "That's *your* daughter. This is *your* business. It has nothing to do with me."

"Get them down here this instant or so help me god—!"

"I said, don't threaten me!" the Wolf shouts. "I'M DONE WITH THIS PLACE! WITH YOU! WITH ALL OF IT! AND HOW'S THIS FOR A THREAT: I HAVE YOUR MISSING FILM!"

"You...*what?*" Willy gasps.

I have no idea what's going on, or what to do. But if Annika is insane, then...well, being crazy sounds a whole lot better than...whatever I've been. Am.

While Doc and the Wolf continue to threaten each other, I put my head through the window.

"Look!" Annika whispers.

Outside, I see the usual: dead lawn, dirt path, hedge wall. Junk on both sides. But it all begins to waver and darken in my peripheral vision as it occurs to me that I could fall. Before I'm seized with vertigo, I lean back into the room, breathing hard.

"Wolfram," Doc says, very calmly. "I am asking you one more time to get those two down here. I promise that if you don't, I will give you what you've always wanted and deserved."

"WHAT I WANT IS TO BE RID OF YOU!"

"We need to jump," Annika tells me, her hand on my arm.

Even though I'm wearing several inches of pads, when her hand squeezes lightly, I feel like I've been Hotshocked. I think of Charlie, the last person to touch me, the last person to tell me to look out this window. I think of my real mother and father, wherever they are. Did they touch me? Surely they did. Didn't they?

The Wolf looks at Doc, then up at us. He makes his way

slowly to the box stack, but with a yellow glove held up—as if to signal that he means no harm.

"Felix," Annika says, locking her electric eyes onto mine, "my martial arts teacher once told me that while it's very important to protect your body—our bodies aren't ours for very long—they're not the real part of us, the part that lasts forever. The most real part of you is your spirit." She takes her hand off my arm and adds, "Don't let them break your spirit, Felix." Then, after knocking out one last shard of glass from the frame, she leans out the window and falls.

"Annika!" I cry, looking out after her. And then I see what she wanted me to see—not across the yard but directly below the window. A bounce toy, the ocean, is right there, and Annika is already bouncing up from its surface, her wig and glasses flying. She bounces a few more times, then settles between two sharks.

"Jump!" she calls up to me.

But I'm just staring at her, dumbfounded. Suddenly another hand, this one in a yellow rubber glove, grabs my shoulder pads. The Wolf has ahold of me, and then his head is out the window next to mine. My breathing goes wild, and everything in my field of vision darkens again.

"Let him go!" Annika cries, standing on the bounce house, her defiant face upturned.

"Bring him down here!" Doc shouts from the attic behind us. "Do not fuck this up, Wolfram! I'm warning you—!"

The Wolf turns his head and puts his hairy mouth right against my ear. "He never told me she had to die," he says, sounding strangely clam. "Time to pop smoke, China."

Then, instead of pulling me back in through the window, the Wolf pushes me out of it.

For some reason, I don't make a peep as I fall to my death.

Above me, I hear the Wolf roar, "CONSIDER THAT FILM FRONT-PAGE NEWS, WILLY. SEE YOU IN THE FUNNY PAPERS! YOU'RE SCREWED!"

I get a glimpse of Annika jumping to the side just before I

hit the bounce house floor on my back. I sink deep into it, then spring up. I bounce a few more times, then come to rest.

Am I dead?

"Are you okay?" Annika asks, leaning over me, eyes wide.

I'm not dead.

I glance back up at the attic window, and see, to my astonishment, a blinding streak of blue lightning.

And then the Wolf falling from the window.

Annika grabs me. She rolls us both to the side just before he hits.

The Wolf bounces like I did, then settles on his back.

Annika and I both scream.

I'm not dead, but the Wolf is. His body is burned beyond recognition. His face is entirely melted to bone and blackened flesh, and his yellow rubber gloves drip from his hands. The charred ruins of his wolf-skin hat smoke on his scorched skull.

I can't stop screaming.

I'm screaming from a place inside me I didn't know existed. Annika pulls me by the hand, down the bounce house's entry ramp, and onto Headquarters grounds.

Sucks are pouring out the front door, gathering around the bounce house to see what happened.

"Come on, we've got to get out of here," Annika says, though her voice sounds to me like it's coming from far away. She helps me into her car, still parked in the driveway, then jumps into the driver's seat just as Doc comes out onto the front porch, yelling and waving his walking stick in the air.

Moments later we're speeding away, and I'm heading, for the first time in my life, down the gravel road, away from Headquarters.

11

THE WOLF'S DEN

We drive through the hedge arch, and I sit, numb, barely able to register my first ride in a motor vehicle. I keep seeing the blackened body of the Wolf falling toward me, his ruined face and smoking hat. The trees on each side of the road whip past in a blur of green, and then, suddenly, Annika swerves onto the side of the road and slams on the brakes. She leaps out of her door and rushes around the car to open mine.

As soon as the passenger door opens, I lean out and throw up on the road.

"Come on," Annika urges, helping me out of the car by my arm.

"Don't pull!" I cry, staggering to my feet. "Why did you stop? Where—?" Then I see a scruffy, patchy-bearded guy in ripped jeans standing by the side of the road admiring the car. Annika, holding out a stack of bills, says, "I will pay you five hundred dollars to drive this car away." The guy flashes a skeptical look at me, but then looks confused to see me dressed in pads, head to toe.

"Take it or leave it," Annika says.

"Sure, hell yeah," the guy says. He grabs the cash and heads for the driver's seat.

"Just drive until someone stops you," Annika tells him once he's behind the wheel. "Then tell them we got into an Uber and headed the other way. Take this too," she adds, handing him her cell phone. "Throw it out the window if you want, once you get down the road a way."

"Whatever you say," the guy says. Then he drives off.

"They'll try to track my phone," Annika tells me before I can ask.

"Why did we give away our getaway car?" I ask instead. "And what's an Uber?"

"Just—follow me," Annika says, taking me by the arm. I pull it away. "Sorry!" she says. But I follow her because…*What else am I going to do?* But she's heading…back toward Headquarters! Annika stops us under the hedge arch. "Quickly," she says, forcing aside some branches and barging right into the hedge. There's a space inside large enough for both of us. I'm in, but my breathing is starting to get out of control again. Along with absolutely everything else in the world.

"It's okay, Felix," Annika says. "We made it. You made it! You handled that fall like a champ."

"You don't understand," I snap. "Any kind of contact, even light contact, can cause hairline fractures in my bones. I may not feel it. And I won't feel it until one of them breaks!"

"Oh my god. I didn't realize it was *that* bad."

"Well, it's not *your* problem."

"Okay, Felix," Annika says. "That's fair. I'm a selfish, spoiled little twit who—"

Just then we hear the roar of a powerful engine and a gleaming red sports car blasts through the hedge, filling the archway with fumes. I could tell it was a Ferrari, and Doc was behind the wheel. In seconds he disappears around a curve in the road.

"Let's go," Annika says. "Eventually he'll realize we outsmarted him."

"Go where?" I ask as we climb out of the hedge.

"Follow me."

She's heading through the arch—the wrong way!

"We can't go back there!" I protest, but Annika veers off the path to Headquarters' front porch. She's heading for the gas pumps.

And the junkyard.

I hurry after her but stop at the pumps.

"Let's *go,*" Annika says, "before anyone sees us."

"But—" I say. Only I have nothing to say. Because I'm speechless to finally be standing here, at the edge of this forbidden world, which rises up in front of me like the remnants of an obliterated city. I can see alleys wind their way through the junk, lined with piles of broken appliances—dishwashers, dryers, refrigerators, stoves, air conditioners, water heaters, microwaves, washing machines. Rusted-out cars are parked like vehicles of the dead. Here and there I see huge heaps of tires rising out of the junk like rubber mountains. I imagine the Wolf strolling through the avenues of his junk city, looking for anything he can hawk at his weekly sales.

Annika heads straight into the junk. I take a deep breath, remembering how I'd wanted to show the Sucks I was brave enough to come to this very place. *Fifty-three seconds was the plan.*

My life has become surreal in just twenty-four hours. I've been sucked into a nightmare, a real-life nightmare. The Wolf is dead! What did Doc do to him? *How* could he have done that to him? What's going to happen to me? What's going to happen to my fellow Freaks?

I take a deep breath, then head off after Annika before she's out of sight. I trail behind as she navigates alley after alley like she knows where she's going. Finally, she stops at a tangled pile of old bicycles almost as tall as me.

"There," Annika says, pointing toward a beaten-up mobile home covered in camouflage colors and partly hidden behind the rusted remains of a pick-up truck with its wheels missing. Annika climbs the porch, opens the door, and walks inside like she owns the place.

Amazed, afraid, awed again, I follow.

The interior is surprising—the walls are covered in flags, military flags from the U.S. Army. Between them, dirty canteens, a camo backpack, a helmet, and a pair of binoculars hang from rusty hooks.

Turning around, I see a sink and a stove and a row of cabinets running along the opposite wall. A little table and two chairs are positioned near a threadbare couch. There's even a shower, I notice, with a camouflage curtain tucked into a dirty tub. The bed looks slept in and dirty dishes are piled in the sink.

Someone lives here.

"Is this…yours?" I ask, stupidly.

"What?" Annika says, flopping onto the couch, trying to catch her breath. "No! I'd die. When I came to the yard sale, I asked the Wolf if he ever felt cooped up living with so many kids all the time. He told me about the 'swanky den' he had in the junkyard not far from the pumps. He asked if I wanted a private tour. I politely declined."

I can't muster up any sympathy for the Wolf, despite his horrible death. None. Less than none. Because I hate him. But now that he's dead, I somehow feel even more vulnerable. How stupid is that?

"I guess we'll be safe here for a while," Annika says.

"What happened to the Wolf?" I ask. "I saw...blue lightning from the attic right before he fell."

Annika shrugs. "I told you my father is obsessed with electricity. He loves electrical weapons. He must have brought one."

"The Wolf," I say, "carried around a cattle prod to shock the kids who made him mad."

"Jesus!" Annika cries. "What a psycho! Is that why he wore those rubber gloves all the time—?" Then her eyes widen and she exclaims, "The walking stick!"

"Had to be," I agree. "But it's no cattle prod. It burned the Wolf's skin right off!"

Annika seems to have blocked this out. She stares at me now, sickened, and for the second time she looks like a normal teenager rather than a goddess-in-training. "Let's just pretend we didn't see that," she says. "Okay?"

"Deal," I tell her. And I mean it. I want to pretend none of this is happening. I feel numb again. I feel lost. I feel helpless.

"I was sure my father was involved in questionable business deals," Annika says. "Something...I don't know, *illegal*, but...I have no idea what I've gotten myself into."

What you've gotten *us* into, I want to say. But I don't.

"I've always known he is a heartless SOB, but I never thought he was a cold-blooded—"

"Wait a minute," I interrupt. "In the attic, the Wolf—he—he *helped* me!"

"What? How?"

"In the window, he said something about how Charlie didn't have to die. It sounded like he was saying your father killed her! Then he pushed me out."

Would I have jumped myself without that push?

Probably not.

Who am I kidding?

Definitely not.

I think the Wolf saved my life.

"Wow," Annika says. "But several kids at Headquarters told me he locked them in bags. And the cattle prod? What the hell?"

"I—I don't understand," I admit. "Maybe the Wolf and your father were working together on developing top secret electrical weapons for the government. Maybe they needed a bunch of people not raised around electricity to test the results. Maybe the Wolf's cattle prod was part of the testing that led to the walking stick."

Annika raises a skeptical brow. "You have quite the imagination," she says. "But I seriously doubt they were doing top secret government research in that lunatic asylum. Speaking of which," she adds, looking around the mobile home, "this army obsession—was your Wolf really a soldier?"

"He said he was, but who knows?"

"Delusional, I bet. This must be his Fortress of Solitude."

"His what?"

"Superman," she says, looking askance. "Wait, you don't know Superman?"

I shake my head.

"Batman? Spiderman?" When she sees my blank look, Annika shakes her head. "You never came across any comic books in the attic? Have you ever seen a movie?"

"The other kids get to go once a year," I say, feeling like an alien, "but the Freaks...well, we never left Headquarters."

"Unbelievable."

"Hey," I say. "Is there anyone you can reach out to for help? Relatives?"

"No," Annika says. "I don't know anything about my real parents, but my adoptive family were all murdered in World War

II, and my father doesn't have friends. Only servants who are terrified of him."

"But he definitely knew the Wolf. Only he called him Wolfram."

"What do you really know about him?"

"Nothing," I admit. "Except he hated electricity and all the kids he was supposed to take care of. Especially me."

"You've got to know more than that," Annika says. "You spent, what, your entire life so far in that house with him? I thought *I* had it bad."

"You know what?" I say—because I've finally decided how to handle this situation—"I'm going to take a nap."

"*Ooookay?*" Annika says.

I lie on the narrow bed and pull the sheets over my head.

And just like that, the Superman of sleep is out.

The Wolf's face is next to mine in the window. His hair is on fire and his skin bubbles grotesquely. He reaches his hand out to me even as the rubber glove and skin melt off it in liquified strips. "Good luck in the Shit Show, China!" he cackles as his face melts away like candle wax. "Not! One! Day!"

"The film!" I shout, bolting upright in bed.

Annika turns toward me, startled. She was tapping on some kind of flat device—a laptop, I think it's called. "What film?" she asks.

"The Wolf and Doc were fighting about some film. The Wolf said it would ruin your father. He said he was going to get it on the news or something. Then—that's when—"

"We need to find it!" Annika cries.

And so we're up and searching the Wolf's den. We ransack the kitchen, the closet, and the bathroom, but find only silver packets of dehydrated food, dirty dishes, and mildewing army fatigues. We search for secret compartments in the walls and beneath the floor, but to no avail.

"It's gotta be hidden at Headquarters," Annika says. "But we can't go back there just yet."

"Is that your computer?" I ask, changing the subject. The last thing I want is to go back into that house.

"It's the Wolf's," Annika tells me. "He's got an thumbdrive too. From what I can tell, he only used it for selling his junk, but finding it was a real stroke of luck. While you were sleeping, I sent a copy of the emancipation papers I had drawn up a few months ago to my father. I told him that unless he promises not to contest my petition, we'll tell the cops that he murdered the caretaker of Wolfgang Law's Great Home for Good Girls and Boys."

"And you're waiting for him to write back?"

"Yeah. I expect it might take a little while for him to see this, but once he does, he'll blow a few gaskets. Then he'll reply with an avalanche of bribes and threats. That's how he rolls. But I've heard nothing yet. Maybe he's still out looking for us."

"I think I'll sleep a bit more."

"Suit yourself."

I'm on the box stack in the attic. Annika tells me, Don't let them break your spirit, Felix, *then falls out the window.* You want to see your parents? *Doc asks. I turn to him.* Yes! *I say,* Yes! *Doc says,* You have to choose. *I look out the window at Annika, who is standing on the bounce ocean like Poseidon. Then I look back into the attic at Doc.* I want to know my parents! *I cry. Doc smiles. He points his walking stick at me and says,* Let me introduce you. *A bolt of lightning hits me in the chest, and I am dust.*

When I open my eyes this time, my first thought is of my parents. What if they're dead? If Charlie was dead, why not them too? Why hadn't the possibility occurred to me before now? What am I doing with this reckless girl?

The futility of my circumstances hits me like a club.

"What are you," Annika asks, "some kind of stress sleeper?"

"It's my superpower."

"Very impressive."

"How long have I been asleep?"

"About six hours." Annika is eating something from one of the silver packets we'd discovered in the cabinets.

"That's nothing," I brag, pretending my life isn't as good as over. "Amateur stuff. How go the bribes and threats?"

"Negative," Annika says. "So to keep from freaking out, I've been doing some research. Except I can't find anything about Wolfgang or Wolfram Law, other than that one article where he's mentioned in connection to Charlotte's overdose in 2008. Otherwise, it's like he doesn't exist. I found the website that lists Purple Heart recipients. He's not on it. Big surprise there."

"What does it say about Charlie?"

Annika clicks on the computer, then reads from the screen: "'Charlotte Law, eighteen, died of a drug overdose the night before she was set to move out of Wolfgang Law's Great Home for Good Girls and Boys. An investigation determined that the young woman found a needle in the back of an abandoned truck in the home director's adjacent junkyard. It was unclear whether the overdose was accidental or a suicide, but Wolfgang Law informed authorities that Charlotte dreaded being on her own and had begged to be allowed to stay. Devastated, Mr. Law has agreed to implement all possible measures to prevent such tragedies in the future.'"

"I have to go back," I tell her, my pulse is racing. "Who knows what's happening there! The Freaks—! Why haven't I been thinking about the Freaks!"

"What?" Annika says. "To Headquarters? Your friends are okay, at least for now. Let's just not do anything rash, okay? We need to go back there, but we need to be smart about it. Here, eat some almonds," she says, tossing me one of the silver packets. "They're nasty."

I duck to the side so the packet doesn't hit me. It smacks the wall behind the bed and falls to the floor.

"Sorry!" Annika cries. "I'm such an idiot!"

"It's okay," I say, kneeling on the floor to reach beneath the bed where the packet rests against the wall. Something mashed between the mattress and the mesh of the bed frame catches my eye—a brown paper bag, decorated with diagonal orange and white stripes. I'm guessing it's not cereal. I leave the almonds and stand up.

Annika looks at me, wondering what's going on.

"Looks like the Wolf was hiding something in here after all."

12.

THE BURN BAG

Together, Annika and I slide the mattress off the bed frame. "Oooh!" she exclaims, grabbing the bag. Printed on the back are the words, *Burn Paper Only Classified Waste.*

"It's a Burn Bag," I say. "I read about them in an old *Military Review* magazine. They're for secrets that should be burned after reading."

"Well, secrets are exactly what we need!" Annika says, opening the bag and dumping the contents onto the kitchen table. Two yellowed pieces of newspaper and a rusty old key tumble out. "I bet whatever this key unlocks is where that film is!" she cries.

"But there are no markings on it," I say. "How are we supposed to know where—?"

"We'll find it," she says. "It's gotta be in the house! But let's look at this other stuff first."

Both newspaper clippings are from the *Reno Gazette-Journal.* Both are old and clearly worn along lines where they were folded, but their print is still legible. The earlier one is dated November 1, 1985. We read it together.

LOCAL BOY MIRACULOUSLY SURVIVES BIZARRE GANG PUNISHMENT

A homeless seventeen-year-old Reno boy (name withheld due to minor status) was subjected by his fellow skinhead gang members to a version of the ancient Roman penalty known as The Poena Cullei (The Penalty of the Sack) after they discovered he was Jewish. The boy was forced to wear wooden clogs and a cap made of wolf skin, then beaten with a rod, after which he was sealed in a waterproof burlap sack with a rattlesnake. The sack was tossed into the

Truckee River in downtown Reno. It was discovered by a local man floating on an inner tube. The man summoned the police, who credited the boy with saving his own life by having enough discipline to remain calm inside the sack.

"The Wolf was Jewish too?" Annika says. "This is—I don't know what this is. Incredibly messed up is what this is."

I'm shocked—both that the Wolf was ever a boy and that he was Jewish. Never once did he ever say anything even remotely religious. And the clogs and the wolf skin hat! The bag! *Discipline?* I don't know what to think. I refuse to feel bad for him. I refuse to feel anything. Then I think of that coin-op machine in his office, the one with the bag on the river. Was he turning those old machines into scenes from his life?

Annika picks up the other clipping. It's dated August 1, 1986.

LOCAL MAN WANTED BY U.S. ARMY FOR DESERTION
Wolfram Adelstein, a local man who enlisted in the army, has been notated by the U.S. military as a deserter, having gone AWOL after a drug-enforcement action in Bolivia. He has not been seen since. If you have any information related to the whereabouts of Mr. Adelstein, please contact the number below.

"Who is Wolfram *Adelstein?*" Annika asks. "And why does he have my last name? What the hell is going on here?"

"Well, if I deserted the army and came back home," I say, "I'd change my name too."

"But from *mine?* Wait—are we related? You don't think he's…my uncle? My father's *brother?* He told me he was an only child!"

"It would explain why your father seemed to know him so well."

"I don't believe this."

"I wonder why the Wolf deserted the army."

Annika turns back to the laptop, taps it to life, and starts clicking and clacking. She types and reads, then types some more.

"Check this out," she finally says. "Google books. Found a page—"

"What's that?"

"Google books?"

"Google?"

"Oh my god. Never mind. It's a search engine—how you search for…anything on the internet. I'll explain later. I'll explain the entire world later. Point is, some guy wrote a book, a memoir, about his time in the army. A page came up where he mentions being part of a drug enforcement action in Bolivia in 1986. See? It found those exact words, 'drug enforcement action in Bolivia.' Angus Spivak is the author. Brilliant that he has such a unique name."

"Why?"

"Hold on." Annika types more, her fingers a blur. "Perfect," she says a minute later. "He counsels military vets. His website even includes his phone, Skype, and Facetime contacts!"

"I don't understand anything you're saying."

"You'll understand this," Annika says. "Just…stand to the side so he can't see you."

"So who can't see me?"

"On the screen," Annika explains without taking her eyes off the laptop. A man's face appears—an older guy with an unkempt beard and an American flag rag-tied around his head. Angus Spivak, I assume. Annika's face appears in a corner of the screen, which I guess he can see. I grab a silver packet from the table and edge a little further away, enough so I can see Angus without him seeing me. The silver packet is full of dried meat—and it's delicious.

"Angus Spivak here," the man says, looking surprised, I guess, to see a beautiful girl with laser-beam eyes on his screen.

"Hello, Mr. Spivak," Annika says. "My name is Annika Adelstein. I have recently discovered that my uncle, Wolf—"

"The Wolf!" Angus blurts, leaning forward and giving a real up-close personal view of his bulging, bloodshot eyes. "The Wolf is your uncle? You're shitting me! Pardon my French."

"So, you remember him then?" Annika asks. "I came across your book—"

"You and about two other people in the last twenty years!" Angus exclaims. "The Wolf. God*damn*. I think about the guy every once in a—pardon my French."

"It's okay. Do you know why he deserted the army?"

"No one has asked me a thing about the Wolf, not one single solitary thing since the army washed its hands of him. Not once in all these years. And he's your uncle! Holy crap. I figured he was dead. Is he alive?"

"Um, no," Annika says. "He...died recently. We think. I mean, no one ever heard from him again."

"Sorry as shit to hear that," Angus says.

"Do you know why he deserted?" Annika presses.

"Look, I wasn't and still ain't any kind of official shrink, even though I think I'm a hell of lot better than half the— Anyway, by '86, we knew what PTSD was."

I know what that means: Post-traumatic Stress Disorder. *Popular Psychology* magazine.

It seems Annika does too. "Did something bad happen to him there?" she asks. "In Bolivia? Something traumatizing?"

"Damn well did," Angus says. "But that guy was traumatized long before Bolivia."

"What do you mean?"

"Wouldn't talk about his childhood much, but he did tell me that he ran away from a screwed-up situation and wound up with a gang full of knuckleheads. He only joined the army after they tried to kill him, 'cause he was sure they'd try again."

"And what happened to him in Bolivia?" Annika asks.

"We went in to bust a narcotics operation. He was staking out a position and got compromised."

"What does that mean?"

"The bad guys grabbed him. Fortunately, at about the same time, we grabbed one of them."

"And...?"

Angus massages his chin, then says, "Look, I don't want

to destroy your youthful belief that your government and its armed forces are run by, well, infallible individuals."

"Mr. Spivak," Annika says, sounding like a woman of the world, "I have no such illusions about any individuals. You can tell me what happened."

"I don't think it's a good idea," he says. "I'm sorry." He turns and looks over both shoulders, then adds, "Probably bring the spooks down on me for all I know."

"I saw a donation button on your webpage, Mr. Spivak," Annika replies. "What if I made a sizable contribution to your cause?"

Angus considers this. "How sizable?" he asks.

"Watch," Annika tells him.

She clicks the laptop and a different screen appears. It has Angus's picture on it under the title *No BS Counseling for Vets*. His web page, I assume. There's a *Donate Now* box. Annika types $5000 into it. A page labeled "Paypal" materializes, and she clicks a few times before a message pops up: *Payment successful*. Then she clicks back to Angus's living face, waiting in the other screen.

"Will that do?" Annika asks.

Angus clicks a few times, then does a double take. "Holy hell," he says. "You're rich?"

"Yeah," Annika says. "But it's not all it's cracked up to be."

"Nothing is," Angus says. "So, you really want to know what happened in Bolivia."

"Please."

"Well, hell," Angus says. "All right. You know the expression, 'When in Rome do as the Romans do?' Well, there's this South American thing, a torture technique, called *parrilla*. You basically strip the target and strap them onto—we used a bed frame—and hook electrodes up to their...I'll spare you the details. But it's often a highly effective way to make people talk. Our bad guy spilled everything, and as a result, we busted the entire operation. And that's how we rescued the Wolf."

"They did the same thing to Wolfram, didn't they?" Annika says.

"They were lighting him up like a goddamn Christmas tree when we got there," Angus confirms. "But the Wolf didn't tell them shit, pardon my French. The army sent him back to the States to recover, but he disappeared from the hospital the day he got back."

"Wait," Annika says. "After all that, they considered him a *deserter?*"

"That's the army for you. Always grateful for your service. But to tell you the truth, I don't think they looked for him all that hard."

"And that was it. You never heard from him again."

"That's was it. I do have a picture of us two somewhere. Want to see it?"

"Sure, that would be great."

"Hang on."

When Angus leaves the screen, I ask, "How did you send him so much money?"

"I've known my father's Paypal password for years," Annika says. "Can't wait till he sees that donation. Paypal is a way to send money using the computer."

Now I can't get the image of the Wolf being tortured out of my head. I think about his Hotshot and his Bags. What did he think he was doing? Getting revenge on innocent children? "I guess we know why the Wolf hated electricity so much," I mutter.

"I guess so," Annika agrees, with a shiver. "So he snapped, went AWOL, and came back to Reno, to his brother—"

"Who had him change his name and participate in…whatever he was doing with Headquarters."

"Right."

"I think the Wolf didn't approve of whatever happened to Charlie," I say. "And I think he didn't want to have any part in it happening to me. That's why he was drinking when we got close to my Discharge day. That's why he was going crazy on the Sucks and Freaks after you showed up. So you wouldn't change your mind about the donation. He wanted out. I think he wanted out any way he could get—"

Angus returns to the screen with a small picture, faded and creased, which he holds up. It's an image of two soldiers in uniform leaning against a jeep, smoking cigarettes. One is a younger, skinnier version of Angus. The other is a large, hairy man, Wolf-sized, for sure.

But it's not the Wolf. Is it?

His face is different. The cheekbones are much more prominent, and they have no scars. And with no beard, a cleft chin is visible. But…it *is* the Wolf. He has the same empty black eyes.

Annika and I glance at one another, perplexed, then back at the photo. Which gets swept away.

"Time flies," Angus says. "Those were the days. Sorry you never knew your uncle. I never saw anyone love the army like he did, until Bolivia anyway. He may not have enlisted out of a sense of patriotic duty, but he was *all in*, if you know what I mean. He loved getting up at the butt-crack of dawn—pardon my French. He loved the training. He loved the uniforms. He loved the food! The guy loved getting chewed out by superior officers. He loved the—"

"Discipline," Angus and I say together.

"He couldn't get enough of it all," Angus says. "The guy found his place in life, you know? But then they broke him. They broke the poor bastard into a million pieces. Pardon my French."

"Thank you, Mr.—" Annika starts to say.

"Call me Angus, sweetie."

"Thanks, Angus. Unfortunately, I have to go. I appreciate the information."

"Any time, darlin'. Thanks for the donation. You can be sure it'll be put to good use. I'm real glad smart young people like yourself are standing up for White Rights."

Annika flashes me a dismayed look. "But," she says to Angus, "I thought you were helping soldiers with PTSD?"

"I counsel vets who've had their brains scrambled fighting these liberal wars with subhumans," Angus explains. "That's what happened to the Wolf! We advocate for total disengagement with savages. Let them kill each other is our—"

Annika slams a finger on a computer key and Angus disappears. Then she frantically opens a new window and clicks until the Paypal page reappears. She clicks a *Cancel payment* button, and a *Cancellation Confirmed* message comes up.

Annika sits back. "I guess I didn't look closely enough at his book," she says. "Or his website. What a douchebag!"

"He did help us, though," I point out.

"True," Annika admits. "But I don't want help from people like him. That's how my father talks!"

"That was the Wolf," I say. "In the picture."

"Before he had amateur plastic surgery," Annika says, still simmering. "And I think we know who performed it."

"The scars!" I exclaim. "Your father gave the Wolf a new name and a new *face*! Speaking of faces," I say, "that can't be good."

"What?"

I point at the laptop screen. A news alert page has popped open, and Annika's face is on it.

"Oh my god!" Annika cries.

The headline reads:

Deranged Girl Assaults Nanny, Kidnaps Boy with Terminal Disease.

There's no picture of me because, I realize, there *are* no pictures of me. Not one in the world.

Terminal?

My pulse spikes as I read the text below.

This is a developing story: Police are searching for a fifteen-year-old girl, Annika Adelstein, prone to psychotic episodes, suspected of attempting to murder her caretaker and of kidnapping a boy, Felix Law (17), from a local group home. The boy suffers from brittle bone disease and is not expected to survive long outside his group home. If you have any information about the whereabouts of these two individuals, please contact authorities immediately. A one-million-dollar reward has been offered for their safe return.

I don't know what to say, so I say nothing. Doc told me many times I could have a normal lifespan if I took care of myself. Was that not true? Maybe this article is just newspaper sensationalism. But maybe not!

Annika doesn't seem to know what to say either. Or maybe she just doesn't know how to say it. Her face is turning purple. "That *bastard*!" she finally rages. "Don't you see what my father has done? He's obviously behind these lies!"

My blank expression assures her that I don't.

"No one will believe anything I say now, and he's provided a good reason for keeping me locked away at home my entire life! And now he can kill you, too, and everyone will think it's your disease!"

"It will *be* my disease!" I cry. I knew this girl was going to get me killed. Why did I get involved with her? *Why?*

"Notice how the article conveniently doesn't mention that my father owns Wolfgang Law's Home for Good Girls and Boys," Annika says. "We have to find that film, Felix!" She grabs the key off the table. "Let's go," she says, heading for the door.

But she stops dead before she gets there. "Shit!" she cries, looking out the window. "Adolf's here!"

13.

SAFE

Annika wheels round, eyes wide and searching. I turn to search too, but for what?

The shower!

I rush into the tub and Annika is right behind me. Just as the front door opens, she whisks the curtain closed in front of us. We hear heavy footsteps accompanied by heavy breathing.

I realize in horror that we've left the laptop open, the silver food bags strewn across the table, and the burn-bag finds right out in the open. We had time only to hide ourselves!

We hear Adolf moving around, opening and closing drawers and cabinets. We hear the screech of the metal bed frame as he shoves it away from the wall, and the sound of him tossing cartons and containers out of the fridge. He's looking for something.

The film!

Annika and I stand as motionless as we can, trying not to breathe. My legs are shaking, and I'm trying desperately not to fall out of the tub.

"Villy?" says a nasally voice with a thick accent. "Da. Okay. I am okay. Going to hospital vas vaste of time. Zey vere here, Villy. In Volfram's junk house. Ya. Doubled back, clever girl. But gone now. Of course. I vill take care of ze boy. Girl vill not be harmed. And Villy, I think zey know you vere brothers. Ya, no matter now. Any news? Good. You stay focused on stone. I vill take care of zis mess. Vill go to house now and have orphans search for film. Ve are close, Villy. So close."

Moments later we smell something burning. Then we hear the gurgle of water in the sink. Now footsteps. The door opens, then slams shut.

Annika and I stay in the shower for another long moment, frozen and silent, before she flings the curtain aside and steps out of the tub. The remnants of the burn bag are scattered in the sink, soaked. The newspaper clippings are ash. The laptop is gone.

"Well, that could've been worse," Annika says. Before I can ask how, she shows me the key, flashing a sly smile. She had it the whole time.

I'm relieved, yet still panicking. "But Adolf's going to Headquarters!" I cry. "What are we going to do now?"

"We're going to get rid of him," Annika says, as if the solution is obvious.

"How?"

"I say we just go out there and take him down. I did it once, so I can do it again."

"I get the impression," I say, "that you like to attack your problems head on."

"Is there a better way?"

"Yes!" I insist. "You outwit your enemy! You fool him with disguises! You're good at those."

"Felix," Annika says, "all I did was wear a wig and sunglasses to bribe an idiot."

"Well, you do other things then. You sneak around your enemy using hidden passages, you confuse him with clever codes, you set traps! You—!"

"Read too much," Annika says. "Look, Felix. I'm just not good with fancy planning. I mean, I don't know, if someone won't take a bribe—and there's no chance in hell we're bribing Adolf—pretty much your only option is to punch them in the—"

The window by the door suddenly explodes in a shower of glass, and we reflexively crouch low to the floor. My heart is wailing in my chest. Some machine part, a large dial of some kind, rests among the shards of glass on the carpet. Annika crawls to the window and peeks out. I'm halfway hyperventilating.

"Boys," she whispers, "from the home. They're in the

junkyard smashing stuff. Perfect!" she says, then starts squirming out of her dress.

"What are you do—?" I start to ask. But I see that under her dress she's wearing dark red pants and a top, both with a multitude of pockets. Annika tosses the dress aside and slips out the front door.

Hesitantly, I go out behind her. Night is coming on, but I can see her moving fluidly, crouched, through the junk piles like a ninja. I hear the whoops and shouts of the Sucks and the sound of things smashing and crashing. I follow Annika between two rusted bumper cars and around stacks of metal ladders. When we reach a small clearing beyond a pile of broken merry-go-round horses, she stops and shouts, "Hey, losers! Over here!"

Ten seconds later, we're surrounded by eight boys, each with one of the Wolf's Bags strapped across their chests. Corkscrew is one of them, and he's carrying the Hotshot.

"Looky here!" he says. "The Fragile Freak! And, oh no, *what?* No Wolf to protect him? Guess what," he says, "the Big Bad Wolf is dead. Burnt toast! And now we're gonna be rich. Who's the girl? Your mom?"

I look around at the circle of faces as Annika edges closer to me. I've Bagged Out every single one of these boys. Many times. And my reward is the little shits are going to stomp me to death. For real.

"Listen up," Annika says.

"Shut up," Corkscrew says. "You're both coming with us. We're not gonna hurt you," he tells Annika, but then points the Hotshot at me and says, "But China here's a different story. First he gets what's coming to him."

"Adolf sent you to find us, didn't he?" Annika asks. "What did he offer you?"

"We should probably Bag you first," Corkscrew says, walking toward Annika, the Hotshot swinging in her direction. "You probably don't wanna see what's gonna—"

Corkscrew chokes on his words, because the moment he's close enough, Annika kicks the Hotshot right out of his hand.

We all watch it sail through the air before clattering into a pile of junk. Corkscrew is stunned, which is why he misses Annika's fist flying toward his jaw. He drops to the ground like a sack of flour.

Then, with a roar, a stocky boy charges us. Annika, pivoting, punches him square in the nose. Then he's down too, bleeding from both nostrils.

A thrill rushes through me at the sight of the Sucks, their mouths agape. I have to admit that Annika's preferred problem-solving technique is very effective. And quite entertaining.

As the two decked boys stagger back to their feet, Annika says, "What. Did. Adolf. Offer. You?" Like she's talking to idiots. Which she is.

"You mean the bald guy?" the stocky boy says, holding the edge of his shirt to his bloody nose. "He said he'd give us a hundred bucks if we found you two. And let us run away after!"

"I'll make you guys a better deal," Annika says. "The bald guy, is he still in the house?"

The boys nod warily, clearly afraid to make more bad decisions. Annika reaches into one of her pockets and brings out a handful of money. The girl is a walking bank. "I will pay you all *two* hundred bucks each to go back and Bag *him,*" she says. "The guy's not in great shape right now. He had an accident. You can easily jump him."

The Sucks look at each other, unsure.

"Here," Annika says. "Half now and half later." She gives everyone a crisp hundred-dollar bill. They look at it, wide-eyed, and the deal is sealed.

The Sucks shove their money into their trouser pockets and start back toward Headquarters.

"Once they take care of Adolf," Annika says when they're out of sight, "we go search the house for whatever this key goes to. Is there a safe in the house somewhere?"

"There's one in his office closet," I say. "But it's the kind that uses a—" I stop short because I've realized something.

"Uses a what?" Annika asks.

"A combination lock. The thing the Sucks threw through the window back there—it was the same kind of lock. Which means they must've found a—"

"And if there's one!" Annika cries, already running, "there might be more!"

I rush after her, and by the time I get back to the mobile home, she's already scanning the nearby piles of junk.

"Help before it gets too dark!" she calls. But then, "No, wait! You're a genius, Felix!"

I hurry to where Annika is standing, in front of a pile of dented and rusted-out safes. There are probably twenty here, and several have had their combination locks bashed off. But many of them take keys.

"It's totally here," Annika says. "It's got to be." She tries the key in a safe, then another. No luck. Then another, and another.

"Try that one!" I exclaim, spotting a black safe with bronze trim around the door. The combination lock is rusted over, and the whole thing is pretty beaten up. But it's got to be the oldest safe here, and underneath the dial is a keyhole—I almost missed it in the rapidly fading light.

Annika tries the key. "Brilliant!" she cries, swinging open the door. She reaches in and retrieves a round silver disk, about a foot across. *Kodak* is inscribed on one side, and a sticker affixed to the other says, *5/15/78*.

"It's a film cannister," I tell her. Which I know for the usual reason.

Annika opens the disk, and we both grin. A wheel of film is nestled inside.

"How are we going to—?" Annika starts to say, but a series of gunshots, one after another, ring out over the junkyard, silencing her.

Afraid, we both crouch down again.

"They came from the house," Annika says, shoving the cannister into the back of her pants. She seizes a piece of iron pipe from a mound of rubble, and, without hesitation, races through the junk toward Headquarters.

"Annika, wait!" But of course she doesn't. And now I'm

hurrying behind her again. I think it's possible she truly is insane. *She's going to get herself killed!*

I catch up to her at the gas pumps, where she's trying to scope out Headquarters. But it's too dark now to see anything other than the fact that the bounce houses are gone. No doubt the Wolf's body is too.

We hear creaking and see Headquarters front door open. And then we see a light emerge from behind it. It's Adolf, holding a lantern that illuminates his bald head and scowling face.

Annika takes off. Just like that, she's a shadow sprinting silently through the darkness, making a beeline for the porch.

But now I see what's in Adolf's other hand. "Annika!" I cry. "He has a gun!"

Adolf sees her now.

But she keeps running right at him.

"I'll shoot!" Adolf shouts, pointing his gun.

Shrieking like a barbarian, Annika leaps up the porch steps and swings the pipe upside his head.

Adolf goes down like a Hotshocked Suck, his gun clattering to the stones.

The lamp smashes on the porch and goes out.

I stand where I am, stuck in place, my breathing frantic.

"Felix! Come help me!"

I force myself to approach the house and climb the porch steps to where Annika kneels at Adolf's side. She's trying to roll his limp form into a Bag.

"You're crazy, Annika! You could have been—!"

"He's not allowed to hurt me," she says, sounding sane again. Mostly. "Can you get some light? And a rope? He's not dead."

I dart into Headquarters, heading straight for the nearest Suck's bedroom. On the way, something wet on the floor sends my right clog sliding. I have twelve heart attacks, but somehow don't fall. The bedroom is dark, but I grab the lamp from where it hangs on the wall and find a box of matches on a nearby shelf.

I light the lamp with shaking fingers, then hurry out of the room, holding it up.

But then I stop in my tracks, horror-struck at the sight of what I'd slipped in a minute earlier. And now I notice an atrocious metallic smell all around me. I can taste it. All at once I understand the authors I've read who've written of a character's blood freezing in their veins. Because my blood freezes in my veins.

A few minutes later—a lifetime later—I hear Annika say, "Felix? What's going—Oh my god."

Bodies are scattered in and around the edges of the pool of light cast by my lantern on the warped wooden floor. Eight boys lie in a flood of blood. Annika sinks to her knees. "This is my fault," she says, her voice strangled. "This is my fault. This is my fault."

I'm in an alternate universe, but I set the lamp down next to Annika and go into another Suck's room to get a second one. Once it's lit I see more bodies in the bed. Franny and the other little girl, the one who got Bagged and hung from a rafter in the Muster room, lie tucked together under the blanket. Franny's arm hangs out, and I can see the red mark left by an injection in the fold of her elbow. Adolf killed them too. Their bodies are cold to my touch.

I check all the rooms on the first floor. If they aren't empty, there's a dead Suck in the bed.

I wait to check Elsa's and Mila's rooms last.

I stand at Mila's door, afraid to open it.

Please no. Please no. Please no.

Breathe.

One. Two. Three.

My clog, on its own, pushes the door open. My hand holds the lamp up toward the bed, and I glance fearfully across the room. *It's empty.* I exhale.

Elsa's room is empty too, as is Klaus's.

From a Bag Room, I retrieve a box of jump ropes and carry them to Annika.

When she sees me, Annika straightens up. In the flickering light of the lamps, her face looks almost demonic. But the electric-blue intensity of her eyes is undiminished. If anything, they look…nuclear. Silently, she sets about wrapping Adolf in his Bag from ankles to shoulders. His head is free, and I see in the lamplight that blood is streaming from a gash at his temple.

"They're all dead in their beds," I say, quietly. "All the Sucks. He gave them shots."

Annika stands up. She has Adolf's gun and his phone, which she puts in her pockets. White-faced, she looks at me with a fearful question in her eyes.

"I think the Freaks got away," I tell her.

"Thank god!" she exclaims, wiping sweat off her forehead with the back of a shaky hand.

"I hope they took their meds with them," I say. "They won't last long without them."

"But where could they go?" Annika asks. "The wheelchair would make it hard to—"

"I know where they are!" I cry. And now I'm racing down the hall and into the Wolf's office. Elsa's wheelchair sits in front of the desk, empty. In the closet, I set the lantern on the floor and lift the trapdoor. Annika is right behind me. We peer down into the pit and see the faces of three cowering Freaks looking back up at us.

14.

FREAKED OUT

Klaus and Annika carry Elsa up the steps. Silent and ashen, they look traumatized.

Am I traumatized? Maybe the four of us always have been.

"Can I borrow your wheelchair?" Annika asks Elsa.

"Who are you?" the Freaks all ask her.

"This is Annika," I say, while she rolls the chair out of the office. "She lives in the mansion I'm always making up stories about. It's right across the way. She disguised herself as the rich lady who came around to meet us all earlier. Doc is her father," I add, "and whatever's happening, he's responsible for it."

"Doc?" the Freaks all gasp.

"What *is* happening?" Mila pleads. "We heard the Sucks saying the Wolf is dead! And a man, an awful man with a gun—he made us all look for some kind of film. Then we heard shots! That's when we came in here and hid."

"I don't know how to tell you this," I tell them. "But he murdered all the Sucks. He gave lethal injections to most of them, but he shot a bunch of boys who…confronted him."

The Freaks are speechless. They look sick. They look scared.

"Doc killed the Wolf," I tell them, making it worse. "That awful man is his henchman."

"But why…" Mila splutters, "did he…kill him?"

"He electrocuted him for helping me get away," I explain.

"From what?" they all ask.

"Doc kills us—when we get Discharged. The Wolf, I guess, didn't want that to happen."

"He kills us Freaks, you mean," Klaus says softly.

"Apparently so," I tell him. *But Charlie wasn't a Freak—was she? Why was she killed?* "There's a lot we don't know," I say, "but we do know that Doc and the Wolf were brothers. The Wolf had a fake name and a fake face, and he's been hiding out here ever since he deserted the army."

Annika rolls Elsa's wheelchair back into the office with the unconscious form of Adolf slumped in its seat, wrapped tightly in his Bag with jump ropes. Two bottles of hydrogen peroxide from the Infirmary Closet rest in his lap.

Annika rolls Adolf to the closet and Klaus helps her maneuver him down into the Brig. She's about to close the trapdoor on him when I say, "Wait! Are we going to let him die down there?"

Annika ponders the question, then says, "I guess not. I'll go back down and loosen the ropes."

While she does that, I discover more silver food packets in the fourth drawer of the Wolf's desk. When Annika comes back up, she dumps the drawer load into the Brig, then tosses down one of the peroxide bottles. "For his wounds," she says. The other bottle of peroxide she slips into yet another long pocket in her pants leg. Then she takes Adolf's gun out of her pocket, ejects the clip, and tosses it down too. Finally, she kicks the trapdoor closed with her sneaker and says, "We need something heavy."

"How about this?" I ask, pulling aside the bags and coats to reveal the black safe in the back of the closet.

Annika and Klaus shove the safe onto the trap door.

"I think we'll be safe tonight," Annika says when they're done. "Earlier," she says, "when Felix was checking the rooms—I texted my dad with Adolf's phone. I told him I found the film and everything was under control. But I said I'd need time to clean up here, and I'd meet him back at the mansion in the morning. I also said there was no sign of Felix or Annika at Headquarters, so they must still be on the run. My dad texted back a few minutes later that cops were watching the airport and the bus and train stations, and that he was confident they would pick us up soon. He said that Adolf shouldn't bother him any more tonight because he *needs to get the kinks worked out in his latest formula before the stone arrives.*"

"What formula?" I ask. "What stone?"

"We'll find out soon enough."

"Why is this happening?" Mila asks, her eyes brimming with tears.

Annika shows everyone the film cannister. "This might give us some answers," she says. "Does the Wolf have an old film projector lying around somewhere? I mean, he needed one to watch that film."

"No," I tell her. "I know the contents of every Bag Room top to bottom. If there were a projector here, I'd know. Maybe the Wolf didn't want one around in case anyone found the film. But we might find one in the junkyard," I add, "although it would probably be broken."

"Well, let's go back to the mobile home and come up with a plan," Annika says. "I can't stay in the house one second longer. It's not a house anymore, it's a…"

"Mausoleum," I say.

"Exactly."

"Where can we go?" the Freaks ask, again all at once.

"The Wolf has a summer home," I tell them, "in the junk-yard."

We get Mila back into her chair and settle Elsa on her lap. Then I push them out of the office into the hallway. Annika follows us with the lantern. Klaus follows her, bobbing up and down like a human piston.

"Freaks," I say when we near the front door, "close your eyes."

No one asks why. They just do it. But from their sickened expressions, I know they can smell the blood.

Annika takes Klaus's hand to guide him, and we maneuver everyone around the massacre. Once we're outside, I say, "Okay, you can open your eyes now." I take the lamp so Klaus and Annika can lift Elsa's chair down the steps.

We roll her over the dead lawn to the pumps.

Once there, the Freaks all peer skeptically down the alley at mounds of debris now lit to silver by the moon. "Oh boy," Mila says with sarcastic cheerfulness, "this reminds me of *The Misfits' Adventures in Junkland.* That's the new title for your book, Felix, and I want ten percent. The best part of the story is when the junk monsters rip us to ribbons. I just hope they got the size right for my Old Tango Uniform!"

"Monsters do want to kill you around here," I tell her as we make our way into the labyrinth by lantern light. "But they're not made of junk."

"If Klaus hadn't…gotten Bagged and…Dragged," Elsa says, "we'd…be dead…right now. How's that for…funny?"

"Hilarious," Mila says. "Pure comedy gold."

"You're welcome," Klaus says.

At the mobile home, we haul the wheelchair through the door and collapse around the kitchen table.

"So what's the plan now?" Mila asks.

Everyone looks at me and Annika. We look at each other.

"Maybe in the morning we can search the junkyard?" I suggest. "Maybe if we find a projector, we could fix it?"

No one thinks that's a good plan.

"We could buy a projector that works," Klaus says.

Annika's eyes light up. "Genius!" she cries.

"Do they even sell them anymore?" I ask.

"My father does," Annika says. "His flagship pawnshop is downtown, in the Reno Casino. If it's old and electric, they have it! And if they don't, they'll know who does. We'll take a bus there first thing in the morning."

"We?" I say. She can't possibly mean me. My palms go clammy at the thought of going to Reno—at the thought of leaving Headquarters entirely. Sweat beads on my forehead. I wipe it off with the back of my hand.

"Felix," Annika says, "you're coming with me. I won't take no for an answer. I need you. Please! Look," she adds, "I know you think I'm fierce, right? Well, the truth is, I'm not. I'm scared as hell, just like all of you. I'm just a good actress. I've never had a friend," she admits. "Not a single, solitary friend. In my *entire life*. At least you all have each other. But you were just as trapped as I ever was. Worse. I feel responsible for you now. I could have grown up with you! And it looks like it's my father who ruined your lives! And—!"

"Why don't we just call the police?" I say, hoping to derail this entire insane idea. "How's your father going to explain a house full of dead kids?"

"With money, Felix. With cold hard cash. If we call the cops, maybe Adolf will go to jail—I'm sure he would—but I promise you my father would not. And you and me and the Freaks? We'll all wind up in an institution, and I suspect none of us will be alive there long."

"So what can we do?"

"I'll text my father from Adolf again," Annika says. "In the morning, when we're on a bus to Reno. I'll tell him Adolf is in the Brig, and he'll rush right over there to get him out. Then they'll have to dispose of the bodies and cover their tracks—which will buy Felix and me lots of time. The rest of you should watch for my dad's car to get to Headquarters, then go straight to my house. Take food packets and lock yourselves in the tower. There are no maids or butlers working tomorrow. The place will be empty, and my father will never think to look for you in his own house."

"I should go with them," I say. "I don't see how I can be of any help to you in—"

"Felix," Annika says, exasperated, "do you really want to put your life—*all* your lives—entirely in my hands?"

Yes, I want to say. *One hundred percent, yes.* Instead I say, "I don't want to put our lives in mine, that's for sure." Which is also one hundred percent true. "How can I possibly help? I can't run fast, or really run at all. I can't fight or defend myself. I will literally be in pieces on the ground at the first hint of violence!"

"You can help by being a second set of eyes and ears!" Annika insists. "By watching my back. By causing distractions if we need one. By coming up with better plans than punching people in the face!"

"I honestly think you'd be much better off without me," I say. "I'm a liability, Annika. It's just that simple."

"Look, Felix," Annika says, "I don't *want* to do this alone. I'll tell you what, when this is all over, and my father actually is rotting in prison for the rest of his miserable life, *I* am going to own the mansion. And you all are more than welcome to move in."

"Wow!" Elsa says. "Thank...you so...much."

"Okay, okay!" I say, defeated. I'm no match for Annika Adelstein's bribes. "I'll do it." I may be useless, but if I'm going to be murdered, it won't be sitting in another tower staring out a window at life passing me by.

Annika flashes a wide, beautiful smile. "Thank you, Felix," she says.

"I'm going to sleep," I tell her.

"Let's all sleep," Annika says. "It's going to be a big day tomorrow."

After we get the mattress back in place, Klaus and I tuck Mila and Elsa under blankets, then I give Mila her shot. Luckily, because she's paranoid, she puts a few full syringes into a little pouch tied to the arm of her chair every morning.

Klaus, Annika, and I find sleeping bags in the closet and we spread them out across the floor. When Annika extinguishes the lantern, I slide down into the bag and fold the top over my head. I welcome the darkness inside—it's the closest thing I know to a safe harbor. But I can't fall asleep.

I try to clear my mind, but I can't help seeing those eight boys lying in pools of blood, and again and again, the Wolf's fried body falling from the sky.

Next to me, Annika reaches out to take my hand. She seems to be having trouble sleeping too. "It's all going to work out okay," she whispers. "I just know it."

No one has ever held my hand before. I don't care if every one of my fingers breaks.

Hand in hand, we both fall fast asleep.

15.

DISCHARGE DAY

I'm in a Bag, up to my shoulders, but it's wrapped tightly with a jump rope that's also an extension cord. I'm swinging from a rafter in the Muster Room over a bare metal bed frame. The Wolf is lying on the frame, burned to the bone. Electrodes are hooked up all over his wasted body, but he's not tied down. Adolf is there too, with his head bleeding openly, his nose mashed in. He throws a switch on the wall and the Wolf's body begins to spasm. Laughing gleefully with every convulsion, he reaches for the end of my jump rope–extension cord and stabs it into his eye socket. The shock travels up to me, and my body seizes with every jolt. Then I see the Sucks standing around the bed, all holding long-needled syringes. They draw close, then stab my quivering Bag. They stab it over and over and over again. Screaming, I look up to see a giant face peering down at me from behind a pane of glass. It's Doc, turning a crank. We're all inside a coin-op machine, and he's the one making us move.

"Felix, are you…okay? Felix, wake up!"

I open my eyes, my heart pounding, my body, in the sleeping bag, drenched in sweat.

"You were calling out in your sleep," Mila says.

"Calling out for what?" I ask, still not fully awake.

"Your mom and dad," Klaus says. He looks embarrassed for me.

"Just a stupid dream," I mutter. "It's nothing." But I'm disquieted by the feeling that none of us is in control of anything happening to us. It seems we've been nothing but cogs in someone else's machine all our lives. The Wolf never got out of his box. And I don't think we'll get out of ours either.

"What do you think?" Annika says.

When I see her, I'm shocked. Her hair is short, all choppy

and short. And blonde. Elsa grins triumphantly, brandishing a pair of scissors. I see the bottle of peroxide on the desk.

"That looks…good," I say. Other than those electric-blue eyes, she's almost unrecognizable.

"I guess I'm ready for my…Promotion," Elsa says. "Long as nobody minds…an hour-long…haircut."

"Sorry you had a nightmare," Annika tells me. "Are you okay now?"

"I'm great," I reply, forcing myself to sound upbeat. "It's Discharge day, and I'm Promoting myself."

"Damn right you are," Annika says, flashing a gleaming smile.

I get up and approach the Wolf's sink, where I splash cold water on my face. I stare at myself in the cracked mirror hanging on the wall and realize that I can't remember the last time I looked at myself closely. I watch water drip from the black curlicue of hair sticking to my forehead down to my too-big chin. I turn back to Annika and ask, "Should I dye my hair too?"

"I don't that'll be necessary," Annika says. "But you are going to need some kind of disguise. They're looking for a girl with braided auburn hair and a boy who walks around dressed like a mattress."

The Freaks howl with laughter at this. I scowl at them. "No way," I tell Annika. "Not happening. I'm not going without my pads."

"Felix, if anyone even looks at you funny," Annika promises, "I assure you, faces will be punched."

"I won't last fifteen minutes," I say. "What's the point of saving my life just to get me killed?"

Annika looks at me, waiting, and I know better than to waste any more of our time fighting another battle I'm going to lose. For better or worse, this cog is leaving his machine.

One by one I unstrap my pads until they're lying on the floor like pieces of a discarded turtle's shell. I feel vulnerable, as if the slightest breeze could break me into a million pieces. I already regret this decision.

"It's going to be okay," Annika says, then stops short at a low roaring sound that I recognize as the engine of her father's car.

"Oh, shit!" Annika cries, fumbling Adolf's phone out of a pocket. She looks at it, aghast. "My father's been texting all morning! I put it on silent so we could sleep!" She drops the phone and crushes it with her heel.

"What…are we waiting…for?" Elsa says. "Let's…go!"

"Wait!" I cry. I grab a duffel bag from the closet and stuff every silver packet of military rations inside, along with my pads so no one finds them here and realizes I'm walking around without them. And because I might need them. Because I *will* need them.

I reach to take the Wolf's laptop, but Annika says, "Leave it. They can track those too." Then she says, "Let's not panic, guys. The plan is going to work."

Outside, we settle Elsa onto Mila's lap. Then, with Annika and Klaus walking ahead of us, I push the wheelchair through the junk all the way back to the gas pumps. Once there, we can see Doc's Ferrari sitting in front of the porch at a crazy angle with the driver's door still open. He's in the house, so we move swiftly to the hedge arch. But once under it, I can't help stopping to glance back at Headquarters, for, I hope, the last time.

"The weary travelers will miss their beloved ancestral home," Mila tells me. "Now, move your brittle ass." Despite myself, I smile.

I push the wheelchair through the hedge, onto the sidewalk, then across the street, where we all stop. The Freaks now see, for the first time, the fairy-tale mansion resting peacefully on the rise ahead of us, its tiled roof gleaming in the morning sun. They are speechless.

"Don't worry. Annika and me, we're gonna figure all this out," I tell the Freaks. "And then we're all gonna live up there. Happily ever after." Of course, I don't believe this one bit, but they need to hear it. And so do I.

"We will," Annika agrees. "We totally will."

"And afterward," I add, "I'm going to find all our parents."

The Freaks' wide eyes turn to me now. They won't look at each other, but they all nod.

But then Klaus suddenly screams, "WE HAVE TO GO BACK!"

The Freaks and I are amazed. He's never spoken that loudly before. But I realize why right away. "Oh, no," I say. "Your cream."

He shows me the tube, rolled up. Empty.

My heart sinks in my chest. "Mila?" I ask.

She shows me two full syringes from her pouch. "They should be okay for a day or so without refrigeration," she says.

I look at Elsa.

"I always keep two extra pills on me," she says. "So I'm good."

"We can't go back," Annika warns. "Not if we want to live."

"How long will that bit of cream last?" I ask Klaus.

"Maybe a day or two," he says, trying to stay calm. "At the most."

I'm trying to stay calm too, but failing. "Then we have less than two days to—fix everything!" I cry.

"We can do this," Annika assures us all, fixing each of us in turn with her electric eyes. "I promise. On my life."

I wish I had one hundredth of Annika Adelstein's confidence.

"You all usually take your meds at night, right?" I say to the Freaks. "Except you, Klaus, I know. So wait as long as you possibly can before you take them tonight. Same with tomorrow night. Maybe we can stretch the time a bit."

"We. Got. This," Annika promises. "Felix and I. We swear. But you have to get to the tower now." Annika pushes the wheelchair toward the gravel path that leads up to the front door of the mansion. She fishes her key out of one of her pockets and hands it to Elsa. I pass the duffel to Mila. "Once you're inside," Annika says, "turn left until you come to the elevator doors. Go to the very top floor, and be sure to send the elevator back down once you arrive. Got it?"

Klaus, Mila, and Elsa nod, clearly frightened but also clearly determined. With a last wave, Klaus pushes the wheelchair up the path.

Annika and I hurry back across the street to the bus stop and sit on the bench under its glass canopy.

"What if your father—" I start to say.

"You're right," Annika replies. "It's back into the hedge for us."

And so we climb back into it. This time we mash branches aside so we can see through the front of the hedge far enough down the street to spot a bus coming. We make sure we can see Headquarters well enough through the back of it too.

"Do you really have an elevator in your house?" I ask when we're comfortable enough.

"What can I say," Annika replies, peering through leaves at the traffic going by in front of us. "I'm a lucky, lucky girl."

I can find nothing to say to this, so I peer through the leaves next to her. Without my pads, I feel totally vulnerable. I'm waiting for that breeze the Wolf told me about, the one that will Discharge me forever. After watching cars whiz by for a while, I begin to fret. "How much time do you think we have?" I ask. "What if the bus doesn't come?"

"It's coming," Annika insists.

At that moment, there's a terrific *crack!* behind us. We both twist round to see a bright flash, like lightning, striking Headquarters. Except this is no ordinary lightning. It emerges from the ground and rises up to envelop the house in crackling blue electricity. Seconds later, Headquarters erupts in flames that send dark plumes of smoke billowing into the bright morning sky.

"He's burning it down to destroy the film!" Annika cries. "And to burn the bodies!"

"Bus!" I wail.

Annika sees it coming and crashes out of the hedge, waving frantically until it stops for her. I'm out on the sidewalk now too.

The doors open with a clank. Above the idling of the bus engine, we hear the roar of Doc's engine.

Annika leaps up into the bus, and I move cautiously up the steps behind her.

The door closes behind us, but the bus has to wait to pull away because a bright red Ferrari bursts out onto the street in front of us, tires screeching. I catch a glimpse of Doc's grim face in the front seat with Adolf sitting beside him, holding a cloth to his still-bleeding head.

PART II

THE SHIT SHOW

16.

BATTLE BORN

Annika pays and I find seats about halfway back. I hear the driver reporting the fire at Headquarters over his radio as we pull out.

The moment Annika sits down beside me, I can't help myself. "What if Doc's going to your house?" I cry. "What if the Freaks didn't have enough time to—?"

"They did," Annika promises. "Besides, he wasn't going toward the house."

"My pads!" I realize. "I left them in the duffel!"

"Don't worry!" Annika hisses.

"Don't worry?"

"Shhhh! If my father does decide to go home, he'll park in the garage. Then he'll go right down to his little Bat Cave to do…whatever evil shit he does down there."

"Bat Cave?"

"Never mind."

I'm on a bus for the first time, so I decide to forget our impending doom and enjoy the ride. Neighborhood streets and tidy little houses with white picket fences roll by. We pass through an industrial area with factories, warehouses, and lots of cars and trucks. The bus stops periodically, and people get on and off. Far off, against the sky, I can see the rising peaks of mountains, bright against the blue sky. It's not a picture torn from a magazine. The mountains are real, and they are so beautiful that I have to hold back tears. And outrage that this has been denied me my entire life.

But wait, where I *really* live—Headquarters—it's burning down! My heart starts to race again and my palms slick over with sweat. *But haven't I always wished for this? To see Headquarters reduced to ash and rubble? Then why the hell am I suddenly panicking about it?*

I realize now that having a lousy place to live is a lot better than having no place to live. Before I start to hyperventilate, I notice we've arrived in what must be downtown Reno, with buildings both historic and new standing shoulder to shoulder. Crowds of people stride down the sidewalk and linger at the lights. They sit at outdoor cafes and walk their dogs. Everyone is rushing to and fro—people of all sizes, shapes, and ages!

I see couples walking hand in hand, and I think of Annika taking mine last night, and how it soothed my fears, and maybe made her feel better too. Drops of sweat bead on my forehead at the thought of holding her hand again. I zone out thinking about when it might happen.

"How long's this gonna take?" someone shouts from the seat behind us.

I snap out of my daze to find that the bus has stopped to allow a parade to pass by. The street outside is filled with people dressed in colorful costumes, riding on top of wheeled platforms decorated with brightly painted scenes. A massive arch of balloons arranged in rainbow colors stretches over us from sidewalk to sidewalk. A marching band goes by with its brass instruments gleaming in the sun. It's followed by troupes of acrobats, cheerleaders, and dancers. People on the sidewalks are waving rainbow flags.

"What's going on?" I ask.

"The Pride Parade," Annika says.

"The what?"

"Burn in hell, sinners!" the same person shouts from behind me. I turn to see a burly, red-faced man in a checkered shirt. "Someone ought to lock them freaks up and throw away the key!" he bellows.

Annika swivels around in her seat, glaring at him. "Why don't you take your medieval thinking," she says, "and shove it up your ass."

Checkered Shirt lumbers to his feet, his gut protruding well out past his belt, and says, slowly, "You want to say that again, little missy?"

"Because you're as deaf as you are dumb?" Annika asks.

"Settle down!" the driver yells back to us.

"Annika," I hiss out of the side of my mouth. "This is *not* a good idea!"

"Wait, I know you," Checkered Shirt tells Annika, smirking. "I remember them eyes. From the TV, maybe. All weird looking."

Uh-oh.

Before the guy can say anything further, all the other passengers start flat-out screaming. And now everyone is suddenly rushing toward the exit all at once, jostling against one another to get out. Outside, I can see that the parade has broken apart. People are running in all directions.

Then I see why—a truck is plowing through the crowd in the middle of the street, knocking pedestrians aside like bowling pins! In shock, I watch it vanish around a corner.

"Everyone off!" the driver yells, opening the doors to allow the press of frantic passengers to get out.

Annika and I wait until the bus empties, then we get off too. I hear sirens sounding in the distance, and then Checkered Shirt accosts us again.

"Hey, you!" he yells, striving to get to us through the fleeing crowd. "Ain't there a reward for you or something?"

"Let's go, Felix," Annika says, weaving around people, finding a path in the crush for us to follow.

Everyone is running, it seems, in every possible direction, and my stress is sky high. Someone is going to collide with me, and then, well, it's game over. But swallowing my fear, I follow Annika as she navigates the sidewalk.

A few minutes later, we're out of the mayhem and standing alone on a street lined with rundown hotels flashing vacancy signs above barred windows.

"What happened back there?" I ask, trying to calm down. "What was the parade for? Why would someone—?"

Annika looks shaken again. Furious, sad, and shaken. "It's

the Gay Pride Parade," she says. "Those people who got hit might have been killed!"

"But—why would—?"

"Because a lot of people are still Neanderthals!"

I still don't understand, but it's not something I have time to process at the moment. "What are we going to do now?" I ask.

"What we came to do," Annika, says, pointing at a building across the street. It's got a huge sign on it shaped like a fanned-out deck of playing cards. Flashing neon letters on the sign spell out RENO CASINO.

Annika strides across the street and I hurry in her wake. We enter the casino through the main entrance, where I stop short, entranced by the flashing lights, the spraying fountains, and the glitzy storefronts. People yell and laugh, and I hear the slap of cards on the table, and the whirring of slot machines as desperate-looking players pull the handles. It's as if an entire city exists within the walls of this one building. I stand, gawking at it all, almost unable to take it in.

"Good god, this is tacky," Annika says. "C'mon, Felix, follow me." She marches me into a nearby shop and tells an employee inside to "Get this guy some cool clothes, and some normal running shoes. Take everything he's wearing and burn it."

Before I know it, we're leaving the store, only now I'm proudly wearing my first pair of jeans, an incredibly soft black T-shirt, and shoes that must be made out of clouds. Three hundred and fifty bucks! The clerk dropped my clogs in a trashcan, which was fine with me.

From there we visit a hair salon, and before long my mop of dirty black hair is blond—and neatly trimmed! The curlicue is gone. I don't recognize myself.

From the hair salon, we wind our way through a maze of halls designed to look like outside streets hosting a fair. Soon enough, we arrive at a large shop with a long, weathered wooden sign over the entrance: *Battle Born Pawn: Since 1955.*

"What's the plan if they don't have a projector?" I ask before Annika opens the door.

"Bribes and threats, naturally," she says with a shrug.

"But what if someone recognizes you again?"

"Then faces will have to be punched. Obviously."

And with that, Annika steps into the store.

Inside, there's a dizzying amount of goods on display—cases of coins, glittering displays of jewelry, gleaming watches, stacks of electronics, guns of all sizes, battered musical instruments, old tools—I think of the Wolf's Bag Rooms and decide this is where all the good stuff came instead. The pawnshop is packed with people, some browsing the shelves, others haggling with sellers stationed behind glass countertops.

We pass a man trying to sell an old painting, and a kid showing off a baseball in a round plastic case. Section after section is packed with old electrical devices and gadgets, even a few coin-op machines. But I don't see a projector anywhere.

Annika approaches a counter in the back of the shop where a skinny man with small round glasses is polishing geodes. "Excuse me," she says. "We're looking for an antique film projector."

"Bummer," the guy says. "We have a collector for those— guy in Tahoe—so they hardly ever make it to the floor."

"You just ship them right to him?" Annika asks.

"Right."

"Any chance there's one waiting to ship now? We'd love just to see it."

"We're old-school cinephiles," I tell the guy.

"Yeah?" the guy says, looking a little bit impressed. Annika, I am pleased to see, looks very impressed. "Well," the guy says, "that'd be the manager's call. I'm just an assistant around here."

"May we please speak with the manager?" Annika tries.

"He's a very busy dude, manages all the shops. Doesn't have time for—"

"We should probably tell him the truth," I say to Annika.

"What?" she says, alarmed.

"Sir," I say. "We'd like to talk to the manager. We have information for his ears only."

"Uh-huh," the assistant says, amused now. "Do tell."

"It has to do with the Holy Grail." I say this as solemnly as I can.

The assistant bursts out laughing. Annika looks at me again, not as if I'm crazy, but as if she's trying to figure out what the hell I'm doing and how she should best play along.

"The *stone*," I say.

The assistant abruptly stops laughing. He glances quickly around before settling a serious gaze back on me. "What stone?" he asks. Testing me.

There's only one stone I know of that anyone would refer to as his Holy Grail. I lean forward and whisper, "The Philosopher's Stone."

The assistant stares me down for a moment, narrowing his eyes. Then he raises a finger, telling us to wait, and picks up a phone behind the counter. While he talks quietly into the receiver, Annika mutters, without changing her expression even slightly, "Friggin' genius. This is why you're here, Felix."

Which makes me full-on blush.

Finally, the assistant gets off the phone. "I told him for sure you two are pulling some kind of stunt, but he wants to talk to you anyway. Follow me."

17.

5/15/78

The assistant leads us through a door behind the counter, which opens into a long hallway. We pass a number of closed doors until we reach a waiting room at the end, with couches situated beside lush indoor ferns. A redheaded secretary sits behind a polished desk, guarding a tall wooden door.

"Wait here," the assistant says, then returns down the hallway to the pawnshop.

"Mr. Royce will see you now," the secretary tells us before we sit down. "Go right in. And don't touch anything."

The office is decorated with dark leather chairs and an imposing desk that has a computer and six small monitors on it. The monitors, I see, show different views of the shop. Glass shelving units line two of the walls, and it's obvious that the various artifacts on them—statuettes, stone sculptures, jewelry made of gold and silver and all kinds of beads—are what we're meant not to touch. There's a miniature museum in here. The man sitting at the desk—Mr. Royce, I assume—wears a neatly pressed suit. He's the bodybuilder type, and his meaty biceps bulge through his shirt and jacket. He presses a button on his desk as we approach, and the door swings shut behind us. And locks. Annika and I both turn, alarmed, at the sound of the click.

"Is this a joke?" Royce asks. "Some sort of prank?"

"I can explain everything," I say.

"What do you know about the stone?" he demands, up and striding around the desk with nostrils flaring. "How did you know I was looking for it?"

Annika and I both take an involuntary step back. Royce grabs my arm, and Annika cries, "Don't! You'll hurt him!"

Royce lets go.

I hold my arm where he squeezed, probing the bones to see if they're broken. I'm about to hyperventilate.

"Wait a minute," Royce says. "You're *them*." To Annika, he says, "You're Adelstein's daughter!" Calm now, he returns to his desk and sinks back into his seat looking thoughtful. "Fortunately for you," he says, "I'm one of quite a few people who know that Willy Adelstein would never pay out a million-dollar reward. Not in a million years."

"You mean," Annika says, amazed, "you know he's—?"

"A lying, backstabbing, two-faced piece of crap? Yes."

Annika and I smile at each other. When we look back at Royce, he says to Annika, "You don't look like a mental patient."

"My father's the psycho," she tells him.

"And I'm guessing you didn't kidnap Bone Boy over here."

"Of course not," I assure him.

"Well, this is all very interesting," Royce says, leaning back, hands clasped casually behind his head. "So what the hell is going on then?"

"We're trying to learn some things about my father's business. We want to—"

"Destroy his livelihood?"

"More than that," Annika says. "Much more."

Royce says, "Must have been a hell of a dad. How can I help?"

"I guess you could start by telling us what this stone is all about," Annika says.

"There was a spectacular gem that came up for sale on the black market in Europe," Royce explains. "The Philosopher's Stone, supposedly. I was in charge of obtaining it at all costs."

"What's the Philosopher's Stone?" Annika asks.

"It can be used to change metal into gold," I say.

Annika scoffs. "Who would sell that?"

"Well, of course, it doesn't actually work," Royce continues, "but the seller has convincing proof that it was at least believed to be the actual Philosopher's Stone in medieval times, which makes it very, very valuable as a historic artifact."

"Are you some kind of treasure hunter?" Annika asks.

"I have a background in archeology, yes," Royce replies.

"And you bought this magical dud of a rock for my dad?"

"For the paltry price of twelve million dollars."

"So, what, you wish you hadn't bought it?"

"If I hadn't bought it, your father would have fired me," Royce replies. "But once it's in his greedy little hands? I'll be fired anyway."

"Why?" Annika asks.

"To be honest, it's evil-genius-level stuff. Your father hires people to complete small parts of his various projects so that none of them sees the big picture. Then he gets rid of them, claiming they screwed something up. Then he coerces them into forfeiting due payment in exchange for not destroying their reputations. See, anyone who works for him signs a nondisclosure agreement as a condition of employment. So after they leave in a rage, they can't say anything bad about him unless they want to cough up a million-dollar penalty. Sadly, I didn't know his history before I took the job running these shops and chasing down his prizes. Anyway, the rumor mill has it that this stone is his crown jewel, his very last buy, and after he gets it, he plans on selling the pawnshop business and retiring. I'd like him to sell it to me. Treasure hunting, as you call it, is a boom-or-bust type of deal. A successful chain of pawnshops is perfect for keeping money in the coffers because people will never stop being broke, and sometimes idiots walk right in with priceless artifacts and sell them to you for a song. So, what do you know about all this?"

"Nothing really," Annika says, "but we do have this." Like a magician, she whisks the film cannister out from behind her back. "And we know my father is very afraid of what's on it getting out."

"Interesting," Royce says. "Let's see what we can see then, shall we?" He picks up his phone and speaks to his secretary, and a few moments later she wheels in a contraption that looks like a giant ant standing on two legs holding a box.

After the door clicks shut behind her, Royce plugs in the

machine and opens the box to reveal a number of complex-looking gears. Annika hands him the film and sets the empty cannister on the desk.

Royce threads the film through the various slots and wheels in the box, then flips a power switch. The projector hums to life as the film moves through its guts. A black-and-white image of a basement workshop appears on the office wall opposite. We're looking at a long metal worktable littered with miscellaneous mechanical parts, as well as an array of gauges and monitors. A jumble of variously colored wires connect the parts to each other and to what looks like a powerful generator.

A large Nazi flag hangs on the wall behind the worktable, and a hefty machine that looks like an old-fashioned hand-crank printing press stands next to it.

"What the hell?" Annika says.

A man dressed in olive-colored overalls moves in front of the camera and takes a seat at the worktable. He looks like Doc, with pale skin and raven-black hair threaded through with gray. His face is very severe, more severe than Doc's. Over his heart is a patch stitched with the name Gerhard.

"Could that be your grandfather?" I ask Annika.

"Oh my god," Annika gasps.

"Didn't you say your family, or Doc, anyway, is Jewish? And that all of his family got killed in the—?"

"My father lied about his brother, so why not about his parents too? Why not about being Jewish?! I don't understand," Annika mutters, totally bewildered.

A young man steps into the scene holding a small chalkboard. And it's clearly Doc—Willy Adelstein—Annika's father. He can't be more than eighteen, but he already wears his sideburns long. The chalkboard has a date written on it: 5/15/78.

"He's so young!" Annika cries. "But…in 1978…he shouldn't be—hold on, can we pause this thing?"

Royce pauses the projector.

"My father says he's seventy-four," Annika tells him. "Can that be true?"

"If your father is seventy-four," Royce tells her, "I'm a

fairy-tale princess. He tells people that because it makes him seem unnaturally vital, like he has secrets to life and living that you aren't privy to. It's just another of his intimidation and one-upmanship tactics. And a way to sell quack 'life-extending' electrotherapy machines to morons."

"So how old do you think he really is?" I ask.

"Sixty, tops," Royce says.

Annika narrows her eyes, gazing thoughtfully at the basement scene frozen on the wall. I know what she's thinking. Or not thinking. She's not *wondering* anymore whether everything her father ever told her was a lie. She *knows.*

"In that case," I say, "he wasn't the original owner of Battle Born Pawn in 1955."

"Maybe he cheated someone out of it?" Annika wonders out loud.

We look at Royce, who says, "Transfer of ownership information is available, but it would take some digging. It's probably on microfiche down at the Secretary of State's office in Carson."

"What do you think the chances are of us finding something incriminating down there?" Annika asks.

"All I can say," Royce says, "is once a shyster, always a shyster. Although, if that's old Willy in this movie, I don't think he's Jewish after all."

"What?" Annika snaps, her hands balled into fists. Though I'm not sure why.

"What are you worried about? Royce asks, unperturbed. "You're adopted, right? It's not in your blood. Although, who knows where they dug you up."

"You anti-Semitic piece of shit!"

"I like you," Royce says, chuckling. "You have spunk. But if you're done defending the Jews, can we get back to Nazi Santa's Workshop and ruining your father's life?"

Annika nods, but her eyes are boiling. Royce starts the projector again.

Under the 5/15/78 date, the chalkboard reads, *Baghdad Battery test.*

Young Willy Adelstein steps away from the camera. Gerhard

moves a clay pot with a rusty cylinder in it to the center of the table. He unscrews the lid from a glass jar and, after putting on a pair of yellow rubber gloves, uses two fingers to remove a dollop of gunk from it, which he proceeds to smear all over the pot and cylinder. He places the clay pot into a white porcelain container, about the size of a milk crate, with dials on the lid, a lever attached to its side, and a single plastic tube protruding from below the lever. Gerhard sets a glass box filled with fluid next to the porcelain container and connects the tube to a stopper in the lid of the glass box. He looks briefly into the camera, nods, then moves the lever on the side of the porcelain box.

The box glows, for just a moment, as a spark lights it up from inside. The dials on the lid react wildly, the needles and gauges move erratically. Examining them, Gerhard jots some notes on a clipboard, then checks another gauge on the side of the glass box and jots more notes. He looks up and nods.

Royce seems fascinated.

After a quick break in the film, the scene returns. Willy stands before the camera with his chalkboard again. This time it reads, *5/15/78: Viking Axe.* After he steps away, Gerhard repeats the same routine. Only this time, he places an old stone axe into the porcelain container, coats it with the same gunk from the jar, seals the lid, then connects the tubing to the glass box. When he moves the lever this time, there is no spark, and the gauges and dials are motionless. Once again he writes on the clipboard, then nods before the film blips.

Willy appears with his chalkboard yet again: *5/15/78: Endromis.*

Before I can ask what *endromis* means, Gerhard puts a pair of old leather strap-up boots into the container. As he's smearing them with gunk, a robust woman wearing an old-fashioned nightgown, her gray hair in tight curlers, enters the scene. She carries a dish piled high with little brown balls.

"Sauerkraut ham balls," Annika gasps. "My father eats those all the time. Could that be my...*grandmother?*"

"But not your real grandmother," I point out.

"I know I was adopted!" Annika cries. "But I have no one else!"

"But, Annika," I say, "if your father lied to you about everything else, maybe your real parents didn't really die in a car crash."

This hits hard. Annika's head literally snaps back, like she's been punched in the face. But before she can speak, the woman in curlers sets the dish of ham balls on the table just as Gerhard lowers the lever again.

Just then, a blinding flash of light makes us all turn away from the wall. When we look back to the film, we see only a smoldering mass of metal. The worktable and all the machines behind it have been literally melted. There's no sign of Gerhard or the woman bearing the sauerkraut ham balls.

Willy steps into view, his expression impassive, maybe slightly curious. He does not seem at all bothered by what just happened. But then we hear a voice cry out, "Mom! Dad!" And then a large, stocky boy, about ten years old, runs on camera past Willy. He drops to his knees in front of the smoking remains of the work area.

"The Wolf!" I cry.

"No! No! No!" the boy shrieks as tears stream down his cheeks. He's clutching at something on the floor, something none of us noticed until now: two piles of ash. His parents were incinerated right in front of him.

"Wolf," someone says. It's Willy, who's just standing there watching his screaming little brother try pathetically to shape the ashes back into his parents again. He seems suddenly to remember the camera is on because he turns and looks directly into it, his face expressionless. He walks straight toward us, and then the picture goes dark.

The three of us stand in stunned silence, processing what we just witnessed. I realize that this scene was reenacted in one of the Wolf's coin-op machines. It seemed he *was* reconstructing parts of his life—the worst parts. Maybe he was trying to change their outcomes?

I look at Annika, who is already looking at me. "The Wolf

told your father that this film would destroy him if it went public," I say. "But did he think your father somehow *caused* that? That he murdered his own parents?"

"I don't know," Annika says. "My grandfather looked like he knew what he was doing. But even if my father did somehow cause their death, this film doesn't prove it."

"As far as I can tell," I say, "all it proves is that he didn't care that his parents got killed right in front of his eyes, and that everything he told you about his family was a lie."

"He turned himself into a big Jewish philanthropist," Annika says. "It wouldn't look too good if his parents were Nazis."

"Hmmm." I'm not convinced that anything on this film would move her father to perpetrate mass murder. Because that's what his man Adolf has committed for him. Mass. Murder. "A good liar could explain this film away pretty easily," I say. "I probably could myself. Why did the Wolf think this is so damaging?"

"Those artifacts he was testing," Royce says, returning to his desk chair, "they're related somehow. I'm just trying to put my finger on it."

We wait impatiently for him to put his finger on it.

"Okay, first," Royce says, thinking out loud, "the Bagdad Battery is an artifact from ancient Babylonia capable, supposedly, of producing electricity."

That sounds promising.

"Then there was a Viking axe, and—"

"Some kind of Greek leather boot," Annika says.

"Endromis," I tell her.

"Endromis," Royce explains, "were rawhide boots that came up to the knee. They were the favored footwear for travel, hunting, and running. The Greeks often depicted their gods wearing Endromis, and they considered the most perfect pairs magical."

"Magic rocks," Annika says. "So why not magic boots? Maybe my father is just straight-up insane."

"Seven League Boots," I say. "I've read stories about them."

"Of course you have," Annika says.

"You could take gigantic steps while wearing them."

"So the connection here is obvious," Royce says, surprising us. "To me, anyway. That is, if we assume the Viking axe was actually Thor's Hammer."

"*Okay…?*" Annika says.

"Thor's Hammer, if it'd been real," I tell her, "would probably have been an axe."

"He *is* collecting magical items," Royce tells us. "But it's not as crazy as it sounds. I'm sure your father doesn't believe in *magic*, but it's possible, even likely, that stories of legendary magical items, like the Philosopher's Stone, were based on some partial truth. It's the battery that gives it away. Very interesting. *Very* interesting."

"How?" I ask.

"What if the Babylonians figured out how to give that pot an electric charge?" Royce asks. "What if at different times in history the same discovery was made and ordinary objects were transformed into something extraordinary by being electrified to some degree, something that would have seemed magical at the time. If so, it's a safe bet that over time, myths would have grown up about those objects, more than likely exaggerating their powers. And certainly the Philosopher's Stone could have been the most powerful object of them all. I mean, the stone I bought is a blue diamond."

"Blue diamonds can conduct electricity," I say.

"You got it," Royce says. "You must read a lot."

In my mind, I see the crash and spark of blue lightning, the lightning that killed the Wolf and set Headquarters on fire.

"Wait—" Annika says. "You said you found the stone—this blue diamond—right? You bought it? You said if you hadn't, you would've been fired?"

"That's right," Royce says.

"But you also said that my father will retire when he gets it. So he doesn't have it yet? You still have it."

"He's going to make your father trade it for the pawnshops," I say.

Royce doesn't deny it.

"You can't give it to him for…anything!" Annika cries. "He

will do something terrible…something unspeakable if he gets that diamond!"

Royce shrugs. "Not really my prob—" he starts to say, before he's interrupted by the ringing of his phone. He picks it up and listens for moment while frowning. "Damn!" he suddenly shouts. "They just left!" And he hangs up. Then Royce looks at Annika and me and says, "We recently installed facial recognition on our security cameras. You were recognized, Annika."

At that moment, someone starts pounding on the door.

18.

THE STONE

"Quick," Royce says, "both of you, hide under my desk. He gets up and moves the chair to let us to scramble underneath. "I'll get rid of them," he says when we're crammed together out of sight. "Take the emergency exit halfway down the hallway. It'll lead you out into the alley behind the casino. Good luck!"

We hear him hit the buzzer on his desk and the door clicks open.

"Sweet Jesus!" Royce cries. "What the hell happened to you?"

"Ver are zey?" someone demands. Annika and I both shiver at the sound of Adolf's voice.

"Those kids?" Royce says. "They just—"

"Vat is this?"

"Just an old film I was—"

A gunshot sounds in the office, reverberating right through the wooden desk. Annika and I clutch each other. A body hits the floor.

"Oh my god!" a woman screams—Royce's secretary. "You've killed him! You've killed him!"

We hear the rattle of the projector. Adolf is rewinding the film.

The secretary is still screaming, but from outside the office now, "He killed him! He killed him!"

"Villy," Adolf says, on a phone. "Good news like you von't believe. I have film. Stone? Royce can no longer help. I'm sorry, Villy. Vas necessary. Ve get stone soon. And all is von."

We hear Adolf leave the office.

I climb out from under the desk.

Annika climbs out behind me, but she's holding something,

a black box of some kind, about the size of her hand. "It was stuck by magnet to the underside of the desktop," she says. "It was jabbing into my shoulder." It's a miniature lockbox with a keyhole in it.

I look at Royce's big body sprawled and bleeding on the floor. There's a key ring clipped to his belt with dozens of keys attached.

I go over and unclip it.

Annika puts the box in a pocket. I put the key ring in one of mine. And then we walk out of the office.

The secretary, blubbering into her phone now, looks at us with tearful incomprehension. Annika takes off down the hallway and I hurry behind her. We go through the emergency exit door and follow a narrow hallway that opens to the street outside. Royce did not steer us wrong.

"Where are we going?" I pant when Annika and I reach the corner.

"Carson City," she tells me. "We're going to look up the transfer of ownership for the pawnshop. We have nothing now without that film."

"We have the box," I say.

"First things first," Annika replies. "Bus station." Before I can ask where it is, she points to a towering pole with a blue-and-white bus balanced on top of it. It's a few streets away, so we head off in that direction. As soon as we get near, we see a police car parked on the curb.

"If the cops don't know what we look like now," Annika says, "they will soon."

Trying to act normal, we walk casually toward the line of buses that idle in the parking lot, wheezing exhaust. We look for one labeled Carson City and find the driver sitting inside, the door shut.

"Don't we need a ticket?" I ask.

Dumb question. Annika walks up to the bus's door, but the driver only looks down at her, tapping his watch. She pulls out a wad of cash from a pocket and holds it up.

The door opens.

"No questions," Annika says, handing the driver the money. He accepts it silently. Is there anybody who won't take a bribe? I wonder, following Annika down the aisle to a long bench at the back. We sit and wait. Annika bounces her leg as we watch the station's rear exit, hoping the cops won't come through it.

Fifteen minutes later a voice calls from speakers on the station's outside wall: "Carson City departing."

All at once, a throng of chatting, laughing passengers make their way over to our bus. There are at least forty of them, and they're all wearing the same white hats embroidered with *Carson City Nugget* in gold letters.

As they clamber onto the bus and take their seats, I realize they're speaking a foreign language, and I listen attentively, fascinated.

The driver puts the bus into gear, and as we begin to move, Annika and I both let out long sighs. But then, to our dismay, the bus almost immediately grinds to a halt. We look out the side windows, where everyone else is looking. A cop is coming.

Annika grabs my hand, but then quickly lets go.

The cop climbs on the bus and says a few words to the driver before starting down the aisle. Everyone has gone quiet. The cop glances up and down between the faces of each person he passes and a picture in his hand.

Breathe, Felix. Breathe.

I look out the window when the cop gets to the back of the bus. In the reflection, I see that Annika is looking right at him! With those magnetic eyes. It's like she's challenging him to recognize her! I hold my breath.

When he reaches our bench, the cop looks between Annika and his picture several times. Then, just when I'm about to vomit, he turns back. He says something to the driver again, then gets off the bus. And I can breathe again.

A moment later we're on our way and the laughing and chattering on the bus start back up, full volume, like someone flipped the switch back on.

Annika takes the black box out of her pocket and I dig the key ring out of mine. The fifteenth key we try turns the lock.

Inside, we find a stunning, sparkling, almost translucent blue diamond, the size of a thimble. It's beyond beautiful. I can't tear my eyes away from it.

Annika discards the box and key ring under her seat, then zips the diamond into a pocket on her thigh. "Can't wait till Daddy finds out we have this," she says. But she sounds more sober than victorious. And I know why. Another person had to die for us to get it.

I try my slow-breathing technique for a while, and it works pretty well. Then I just watch the downtown streets turn to highway.

When Annika and I realize we're hungry, we share several packets of the Wolf's dried meat rations. I feel much better after eating a few pieces of the jerky, and I can tell Annika does too, even though she doesn't like it.

"I thought for sure that cop was going to recognize you," I tell her. "Why did you look right at him like that?"

"So I wouldn't look like someone who didn't want a cop to look at them," she says.

"Ever punched a cop in the face?"

"Can't say I have, no. But I wish I'd punched that meathead Royce. I mean, I'm sorry he's dead. But he was just as bad as that Angus guy. I know—they both helped us."

"About your real parents…" I venture. "We can find them too…if they're still—"

"No," Annika says, and adamantly. "I guess I'm not as optimistic as you and the Freaks are. I don't want to put my hopes in something like that."

I want to say I totally understand, but before I can, the crowd on the bus bursts into song, although I can't understand a word of it. They cheer and laugh during the chorus. One man gets to his feet, waving a pretend baton to summon louder singing from the shyer members of the group. I can hardly hear Annika over the raucous noise.

"I wonder what everyone is so excited about!" I shout in her ear.

"They're the housekeeping staff at the Nugget Casino in

Carson City," Annika explains. "They had a free night's stay last night at the Reno Nugget and are going home now. They had a great time."

"How do you know that?"

"I speak Spanish," Annika says, smiling. "Yes, Spanish lessons. But never mind that. Are you okay? You're holding your arm. Is it hurt?"

"I don't know."

"I'm sorry, Felix. For being such a—"

"Don't worry about it," I say. "I'm going to take a nap."

"Okay."

Annika and I lie on the Wolf's bed in the mobile home, which is being dragged behind a bus. The mobile home is on fire. Annika reaches for my hand, linking her fingers between mine under the covers. She squeezes and my bones crack like twigs. Then, she turns over and kisses me, and my jaw breaks like glass. She rolls over on top of me, and my entire skeleton splinters into shards of brittle bone.

"Felix! Shit! Felix! Wake up!"

I open bleary eyes to see a man in a red baseball cap standing in the aisle.

"Just…stay calm," Annika says under her breath. I think she's talking to herself.

"Sir, please take your seat," the driver says over the PA system.

"This is America!" the man hollers. "I can't take this shit no more from you illegals!"

I assume he means illegal immigrants? How would he know if any of us were illegal? Am I legal? If the Wolf even had any official paperwork regarding my existence on this planet, it's surely up in smoke.

"We speak American in America!" the man shouts to the now quiet crowd.

"Well, you obviously also speak Dumbshit!" Annika yells, leaping to her feet. Her eyes are radiating blue fury and I know we're in trouble.

The casino crowd claps for Annika, roaring in approval.

Red Cap is fuming. "I'm doing this for people like me and you!" he shouts at Annika.

"I'm not anything like you!" Annika shouts back.

"Please take your seat, everyone," the driver says again. "Or I will have to stop the bus."

"The hell you will!" Red Cap roars, reaching under his leather vest. He pulls out a gun!

Cries of alarm erupt from all over the bus as passengers duck down in their seats. Annika sits back down next to me, her face flushed.

"Only way you illegals is getting off this bus alive," Red Cap announces, waving the gun around as he moves down the aisle, "is in Mexico! Driver! Change of destination. We're taking out the trash!"

"Cops!" someone cries.

Red Cap looks out the front window and shouts, "Goddamn conspiracy!"

On the shoulder of the highway up ahead, we see a policeman standing next to his car, lights flashing. He gestures for the bus to pull over.

"The cops aren't here for him," Annika whispers. "They have no way of knowing what's happening in here. They have an updated picture of me, I just know it."

Red Cap puts the muzzle of his gun to the driver's cheek and says, "You stop this bus, you die."

"Easy!" the driver cries. "Take it easy!"

"Floor it!" the man demands.

The driver steps hard on the accelerator. Our tires screech against the road, lurching us forward.

Ahead, we see the cop talking into his radio, the mic of which he has stretched out through his open window. I can tell that he can tell the bus isn't going to stop.

Half the passengers scream for our driver to stop, and the other half just screams.

As we speed toward the cop, I can see him pulling his gun out of its holster. He aims it at our driver!

Just before we reach him, Red Cap grabs the wheel and swerves us right at him. The cop dives into the grass embankment as we smash into the side of his car, sending it hurtling off the road. Everyone on the bus is hysterical now. Some are crying. Some are praying. Only I am silent as, once again, I await certain death.

The bus swerves back onto the highway when Red Cap finally lets go of the wheel. "You're all going back where you came from!" he wails.

Annika and I look at each other in disbelief. This lunatic is actually saving us from the cops! The passengers have gone quiet again. They're holding hands, whispering prayers, and huddling in their seats. Ahead I see a sign for Carson City.

"What in hell?" Red Cap shouts, leaning over to look out the driver's side window.

Looking to our left, Annika and I see a black convertible racing alongside of us. The top is down, and I can see a crisscrossing railroad of stiches on the driver's bald head and, around his sunglasses, a face bruised in lurid shades of black, blue, and yellow.

"Adolf!" Annika cries. "Goddamn it!"

Red Cap grabs the wheel again, jerking the bus off the highway onto a long exit ramp. Adolf hits his brakes before passing it, and now he's roaring by us again on the left shoulder. A few moments later our driver hits the brakes, and we're all thrown violently against our seat belts. People are screaming again. This time I am too. Because I'm sure I've broken every rib in my body.

"What. In. Hell!" Red Cap rages.

We can see through the front windows that Adolf has stopped his car sideways on the ramp ahead, blocking the road. He sits in the driver's seat. Waiting and watching.

"He didn't see what happened with the cop," Annika says, "and he has no idea what's happening in here either! Hold on, Felix."

"Drive!" Red Cap orders. His gun is at the driver's cheek again.

The engine revs and the bus leaps forward. We hear sirens blaring in the distance.

"Everyone get down!" a woman shrieks.

Annika reaches over and puts an arm in front of me.

And then we hit.

The world fills with screams and the sound of metal ripping metal. The windows shatter all around us. I'm slammed forward, then back. The bus reels, tilting over—we're going off the road!

The bus turns, slams on its side, and slides down into a ditch full of tall grass. In what seems like slow motion, I see the overhead bins fly open, and all at once, bags and purses go sailing in all directions. Passengers also float by with stunned expressions frozen on their faces. Then the bus topples over and we're upside down. I breathe faster and faster, clenching my eyes shut.

This, finally, is the end of my life. Which only just started.

Did it start?

Somehow, we're back right side up again, skidding toward a stand of trees.

Everything is unnaturally quiet.

I try to control my breathing, but it's coming faster and faster and now I can't breathe at all. The world is a blur, and just before we hit the trees, it all goes black.

19.

MY BONES

Annika! I call, but she doesn't hear me. She's walking down the road, and behind her I can see the bus driven by the madman in the red baseball cap. Adolf, in his convertible, races alongside, and dozens of police cars pursue her from behind, sirens screaming. Everyone is chasing Annika. "Run!" I cry. But she just walks in her confident, athletic way. They can't catch her. As she walks, wires snap off nearby telephone poles and spit sparks in her direction, but they cannot touch her. Dark clouds roll in and lightning strikes at her heels. It cannot hurt her. Annika just walks.

"Annikaaaaaa!"

"Felix? Felix!"

I open my eyes and see thick billows of smoke shot through with red-and-white flashing lights. Passengers, some in their seats, some thrown across the aisle, cry and moan. The front of the bus is buckled against the trunk of an enormous oak.

"Felix! Are you okay?"

It's Annika. "Where are you?" I croak, choking on the smoke.

"I'm here," she says. "Behind you."

I turn my head slowly toward the emergency exit behind my seat. It's open and Annika stands outside, her face smudged with smoke and her hair in wild disarray. But her eyes, as ever, crackle blue. Behind her, near the exit ramp, I can see at least three or four vehicles that have crashed. Police cars are everywhere. Several ambulances wait as medical personnel carry bodies uphill to them on stretchers.

"Please tell me you're okay," Annika begs.

"I don't know," I tell her. "I don't feel…anything."

"I think you're in shock."

Yes, I think. Of course I'm in shock. When have I not been in shock?

"Felix, do you trust me?"

"What?"

"I'm going to leave you here."

"What?"

"Adolf was just pulled out of his car, covered in blood. I think he's dead. The driver and the hijacker are definitely dead. And, like, six cars crashed behind us. But we're alive. We have the diamond, and we're alive."

"But—"

"They're looking for *me*, Felix. I spotted a cop with a new picture of me, from the pawnshop video. He didn't have one of you, so let the paramedics take you to the hospital. Make sure you're okay. Just don't tell them who you are. Make something up. *That's* your superpower."

"But what—?"

"I'm going to the Secretary of State's office in Carson City to get the information on the previous pawnshop owner. They close in an hour, so I have to go right now. When I'm done, I'll come find you at the hospital. And then we'll decide what to do. I'll come back for you. I promise. Do you trust me?"

"I do."

"Good." Annika makes binoculars with her hands and peers through them at me.

I form a spyglass with mine and peer back.

Then she turns and walks away.

I watch Annika's peroxide-blonde bob move off through the billowing black smoke, past the rushing rescue crews and the hovering cops, up the embankment, and back toward the road. Then she vanishes into the chaos.

At that moment I decide Annika Adelstein is not real. Has never been real. Will never be real. I decide that all this time, I've been sitting in the attic, staring through my spyglass, fantasizing like the hopeless case I am—and I fell asleep. And then tumbled down the box tower to the attic floor below. And now I'm dying, seeing the life I never had flash before my eyes.

A woman's voice comes to me out of the smoke, a paramedic. "Young man, are you hurt?"

"I—I don't know," I say. And then I hear myself shouting, "I don't know! I don't know! I don't know!"

A second paramedic joins the first, pushing a wheelchair toward the bus. He climbs up next to the woman, feels around my neck, then prods me gingerly here and there, on my torso, my arms and legs. "It's okay, buddy," he says. "Anything hurt bad?"

"I can't feel anything!" I hear myself bawl. "My bones!"

"What about your bones? Is something broken?"

"My bones!" I bawl again, unable to stop myself. "I have brittle bone disease!"

"It's okay, buddy," the female paramedic says, "we're going to get you out of here." Her partner unlatches my seat belt, then places a soft brace around my neck. Then the two of them carefully maneuver me out of the seat, through the emergency door, and into the wheelchair, which then converts somehow into a flat stretcher. They carry me up the embankment and into the back of an ambulance waiting on the exit ramp.

"This is the fellow with brittle bone disease!" the male paramedic tells a white-coated woman waiting inside. "Possible concussion. Probable shock. No clear signs of fractures, but multiple possibles."

"Got it!" the woman in the ambulance says as they close the doors. When the vehicle starts moving, she says, "What's your name?"

"I—I—my bones!"

"It's okay. It's okay," she says. "Don't worry about that right now. Don't worry about anything."

"My bones!" I wail, completely out of control. "My bones! My bones! My bones!"

"Breathe!" she tells me. "Try to breathe!"

But I keep wailing until she puts a needle into a vial and draws out some clear liquid. Raging like an animal at the sight of it, I struggle against my straps, thrashing in protest until she sticks the needle in my arm.

And then, again, everything goes black.

I'm lying naked on a bare metal bedframe as Doc's face hovers above mine, peering at me through a blue-diamond monocle. He dumps the contents of his black doctor's bag on the floor and a mess of broken bones spill out. Doc smiles, and I know the bones are mine. I look down and see that I am an empty bag of skin, a living leather bag.

"Annikaaaaaa!"

This time I open my eyes to find myself lying in a hospital bed. A curtain blocks my vision of the rest of the room, but it suddenly whips open, scaring me half to death. A haggard-looking man in a white coat comes toward me.

"You're awake," he says, with an angry edge to his voice. "Great. I'm Doctor Danson, and you have some serious explaining to do, young man."

I have no idea what he wants me to explain. Everything?

"Well?"

"I—I don't know what you—"

"Claiming to be someone you're not is a despicable thing to do," the doctor says. "We've got all manner of crises going on here with limited resources to effectively handle them all."

"But—what time is it?"

"Almost four."

"What?"

"You were sedated in the ambulance, which no doubt contributed to your…mental confusion. Though we didn't expect you to sleep for nearly twenty-four hours."

Twenty-four hours! Where is Annika?

"How old are you?" Dr. Danson asks.

"Eighteen."

The doctor shakes his head, exasperated. "The cost of giving you a full bone survey—do you have any idea of the time and resources we wasted on conducting useless tests? Let me guess, you have no insurance, right? What's your name?"

"I don't understand. What did the bone scan—?"

"If you have brittle bone disease, I'm a fairy-tale princess."

For this, I have no words. I just stare at him, dumbstruck. The entire world—the entire universe—is imploding around me, crushing me. I can't breathe again.

This cannot be true.

This. Cannot. Be. True.

What does it mean if this is true?

"Are you okay?" the doctor asks, concern creasing his brow. I'm full-on hyperventilating, sucking in huge amounts of air and gasping it out. "Just breathe calmly," he says, "in and out—"

Then, before I can do much of anything, the curtain whips open again, and Annika is there. "Hurry, help!" she cries. "There's an emergency out here!"

Dr. Danson rushes off past her and I can breathe again.

"Are you okay?" Annika asks, pulling the curtains closed behind her.

"Yes," I say, struggling to sit up. "I'm...okay."

"Oh, thank god," Annika sighs. "I've been sitting out there all night and day. It's complete madness out there! They've got people injured from the bus and patients from the cars that wrecked behind it. And then someone shot up a summer school program in Carson City a few hours ago!"

"What? Why would someone shoot school kids?"

"Happens all the time, Felix."

"What?" This is too much for me to deal with, so instead I ask, "Why didn't you wake me up?"

"I was afraid to," Annika says. "I thought if you were really hurt, you'd need the rest, so I've been out there trying to figure out what was going on in here. I didn't want to ask anyone anything, though, because they knew who you were, or thought they did. I didn't want them to figure out who I was!"

"I'm sorry. I didn't mean to—"

"It doesn't matter," Annika says. "Let's just get out of here because we are seriously running out of time."

"But my clothes," I say. "I think they cut them off—"

"Don't worry about it!" Annika gently helps me out of bed. "Oh, good," she says. "You got a gown that ties on the side."

Just then our curtain whips open again. Dr. Danson is back. "It's you!" he says to Annika. "You need to stay right here!"

He steps away and calls out, "Security!"

And that's when we run.

Annika wasn't exaggerating. The hospital is a complete madhouse. Cots with injured kids are set up around a large open area that's been converted into a triage unit. They even spill out into the hallways. The kids are yelling. Their parents are yelling. Nurses, doctors, and orderlies running around between them all, yelling.

"Hey!" Dr. Danson shouts at us.

We race toward the exit sign at the far corner of the triage center, keeping close to the walls to avoid the maze of moving beds being wheeled around.

"Stop them!" Dr. Danson yells. "That's the girl everyone is looking for!" This gets the attention of all sorts of people, including a security guard already trying to pick his way toward us through the pandemonium. He sees where we're headed and cuts us off.

That's the only way out, so we stop, uncertain what to do.

"The stairwell," I say, pointing at a nearby door. But before we can move, a hospital room door flies open right next to us. A gowned figure, with a gauze-wrapped head and plaster casts on his arms and legs, bursts out and tackles Annika to the ground.

Adolf!

"Get him off me!" Annika cries, flailing beneath him.

Two female nurses and a male orderly rush over and try to do exactly that.

"This is not possible!" a nurse cries. "He can't be able to—!"

A full-scale scrum ensues because three adults cannot seem to get Adolf off Annika. I don't know what to do. Other than what I always do: watch.

Finally, with the help of the security guard and another orderly, Adolf is dragged away, struggling like a madman. He is truly gruesome to behold. "I vasn't going to hurt her!" he yells.

This hallway tackle, this chaotic insanity, it keeps all eyes focused on Adolf, which allows Annika to scramble to her feet and run with me for the exit. Then through it. Outside, we sprint across the parking lot. After a minute or so of dashing between cars, Annika stops behind a green van and waits for me, breathing hard. I stop too, realizing that I've just run faster and harder than I ever have before. In bare feet. Which makes me remember: *I don't have brittle bone disease!*

"I don't think anyone's chasing us," Annika pants as we catch our breaths in the late afternoon breeze. Looking back at the hospital, I think she's right. They have bigger problems to worry about than two runaways. Even two runaways with a price on their heads.

"Are you really okay?" Annika asks.

"I'm worried about the Freaks," I tell her. "I'm not sure we did the right thing sending them to your—"

Annika presses a finger to her lips when a woman in a purple jogging suit and purple sneakers appears from around the side of the van.

"Goodness!" she says when she sees us. Her white eyebrows almost disappear into her white hair as she looks me over. "Is everything all right?"

"We've just had a hard few days," Annika says. The understatement of the year.

"I probably look like I'm running away from the hospital or something," I tell the lady. "But I was part of that bus accident yesterday, and they had to cut off my clothes. But I'm from Reno and lost my luggage in the accident, so…" I'm rambling, I know, but I can't help myself. So I go on, even though Annika is shooting daggers at me. "I was released from the hospital and my sister took a bus down to pick me up. But to be honest, the last thing I want to do is get on another bus right now. But I don't know how else we'll get home."

"Would that help?" the lady asks, pointing a finger over our shoulders.

We turn to see a bright pink RV with the words *Good Deed Ferry*, stenciled on the side.

"Are you serious?" Annika says. The daggers are gone. Now she shoots me an I-cannot-believe-our-luck grin.

"Of course!" the lady says. "The Lord has put me on this earth to do good deeds. I was on my way to help these poor children who got all shot up, but you kids look like you're in sore need of assistance too. My name is Leonora, but my friends call me the Good Deed Fairy! As you can see, I call my rig here the Good Deed *Ferry*, if you get my meaning. Where can I take you?"

"My name is Amy," Annika says, "and my brother here is Fred. We live at 1 Sparks Circle…in Sparks."

"It'll be my pleasure to ferry you there," Leonora says. "Thank goodness for GPS! This way now," she beckons, leading us to the shockingly pink vehicle. When we reach its back door, she says, "You'll find it quite cozy. Help yourself to all the food you like!"

"Really, we can't thank you enough," Annika says as we climb inside.

"We'll be there in a jiffy!" Leonora promises, closing us in. "But I'm a law-abiding citizen, so you won't catch me breaking any speed limits!"

20.

THE GOOD DEED FERRY

The RV is cozy—it's much smaller than the Wolf's mobile home but more up to date. A raised bed runs along one side of the interior, and a couch lines the other. A kitchen nook contains a table, microwave, and refrigerator. The windows are draped with pink lace curtains, the couch piled with pink cushions, and the bed covered in an old-fashioned pink stitched quilt. A number of silver crosses decorate the walls, and all are polished to a gleam. This time, there's a wall between us and our driver.

Annika heads right to the fridge when we get moving. "Chinese food!" she cheers, after looking inside. She opens a few white boxes and sniffs them. "You like chicken fried rice?" she asks.

I shrug. I have no idea. Sounds like a good fit for someone called China, though. Although, if it's true that I don't break easily, I never want to hear the word again.

Annika hands me the container along with a fork, and I dig right in.

"This is the best thing I've ever eaten in my entire life," I tell her, mid-chew.

"You saved me from bribes and threats," Annika says, her mouth full of noodles.

"Wouldn't have been cool to punch an old lady in the face."

"I hope you never run out of—"

"Lies," I say, heading to the fridge. I find cans of apple juice and give one to Annika. We sit and eat and drink until everything is gone.

"We're driving at, like, thirty miles an hour," Annika says, glancing out the window.

"I guess beggars can't be choosers," I tell her.

"True. Leonora is the lucky break we needed. Even if she's a bit of a religious nut. Speaking of breaks. What did they tell you at the hospital? No breaks at all? No hairline fractures even?"

"No breaks. No fractures."

"Talk about lucky!"

"They told me a little more than that."

"What do you mean?"

I'm having trouble saying the words because they haven't sunk in yet. And I just can't believe it. And I can't face what it means.

"Felix?"

"They told me I don't have brittle bone disease."

"*What?*"

"They did a bone scan and found nothing. The doctor was mad at me for claiming to be the brittle bone kid."

"You're serious?"

"That's what he said."

"Well that's…incredible!" Annika's face lights up. Her eyes sparkle like the blue diamond in her pocket. "Aren't you *ecstatic?*" she asks, sitting down next to me on the couch.

"Yes," I say. "No. Maybe. I just don't understand. My whole life—"

"Why did they tell you that?" Annika cries, eyes flashing now with indignation. "Why would they steal your entire childhood! They stole it!"

"I'd like to know."

"You're going to know," Annika promises. "You're going to know soon. And everyone involved is going to pay!"

"I'd also like to know who my parents are. All the Freaks want to know who their parents are."

"You don't know anything about them?"

"Not a thing."

"Faces are going to be punched, Felix. Many, many faces. All the faces!"

I hope so, but I don't want to talk about this anymore, so I ask, "Did you learn anything in Carson City?"

"Yes!" Annika cries, jumping to her feet. She has to take a

few deep breaths to settle down before explaining. "Yes!" she says again. "I found the record on microfiche. I told the lady I was a journalist investigating Willy Adelstein, the owner of Nevada's most successful pawnshops, because I think it might be a secret criminal enterprise. She got super excited because I was an 'engaged young woman.' She said she was sick of mediocre men running the world and was willing to do anything she could to help a strong female find her voice and topple the patriarchy. She was so into it that she stayed late to help."

"Wow. What's microfiche?"

"It's—doesn't matter."

"What's the patriarchy?"

"It doesn't matter! The point is that the original owner of Battle Born Pawn was, get this…Gerhard Adelsberger."

"Your grandfather was Gerhard," I say. "But… *Adelsberger?*"

"Hold on," Annika says. "It gets better. There was a transfer of ownership in 1978, when the business was inherited by, get this… *Wilhelm Adelsberger.*"

"But—?"

"Hold on. There was another transfer of ownership in 1985, when the business was sold to, hold on to your hat—"

"William Adelstein."

"Bingo."

"Wilhelm Adelsberger sold it to *William Adelstein?*" I say. "That's pretty—"

"His brother changed his name," Annika says. "Why not him too? But he was too narcissistic to give up his name completely and didn't think anyone would ever look into his past. William Adelstein—give me a break!"

"But that would mean he sold the business…to himself?" I say. "Why would he do that?"

"Because," Annika says, "Willy Adelstein wanted to pretend he was Jewish. And that meant not having anything to do with Wilhelm Adelsberger, who was apparently the son of a Nazi. We need to figure out why."

"Let's do a search," I say.

"What do you mean?"

I point toward a shelf above the couch where a pink laptop sits atop a stack of Bibles.

"Genius!" Annika grabs the laptop, powers it up, then starts a search. I go over and watch her fingers fly across the keyboard. "So," she says, still typing away, "my father pays a company to scrub the web for him, which means they make sure there's nothing bad about him out there. But the thing about scrubbing the web—is that it really can't be done, not completely. I learned that from my tech tutor."

"Tech tutor?"

"I know, I know! Anyway, there are two main things you can do. One is threaten people with lawsuits to take down material you don't like, a technique my dad is a big fan of. But mostly what these companies do is flood the web with positive stories that will come up when someone searches you, pushing anything negative way, way down the list. Further than any normal person would ever bother looking."

"But we're not normal people."

"Exactly. We're Freaks." Annika looks at me uncertainly. I can tell she's hoping she hasn't overstepped this time.

"And now we know what we're *really* looking for," I tell her, and she looks relieved.

"Right," Annika confirms, scrolling through entry after entry on the computer screen. *Adelsberger* appears somewhere in every one moving swiftly by. But neither of us sees a *Wilhelm* anywhere.

"Stop!" I say on, maybe, the fiftieth screen. I point to a line.

"But that says *Gertrude Schmidt* Adelsberger," Annika points out.

"No, look." I point further along the same line of text, to where it says *Nazi Death Ray*.

Annika clicks on the link. After looking over what comes up, she says, "It's an archived Reddit thread from 2010 about university research projects."

"A Reddit thread?" I ask.

"Just a place online where people have discussions on pretty much any topic you can think of." Annika clicks again and the page changes. I lean over her shoulder to read the paragraphs that pop up. People were sharing ideas for history research papers. The one we clicked on was written by Hannah Schmidt. She wrote, "I need some advice, everyone. My mother won't discuss our family tree because I think we might have Nazi roots. I've wanted to know the truth, so for years I've been reading everything WWII I could get my hands on, searching for the name of my great-grandmother, Angela Schmidt. I found a ring with Angela's name engraved inside it. It said, in German, 'To my dear Angela, Love, Gerti.'

"I buy books, read websites, and even go to the library just to check indexes for her name. So, anyway, a few weeks ago I stumbled across a wacky conspiracy theory book about the Nazi Death Ray, with a lot of crazy stuff about Hitler and Tesla and the Kellogg's cereal guy and alien technologies. But the book also included an alphabetized list of 5,000 workers killed during an RAF strike on the Death Ray facility the Nazis were building in Vatan, France, which really happened, and I spotted the name Gertrude Schmidt Adelsberger. *Gerti!* So, is it a crazy idea to possibly expose your own family as Nazis? I suppose I could do it just for myself, but I have to pick a thesis topic soon, and they go gaga for anyone who can 'connect the historical to the personal' at UNR."

Below, we read people's responses—*Best to let sleeping dogs lie*, and *Bury the past or it will bury you*. Others encouraged her to find the truth at all cost.

"What's RAF?" Annika asks.

"Royal Air Force. England," I tell her. Then I add, "Military history book on the British Empire."

"I think you had more tutors than I ever did," Annika says.

"Maybe so," I say. "What's UNR?"

"Oh my god!" Annika yelps. "That's the University of Nevada, Reno! Maybe Hannah Schmidt lives here! But let's see what this Death Ray nonsense is all about, shall we?" She types in *Nazi Death Ray*, and we spend the next twenty minutes learning that the Nazis planned to build a "directed energy weapon" capable of destroying entire fleets of airplanes mid-flight and burning cities to the ground. Apparently, Nikola Tesla had perfected the technology for harnessing energy of this kind, and the Nazis wanted to steal it from him. Engineers worked in secret, night and day, to perfect the weapon, but their facilities were repeatedly bombed, so they were unable to complete the project.

"So, did my father manage to perfect this Death Ray weapon?" Annika asks, chewing her lip. "What he did to the Wolf and Headquarters…"

"I don't think so," I say. "If he could destroy fleets of planes and burn cities to the ground—"

"He wouldn't care about two nobodies like you and me."

"And that video—Gerhart, he seemed to be—"

"Trying to extract energy, not shoot it."

"But all of this has to be related somehow."

"Felix," Annika says, gripping my hand—I instinctively flinch before remembering I don't have to flinch anymore. "We're getting close."

"I think so too."

We look at each other for a long moment, one that stretches into weirdness. I find myself riveted by her eyes. My hands are instantly damp and my heart races.

But then, all by itself, my head leans toward hers. And we kiss.

Her lips are soft.

We part, then stare at each other, blinking.

"Hmmm," Annika says. "Was that your first kiss?" I nod, not bothering to lie. "Mine too," she says. "I think there's supposed to be more…"

"Electricity?"

Annika smiles awkwardly, and I feel a horrible sinking feeling in my gut. *Did I do something wrong?*

"Let's see what else we can find on this Reddit thread," Annika says, clicking on the history tab at the top of the screen.

"Good idea," I say.

Annika says, "Oops" when a window pops up with the *Reno Gazette Journal* banner at the top. The headline screams, in bold capital letters: *Five-million-dollar reward offered for Safe Return of Vulnerable Runaways.*

"Oh shit," Annika mutters, clicking on the link to the newspaper article. Below the headline is a security-camera picture of her entering the pawnshop.

"OH SHIT!" she cries, slamming the laptop shut.

"What?" I ask. "We already know they have your—"

"That page from the *Reno Gazette* was in the browser history!"

"What does that—?"

"It *means*," Annika says, "that our Good Deed Fairy visited this page. She knows who we are, Felix! We have to get out of this truck!"

21.

PSYCHO BITCHES

"What can we do?" I ask.

Annika peers through the curtains on the backdoor's window. "Maybe we can find a *real* good Samaritan," she says, then heads to the kitchen area and shuffles through the contents of the drawers. She finds a book of crossword puzzles and a thick black marker. Folding the book in half, she writes HELP! in giant black letters across the page. Then she goes back to the door and tears the curtains right down. She presses the book up against the window.

I can see the road behind us. Cars move from one lane to the other, speeding up to overtake us. Nobody seems to take any notice of us or our sign.

"Help, goddamn it!" Annika shouts.

I need to help! Suddenly, I have an idea that might pay off if we can get out of this latest nightmare. I grab the laptop and type in a name. After only a few clicks, I have what I need.

"Help, you jerks!" Annika shouts. "Oh, hey! Hummer guys! Help!"

A gigantic black jeep approaches the RV from behind. It looks like a convertible tank with its top down, and two guys with sunburned faces wearing orange and brown hunting vests occupy the front seats.

Annika throws open the back door, letting wind and road noise rush in. She waves the sign.

"Careful!" I shout.

The men in the Hummer look at each other, then whip to the other lane and pull up alongside the front of the RV. Annika closes the door and we move to the side window to see the Hummer's driver honking wildly at Leonora. The passenger yells, gesturing for her to pull over.

Leonora, steadily driving at her snail's pace, seems to be ignoring them.

The Hummer swerves toward us a few times, and Leonora swerves away.

The guy in the passenger seat of the Hummer reaches into the back seat and comes back up with…a rifle! Which he aims at Leonora! She slams on the brakes—Annika and I lose our balance and go tumbling onto the couch.

The moment Leonora stops on the shoulder, Annika throws open the back door again. We scramble out onto the road and run toward the Hummer, which is parked on the shoulder too. Both men jump out—one runs to me and Annika, the other approaches Leonora's window, pointing his rifle. But at that moment, she hits her accelerator and peels back out onto the highway with her tires spitting gravel.

The Good Deed Ferry speeds off—slowly—into the night, with its back door still open.

"What's going on?" the jeep driver asks as his friend comes back to join us. "Are you two okay?" He looks confused by my hospital gown. "I'm Jimmy," he adds. "This is Dave."

"That was our abusive stepmother," I tell them. "Our parents are divorced and fighting over custody, and she tried to kidnap us while my sister was visiting me in the hospital."

"Thank you so much for saving us!" Annika adds, overdoing it a bit. "You're heroes!"

"That psycho *bitch*!" Jimmy practically spits. "You hear this, Dave? Sounds like *your* psycho bitch wife!"

"She'll probably get custody," Dave tells us. "The psycho bitches always do. No questions asked."

Annika's eyes narrow, and I brace myself for what I know is coming. "Not *all* women are psycho bitches," she says calmly. I try to give her a look that says, *Leave it alone for once!*

"Well, I'm sure you'll make some man a delightful life-partner," Jimmy says with just a hint of sarcasm.

"Can we take you home?" Dave asks. "Where do you live?"

"1700 Sagebrush Mountain Road," I say before Annika can respond. She looks at me, confused.

"I'm Fred Schmidt," I say, "and this is my sister, Amy. Our aunt Hannah lives on Sagebrush, and she can help us with all this family drama."

"Happy to oblige," Jimmy says.

A few minutes later Annika and I are riding in the back seat of the Hummer with the whooshing rush of wind in our ears. My feet are literally resting on the rifle, which Dave has laid behind the front seats. *It's like the Wild West out here!* Not counting Charlie, I'd never known of a single person who'd died…until I left Headquarters. I never even *thought* about people dying. Other than myself, of course.

I'm suddenly sure that my parents, whoever they are, are dead. The thought floods me with despair, and I'm overwhelmed by a desperate need to find them. With a jolt, I realize Annika and I are holding hands again. I keep my eyes on the yellow-lit windows of the houses flashing past, thinking about our first kiss. If I get another chance, I will do it better. I concentrate my entire being on not letting my palms sweat. The whipping wind is a godsend.

It's a warm, beautiful night, and I can see on the dashboard clock that it's past 8:30, which makes my stomach knot up and my palms sweat, despite the breeze. The Freaks will take their last meds soon. Then what?

We have to help them before it's too late!

At nine o'clock, we're off the highway and driving down a busy street, which eventually winds back into a neighborhood tucked behind some rolling brown hills. I see a sign saying, *Welcome to Hidden Valley.*

Two minutes later, it feels as if we've left the city entirely behind. The road widens, giant trees line the sidewalks, and the houses retreat from the streets, lit only by porch lights. The houses here are rustic, roomy, and inviting, and I can't help wondering about those who live inside.

We stop in front of a long, one-story ranch house with two garages. Annika and I trade worried looks as we reluctantly unlock our hands. Jimmy and Dave turn around to look at us. Jimmy opens the glove compartment, where I see a handgun.

Annika and I freeze, but then relax when he reaches in for a scrap of paper and a pen. After scribbling on it, he hands it to me. "I hope you two are going to press charges," he says. "But in any case, if it comes to it, and you need legal representation, I'll be happy to help."

"You're a lawyer?" Annika asks, shocked.

"I am."

"Thanks very much," I say, tucking the card into my pocket. I shoot Annika a pleading look that means, *Please, just let us move on.*

"If I were your dad," Dave says, "I'd handle it with a bullet."

"Don't get married," Jimmy says, looking me in the eye.

"Thanks again," I say.

Annika, about to explode, slams open her door and practically hurls herself out onto the sidewalk.

Holding my breath, I get out behind her, then gently close the door.

The Hummer drives away.

"ASSHOLES!" Annika shouts after them.

"Good job holding that in," I say. "I thought you were going to have to punch yourself in the face."

"I nearly did!" Annika fumes. "How is it we keep getting help from jerks?"

"I don't know. What I do know is we're running out of time to save the Freaks!"

"I know," Annika says, "which is why we're going to ring this doorbell. Which is why Hannah Schmidt is going to open the door. Which is why she'll be thrilled to meet us. Which is why she's going to tell us everything we need to know."

"All right then," I say. "Just don't punch *her* in the face. Even if she's a jerk."

"If you insist," Annika says, ringing the bell.

No one answers.

I ring the bell.

No one answers.

Now what?

"There's a gate," I say, pointing to a wooden door in a fence to our right. We head over to it and pass through. I close it behind us. Tall wrought-iron lamps throw soft pools of light around the backyard, illuminating a long oval of grass, three chairs around a glass table, and a fire pit. A small shed is tucked along a tree-lined back fence.

A long sliding-glass door runs along the back of the house, but drawn curtains prevent us from seeing inside.

"She'll be home soon," Annika says, collapsing into one of the chairs.

"She better be," I say, joining her.

We wait. And we wait some more. And the longer we wait, the more I feel my throat tightening up. I take in deep breaths, trying to calm myself, trying not to think of Mila spasming without her medication or Klaus scratching his arms raw.

"So," Annika says, noting my distress, "you never had a girl-friend at Headquarters?"

"No," I admit, feeling my anxiety spike. I pray it's too dark for her to see me blushing. And sweating. I'd rather just wait in silent stress than talk about this after our failed kiss.

"Did you want one?"

"I'm—I—" I splutter. "I guess I didn't think about it too much. I guess I didn't think about anything too much, to be honest. At least until you barged in. You probably never had the chance either to—"

"I've had wicked crushes on lots of my teachers," Annika says. "Tried to get my acting coach to kiss me in a scene we were doing once, but he was way too scared of my dad. That, and I was thirteen. Minor details. Ha! Minor. Get it?"

I get it.

She takes my hand again, and we lean into one another.

We kiss again, but only for a moment.

"I'm—sorry," I say. "Something doesn't feel right."

"There's supposed to be chemistry, I guess," Annika says. She smiles ruefully. "I'm sorry, Felix."

"I love you anyway," I tell her. "I love you twelve times for-ever."

WHY THE HELL DID I JUST SAY THAT?

My mouth—the words—they just came out on their own!

"I love you anyway too," Annika says, her eyes locked on mine. "And I will love you till the day I die."

We smile at each other.

"Now what do we do?" I ask, eager to change the subject—because this moment is too big for me to handle. "It's got to be close to ten o'clock. For some reason I'm not even tired."

"That's because you aren't depressed anymore," Annika says, and I realize, with astonishment, that she is right.

"And neither am I," she adds. "Except about the fact my father was right."

"About what?"

"The world is full of vermin I need to be protected from. Vermin like him."

Again, the truth seems to require no commentary.

Suddenly, a light on the side of the house flickers on. Inside the house, the curtain is moved aside, and the door slides open a crack.

"Who are you?" a woman calls. "If you kids are drunk—it's time to go home."

"Um—" Annika says.

"I'll call the police if I have to," she warns, sliding the door slowly closed.

"Wait! Please!" Annika cries. "You're Hannah Schmidt, right?"

To door stops sliding. "How…do you know my name?" Hannah asks. "I think I better call—"

"We saw your posts about your great grandmother, Gertrude," Annika says. "We just want to learn the truth about her."

"Who are you?" Hannah demands.

"My name is Annika Adelstein," Annika says, rising to her feet. "I'm adopted, but I think my name should be Adelsberger. I think we're related. I'm the girl everyone's searching for. I'm not insane. I'm not dangerous. It's all lies. The guy in the dress here is Felix."

"The boy with—?"

"Also lies," Annika says, and as if to prove her point, she punches me hard in the shoulder.

"Ahhh!" I cry. All my fears have been triggered and my body is flooding with fear. But then I realize it didn't hurt, so I grin. Annika grins back.

"Come inside," Hannah says. "You both look like hell."

22.

69 GERMAN DIARIES

Annika and I step into a cozy living room. A leather couch sits on a checkered rug, covering wide-planked hardwood floors. Shelves full of books line the walls to either side of a brick fireplace, and a cup of steaming tea sits on the coffee table in front of the couch. I'm mesmerized by the hominess of it all.

"Are you okay?" Hannah asks me. I can see her clearly now in the light of the living room. She's a wiry woman, maybe thirty, with bright brown eyes and yellow hair pulled tightly into a bun.

"I—I was—"

"Raised in the sixth circle of hell," Annika says. "So was I, but in a nicer neighborhood."

Hannah smiles sadly and closes the sliding door. "Come upstairs," she says. "Before we talk, you two need showers and clean clothes." It was true, I smelled awful. Annika's T-shirt and pants are smeared with dirt, her hair a tangled mess. We've had other things to worry about, I guess.

On the second floor, Hannah disappears into a bedroom—Annika and I glance apprehensively at one another, both wondering, I bet, if she's going to return with a machine gun and mow us down. But she comes back out with a pair of jeans, boxer shorts, socks, a button-down shirt, and some running shoes. "My ex-boyfriend's," she says. "He's about your size." She hands me the pile and points me toward a door down the hall.

"Thank you very much," I say, clutching the clothes to my chest.

"You can use the shower in my bathroom," Hannah tells Annika. "While you two clean up, I'll gather up a few things."

In the bathroom, I shrug off my hospital gown and step into the shower. I turn the water on super hot and let it stream onto my head and run down my face. So this is what a hot shower feels like. I'm actually shaking from the pleasure of it and stand beneath the scalding flow for I don't know how long. Then I realize I don't have time for this. What am I doing? The Freaks need me now!

I quickly wash with soap that, miraculously, doesn't feel like sandpaper, and lather my head with shampoo for the first time. Then I dry off with a towel that doesn't feel like steel wool. After dressing quickly, I head downstairs to find Annika sitting on the fireplace couch with Hannah beside her. A large black plastic crate with a white lid sits on one end of the coffee table, accompanied by tray of fruit and delicious-looking pastries.

"There he is," Hannah says when I join them.

"Sorry I took so long," I say, sitting cross-legged on the floor. I take a donut, and after my first bite, tears spring to my eyes. *This* is now the best thing I've ever tasted.

"Annika told me about her father and your…stay at the group home," Hannah says. "I am so sorry for you both, and I hope I can help. As you know from the Reddit thread, I wanted to learn the truth about my family's past—because my mother would never tell me anything about our extended family, only that we were related to some horrible people. I desperately wanted to believe that wasn't true."

"Are you Jewish, Hannah?" Annika asks.

"No," Hannah replies. "Why do you ask?"

"I don't think I am either," Annika mutters to herself. Then, more loudly, she says, "So, we're guessing you never wrote that thesis."

"I did not," Hannah confirms. "A few weeks after I wrote that post, a man came to my door. He said he was a lawyer who had been hired to protect the interests of parties he chose not to name. He told me, in no uncertain terms, that if I pursued the line of inquiry I had proposed online, I would be buried in lawsuits that would ruin my life."

"My father's standard operating procedure," Annika says grimly.

"So I dropped it," Hannah explains. "At least until I found this." She gestures toward the crate, and our eyes turn to it. It suddenly looks like a treasure box.

Hannah removes the lid of the crate and lifts out an old leather-bound book tied with a lavender ribbon. Annika and I lean over to look inside the crate: it's full of similarly old books.

"I was trying to get things in order when my mother was dying from cancer last year," Hannah tells us. "I found this crate in the attic and asked her about it. There are sixty-nine of these journals altogether, diaries with dated entries, all written in German. My mother, too weak from chemotherapy to lie anymore, told me they had belonged to her mother, who kept them even though she was too frightened to find out what they said."

Hannah unties the ribbon and opens the journal. She shows us a black-and-white photograph tucked inside the front cover. It's of a young man in an old-fashioned suit and a young woman in a long black skirt and blouse. They're standing in front of a domed brick building festooned with Nazi flags. The couple beam happily, holding up their clasped hands to reveal wedding bands. A heart had been drawn on the photograph around the man's face, and an *X* has been drawn on the woman's ring finger. Hannah flips the photo over and shows us some scrawled writing in German, along with a date: 10/10/33.

"I got the inscription translated," Hannah tells us. "It says: *Oskar and Gerti Adelsberger. First day of classes at the University of Gottingen.*"

"Do you know who wrote on the photo?" I ask.

"My great-grandmother, Angela," Hannah says. "She took the picture. She was Gerti's younger sister by five years, and she was in love with Oskar."

"How do you know that?" Annika asks.

"I know that because after my mom passed, I spent nearly a year learning German."

"So you've read all the journals?" Annika asks.

"I have," Hannah confirms. "These diaries were written by Angela. This one, started in 1933, when Angela was fifteen, is the first one. The first entry dates to the day before that photo was taken, the day Oskar and Gerti got married. Angela writes of her devastation that Oskar married her sister instead of her. She writes of how terrified they all were of Hitler and what was becoming of Germany, and how Jewish professors were fired from the universities. She paints a pretty bleak picture of what life was like for them in 1933."

"So they weren't Nazis then?" Annika says, relieved. "Just young people trying to survive a terrible time in history?"

"In a very real way, yes," Hannah says. "Gerti and Angela's parents died of tuberculosis, so they were on their own. Then, five years after Oskar married Gerti, they had a baby boy, Gerhard—"

"Gerhard!" Annika and I both exclaim. Hannah looks surprised.

"Gerhard was my grandfather," Annika explains.

Hannah stares in disbelief for a moment, then pulls her into a long hug that brings tears to Annika's eyes. I turn away to give her a moment of privacy because I can see how badly she longs to make a real connection with this real family member, one who's alive and right here and not a childish figment of wishful thinking. And who is also not her father.

When Annika finally lets her go, Hannah says, "We'll have time for that, my dear. But first let me tell you the rest of the story. Angela left school so she could take care of Gerhard while Gerti finished her education. She loved Gerhard desperately but writes in her diary that she also hated him, at times, for not being her own. She was horribly jealous of Gerti, not only for marrying Oskar, but for attending university. Gerti and Oskar both studied electrical engineering. It was very rare for a woman to be allowed to attend university then, but evidently Gerti was incredibly smart."

"Wow," Annika says.

"Over the next few years," Hannah continues, "Angela

writes obsessively about Oskar, and how he and Gerti became fascinated with Nikola Tesla. Are you familiar with his work?"

Annika and I both nod, eager to hear more.

"Well, Oskar and Gerti both graduated at the top of their class and, in 1940, after graduate school, they moved to Berlin to work for a company called AEG, an electric company. Over the course of the next few years, Angela divulges some pretty dangerous stuff."

"Like what?" Annika asks.

"Amid her endless praise of Oskar, she reveals that he, like Tesla, wanted to discover the ultimate energy source, and also like Tesla, not for the good of the Fatherland, but for the good of the world."

"Wow," Annika says again. "Oskar could have been killed if that diary had been discovered!"

"It was reckless of her to put that on paper, for sure," Hannah agrees. "But then the focus of Angela's diary shifts almost entirely to Gerhard. Oskar and Gerti enrolled him in kindergarten, which began at age three so children could receive a 'proper Nazi education.' Angela kept house during the day while Gerhard was in school. She spent most of that time, it seems, worrying herself to death about the child getting brainwashed. And she was right to worry. Within eight months, Gerard was spouting pretty vile things about Jews, parroting phrases he heard at school. Then, in 1944, Oskar and Gerti were both recruited to work on a secret project in France, a secret they either didn't hide from, or couldn't keep from, Angela."

"The Death Ray," I say.

"Right!" Hannah says. "They left Angela and Gerhard in Berlin and went to France. Angela describes, however, their true intentions, which were to steal the Death Ray technology and give it to the world. In her last entry, dated September 7, 1944, Angela writes of her fear for Oskar and her fear of Gerhard—who was by then, it seems, a proper little monster. Then there's nothing in the diary for six months. The first entry, when it starts again, was written in Reno."

"What happened?" I ask. Like me, Annika is leaning forward

to hear every word, eyes wide, half of a croissant forgotten in her hand.

"Oskar and Gerti were caught trying to steal data from the Death Ray facility," Hannah says, "but as they were being arrested, the RAF bombed the building, killing almost everyone, including Gerti. Oskar survived and made it back to Berlin. He, Angela, and Gerhard managed to obtain berths on a boat for America. During the trip, Oskar befriended a fellow German going to Reno to work for Sierra Nevada Power, so they accompanied him. In a matter of months, Oskar had a good job and a home."

"Amazing," Annika says. "Did Angela end up marrying Oskar?"

"Unfortunately," Hannah says, "there was no happy ending for Angela. Things went from bad to worse in America. Her diaries from 1945 onward demonstrate a steady decline. She writes of a terrible guilt for not having adequately supported or loved her sister. She fears, too, that Oskar was becoming obsessed by the electricity experiments he was conducting in his basement. Eventually, Oskar confides in Angela that while in France he discovered that the Nazis were not, in fact, attempting to execute Tesla's theories on electricity. That was a cover-up for their *real* investigation, which was into some Jewish mystical mumbo jumbo about godlike Sparks of divine energy." Hannah shrugs. "I know, crazy. Anyway, Gerhard, who was now nearly eleven, had become an irredeemable little Nazi clone who blamed the Jews for his mother's death. In 1947, after he was expelled from school for attacking a Jewish classmate with a hammer in shop class, Angela couldn't take it anymore. She just left. She moved to Fallon, bought a house, and opened a day care. She had a child, my grandmother, Maria, out of wedlock. She recorded entries in her diary until 1960, but she never mentioned Oskar or Gerti or Gerhard or Germany again. Her last entry was a suicide note to Maria, apologizing for not being able to go on. Maria Schmidt eventually married—a man also named Schmidt, funnily enough—and had my mother. My grandmother never mentioned the diaries, and my mother inherited them pretty much the same way I did from her."

"That's an incredibly sad story," Annika says.

"What happened to Oskar?" I ask.

Hannah reaches into the crate of diaries and pulls out a yellowed piece of newspaper from the *Reno Gazette Journal*, dated 1950. The headline reads *Local Man Electrocuted in Bizarre Basement Ritual*. Under the headline, the article features a photograph of a basement, not unlike the one we saw on the Wolf's film, with containers and gauges linked by wires scattered about the room. A large symbol had been drawn in chalk on the concrete floor comprising ten circles, each connected to the other by straight lines. The circles all contained a word in German. The article was brief:

Local electrician, Oskar Adelsberger, was electrocuted while performing bizarre electrical experiments in his basement yesterday morning. Pictured here is his laboratory with the Jewish Kabbalistic symbol known as the Tree of Life drawn on the floor. Authorities have ruled the death an accident.

"I did some follow-up research on Gerhard," Hannah says, tucking the article back into the crate. "He became a Neo-Nazi and published a white nationalist magazine for years, and he got rich opening—"

"Pawnshops," I say, remembering the printing press we saw on the Wolf's film of Gerhard's basement.

"Right. You two are serious researchers!"

"Do you know anything else?" Annika asks.

"Yes," Hanna says. "He married someone named Klara Becker, and they both died in an explosion in their home in 1978."

"Yeah," Annika says, "We know—"

"Along with their three-year-old daughter, Emelia."

"What?" Annika and I both gasp.

"It wasn't in the papers," Hannah tells us, "but I found a police report about it. They called the accident an 'incineration incident' that made positive identification of the bodies impossible. But it said the only survivors of the family of five were two boys: one, William, eighteen, and the younger one, Wolfram, ten, who was left in his brother's charge."

"We saw what happened in that explosion," Annika says. "It was all recorded on an old film. There was no sign of a little girl in that basement."

"Did the police report say there was damage to other parts of the house?" I ask.

"Actually," Hannah says, "it noted that no one could explain how such a powerful explosion could have damaged only one section of the basement."

"That's why the film could hurt him!" Annika exclaims. "He lied about his sister being killed. But *why?*"

"Hannah," I say. "This Jewish mumbo-jumbo stuff about divine Sparks you mentioned. Do you know anything about it?"

Hannah retrieves a book from one of the shelves by the fireplace. Its title gleams in gold across a blue spine: *Mystical Secrets of the Kabbalah*. "Short answer is no," she tells us. "The diaries provided the answers to what I was looking for—that my German ancestors were not Nazis, except for Gerhard, of course. I was going to delve into the mystical stuff too, so I bought this book a few months ago. I never read it though. I decided I'd rather had enough of it all, and I wanted to move on with my life."

"Have you told anyone about any of this?" Annika asks. "I'm guessing you haven't posted anything online, right?"

"No," Hannah says, emphatically, "and I haven't felt the need to. That lawyer may have bullied me out of publishing anything about my family history, but he damn sure couldn't stop me from learning about it for myself. I know the truth now, and that's good enough for—Oh my god!" Hannah suddenly shrieks, dropping the book. She's staring out into the backyard, face drained of blood, petrified. "Is that...*him?*"

Alarmed, Annika and I turn to see what she's looking at, and there in the shadows of the backyard, we see the hulking figure of Adolf.

Or what's left of him.

23.

A METAPHOR OR SYMBOLISM OR WHATEVER

Horrified, we stare through the glass at Adolf, who stands staring back at us from the patio. His casts are mostly gone, but jagged sections of plaster remain, partially encasing one leg and both arms. He's wearing doctor's scrubs that are too small for him, and we can see broken ribs bulging grotesquely from his chest. Black-threaded stitches cover his face, and dark blood has crusted across his head and cheek.

He's a monstrosity.

"Oh my god," Annika gasps.

When Adolf lurches toward the sliding glass doors, we all wheel round and run for the front door. But before we get there, three men in dark coveralls kick it open. They point guns at us. "Get back," one barks, gesturing for us to return to the living room where Adolf now stands—though *stand* is not the best word for the sickening way he keeps himself upright. There's a revolting scar from the corner of his mouth to his ear. When he talks, his voice sounds slurred and wet. "Virst things virst," he says, spitting blood and mucus from torn lips. "Zey might have veapons."

Hannah bends over and vomits on the floor.

One of the gun-toting goons starts to pad me down. I flinch at every touch, because that's who I really am and who I'll probably always be. Then he turns to Annika, whose face goes white.

The diamond!

I don't know what to do!

The goon pats her down, then pauses when he feels the diamond in her thigh pocket.

"No!" I cry.

Annika twists around, trying to prevent the goon from unzipping the pocket, but his fellow goon wrenches her arms behind her back until she can't move.

"Leave her alone!" I cry, but before I remember that I don't have brittle bone disease, I feel the cold barrel of a gun against the nape of my neck.

The second goon takes the diamond out of Annika's pocket and, with a low whistle of appreciation, holds it up to the light.

"Vell, vell, vell," Adolf remarks, snatching the diamond from the goon's hand. "Anozer vonderful surprise! Vat a vonderful daughter to get her father such vonderful gifts."

"Go to hell!" Annika screams. "All of you go to hell!"

"Take care of zis," Adolf tells his men, then turns to the kitchen, where the light shines brightly, to better admire the diamond. One of his goons takes a menacing step toward Hannah, who backs fearfully away.

"Please!" she cries. "Leave me a—!"

The goon seizes her by the neck and lifts her right off the floor. He's strangling her! But what I can do with a gun at my neck!

Annika lets out a primal scream before throwing herself at the goon. But he twists around when he sees her coming, drops Hannah to the floor, then punches Annika so hard in the stomach that she drops soundlessly to her knees.

"Not ze stomach!" Adolf cries. "Dummkopf!"

"Annika!" I cry.

Now this animal picks Annika up as if she were a rag doll and tosses her on the couch. The goon with the gun at my neck forces me over to the couch, where I sit down. Annika is doubled over, gasping.

"Count your breaths," I urge her. But she doesn't seem to hear me.

One of the goons drags Hannah over to us.

"Let her go!" I scream.

Adolf, who is casually flipping through one of the diaries, says, "Zis vould be a good time to tell me vere ze other three children are. I'm sure Felix here knows vat vill happen if zey do not get zeir medicines. I think maybe zey have a few hours left before bad things start to happen, no?"

Annika, upright now, stares impassively at Adolf, mouth tightly compressed. She will tell him nothing.

"They're in the junkyard!" I cry.

"Try again," Adolf says. "I have been zere already."

"There's a bunker!" I lie. *He has to believe this story!* "The Wolf thought the army would come after him one day. He was paranoid, so he built a secret bunker under the mobile home in the junkyard."

Adolf considers this for a moment, then nods at the goon still manhandling Hannah, who proceeds to squeeze her neck until her eyes roll back in her head. He drops her to the floor.

"You goddamn bastard!" Annika screams at Adolf.

Adolf starts laughing uncontrollably, his ruined mouth puckering and flapping repulsively. Then, abruptly serious again, he slaps Annika so hard that she's thrown from the couch. One of the goons puts his gun to my temple, and I all I can do is look on with horror.

"As you can see," Adolf spits, "ze don't hurt precious Annika rule is no longer in effect."

The goon drags Annika to her feet and shoves her back onto the couch.

"What do you want!" I hear myself shout. "Why can't you just leave us alone! Why do you want to kill the Freaks?"

"If ve vanted ze Freaks dead," Adolf says, "ve'd kill you right now, yes? So listen, both of you. In thirty seconds, you vill both valk calmly out of zis house and get into ze back of ze van parked in front. If either of you deviate from ze plan, we vill shoot Felix in ze head. Von dead Freak iz okay." Then he adds, "And ve vill shoot Annika in both knees." We look at him mutely, certain he'll do exactly as he says. "Throw zis crate in ze back," he tells a goon. To Annika he says, "Your daddy is anxious to see you." And then to both of us, he snaps, "Now move."

We walk unsteadily toward the front door and down the driveway toward a white van waiting ominously at the curb. I look up and down the street, but the neighborhood is as quiet as can be. Without streetlights, it's as dark as can be too.

The goon ahead of us opens the rear doors to the van and waves us inside. We climb in and sit down on the metal floor while the second goon shoves the crate of diaries in after us.

"You two come vith me in front," we hear Adolf say. Then, to the third goon he says, "You go back and dispose of ze body."

The doors are slammed shut and locked.

When we pull away from the curb, Annika starts to sob beside me. I reach out for her hand, but she won't let me take it. I want nothing more than to return to the ruined remains of Headquarters, find every Bag the Wolf ever had and zip myself into all of them, one after the other.

"It's my fault," I say. My voice sounds hollow. "I left the window open on the laptop in that lady's truck. It had Hannah's address."

Annika doesn't reply. She doesn't care anymore. They've broken her. She sobs and sobs and sobs.

They've broken me too. My spirt. My will. Myself. My short life outside Headquarters has been a series of rides in moving vehicles transporting me closer and closer to my inevitable death. I was crazy to think I'd ever escaped Wilhelm Adelsberger's execution machine. The gears have never stopped turning, but when they do, I'll be dead.

And the worst part of it is, the Freaks are going to die too. Probably in agony. And it will be my fault for going along with this stupid scheme. For imagining I could help anyone. We gave the film to Adolf, and now the Philosopher's Stone as well. We might as well have delivered them to Willy's door. The Wolf was right about the world. It's a Shit Show.

The van bounces us along for a while, then takes a sharp turn around a corner, tipping the crate over and spilling its contents across the floor of the van. Annika doesn't even seem to notice, but one book catches my eye—it looks different from the others.

It's the book about Jewish mysticism Hannah dropped when she saw Adolf.

I reach for it and show it to Annika, who barely glances at it. She has stopped crying, but I can't bear to see the light gone out of her eyes. They're empty now, like the Wolf's. To avoid looking at them a moment longer, I flip to the index of the book and search for the word *Sparks*. It sends me to page nineteen, where I read aloud to Annika, hoping for…anything.

"'At first there was nothing but God. To make room for the universe, he contracted himself, creating darkness. When God summoned the Light, it came forth in ten vessels, which could not contain it. The vessels shattered, scattering the Sparks of primordial light. Most of this divine energy returned to God, but the Sparks that did not adhered to the broken vessels, which constituted the material world. It is the mission of the Jewish people to repair the world by releasing the trapped Sparks through a combination of contemplation, prayer, and good deeds.'"

Annika's dead expression does not change while I'm reading, but at least she appears to be listening. It occurs to me, now that I'm on my way to meet my maker, that I've never thought about God in any meaningful way. I read the Bible the Wolf made us keep in our rooms, but I guess I read it like all those novels in the attic—as an entertaining collection of stories.

"So," Annika says, but with little enthusiasm, "all that is a metaphor or symbolism or whatever—for something true. Some sort of energy from the Big Bang was trapped in the artifacts my father hunts down, or I guess, in the materials they were made from."

"So, Oskar, your great-grandfather," I say, "who was inspired by Tesla to give free energy to the world, learned that the Nazis believed in these Sparks. And then Oskar himself discovered them during his basement experiments, and Gerhard witnessed his death when those Sparks were somehow released."

"Then," Annika says, "Gerhard continued his father's experiments, but in order to get revenge on the Jews for supposedly killing his mother."

"And then Gerhard's son, Wilhelm," I say, "saw him die succeeding in releasing even more Sparks. And so *he* took over the experiments."

"He learned how to create a weapon with the Sparks," Annika says, coming slowly back to life, "and he pretended he was Jewish so no one no one would ever dig up his Nazi connections and interfere with his work. But—why? What does he want?"

"I'm sure we'll find out just before he kills us," I say. "Or kills me anyway. That's always how it goes."

"Why does my father even still want me alive at this point?" Annika snaps. The heat and fire are back in her eyes. "He doesn't love me. He doesn't care about me!"

"You're somehow part of his plan," I tell her.

"How could he possibly think I'd help him? Does he think I'll take over this psychotic quest from him someday? Over my dead body!"

The van slows down, jolting from side to side as we hit potholes in what seems to be a rural road. The reassuring sounds of city life and traffic are gone, and the world outside the van seems eerily quiet.

"Whatever happens," I say, trying to stay calm, "we have to figure out how to get the Freaks safely out of your house and send them somewhere they can get the treatments they need. Maybe Dr. Danson would—"

"But Felix," Annika says, "if you don't have brittle bone disease—"

For the first time in I don't know how long, I feel a surge of hopefulness. "You think—?"

"If we're going to my house," Annika says, fully animated again. "We need to somehow tell the Freaks *not* to take their meds. What if my father and the Wolf were experimenting on all of you? And what if the experiment ends when you turn eighteen? Maybe he's trying to create soldiers who are immune to his weapon!"

"And he has to wait until his subjects reach adulthood to know if the effects are permanent?" I guess. "Maybe he wants to create his own army. Maybe he wants to be the new Hitler."

"How can we get a message to the Freaks?" Annika asks. The energy fairly crackles from her now, and I, too, feel ready to keep fighting.

"I have an idea," I tell her. "I need you to create a distraction when they open the van doors."

Not a moment later, the van lurches to a stop, so I hurry to the rear doors, crouching in front of them with my arms outstretched.

"Felix?" Annika says. "What are you—?"

Just then, the doors open.

24.

THE GREATEST SCIENTIFIC
ACHIEVEMENT OF ALL TIME

It was one of the goons who opened the doors, but just as I hoped, Adolf is there too. Lunging forward, I reach out and wrap my arms around him. Then I wrap my legs around him, too, like I was an inconsolable child and he was my mother. Like he was Charlie.

"Get off me!" Adolf shouts, squirming to get free.

His body is a sack of broken sticks—the future I've always expected for myself. I tear at the stitches that cover his head and wonder that he hasn't collapsed under my weight. The goons grab me, and I don't resist as they pull me off.

"What ze hell do you think you're—?" Adolf yells at me, but he stops short and grabs for his pocket. When he finds the diamond safe and sound, he looks at me and laughs. Just then, from the van behind me comes a bloodcurdling yowl, a war-cry I now know only too well. Annika leaps past us, out of the van, whooping like a tribal warrior, and bolts away toward the dark mansion at the top of the driveway.

"Get her!" Adolf shouts. "But no shooting!"

The goons chase Annika, hollering with their guns drawn. And while Adolf is distracted, I take a step toward the side of the van, work quickly to complete my task, then I run.

"Stop!" Adolf shouts at me now.

I race after Annika toward the mansion, praying not to be taken down by a shot in the back. Fortunately, no one shoots me. When I reach Annika on the front porch, we stand there catching our breaths, waiting for the goons, who reach us a minute later.

Adolf stumbles over like a malfunctioning robot. "Games!"

he spits. "You play childish games with your lives! Inside! Now!" He opens the front door and waves us angrily through.

I risk a quick glance behind me as I enter the mansion. Although I'm blinded for a moment by the exterior spotlight sweeping by, I see my handiwork scrawled on the side of the van, which is dimly lit by the interior mansion lights. A message written in Adolf's blood: DON'T TAKE MEDS. The spotlight sweeps by again as I wipe my hands on my jeans. Showtime, I guess.

The door closes behind us.

My momentary sense of victory drains right away, replaced by a certainty that now that I'm inside the house I've dreamed about my entire life, I won't be leaving it alive.

But what a house.

It's a palace. Or a museum. Or both. We've stepped into a grand entry room. The floors are covered with thick Persian carpets, the tall windows hung with dark velvet curtains. Gold-thread upholstered chairs and couches are situated around a wooden table on fancy metal legs. The walls are lined with dark wood bookshelves, richly polished and filled with old, odd-looking devices—strange boxes with gears and dials, and circuit boards with electrical wires and devices protruding in all directions. One resembles a fan and a microphone. Among the comfortably plush furniture are metal machines clearly made to sit on, or even in.

I understand why the Wolf would never step foot in here.

At gunpoint, we're propelled through the foyer to an enormous kitchen with gleaming appliances and a long, narrow island. Here, too, boxed shelving units are built into the walls, each cubby filled with a different kind of electrotherapy device.

From the kitchen we enter the dining room with a table so large that it could fit every Suck and Freak around it. It must be hewn from the biggest tree in the world. Here and there are metal devices that look like torture chamber versions of fitness machines and old electric chairs from Death Row. One has a helmet resting on top, another, a belt.

"Move," a goon growls behind us.

From there we're herded into in a spacious library with floor-to-ceiling bookcases, all filled with beautiful leather-bound books. Wheeled ladders attach to rails that allow access to the highest shelves. I take a long, deep breath, reveling, despite our dire circumstances, in the gloriously musty smell of leather that has defined my life.

Here, too, every nook and cranny contains an electrotherapy machine, large or small. And behind a large, polished desk, half-hidden by the window curtains, is a door to a vault. Adolf spins the combination lock on the metal door back and forth, then swings it open. So many safes in the life of someone for whom the word has never had meaning. Beyond, I can see a flight of wooden stairs descending into gloom.

One last set of secret steps. Safe Steps, I think, darkly.

"Oh, joy," Annika says. "I finally get to see the Bat Cave."

"Take zem below," Adolf says. "I vill stay here—Vait!" He takes the diamond out of his pocket and hands it to one of the men. "Give to Villy."

The two goons force us down the steps, guns at our backs. The flight of stairs winds around for some time, and as we descend, I notice the walls are covered with a thick layer of rubber.

When we finally reach the bottom, I see we're in yet another workshop basement, not unlike the ones in the Wolf's film and that old newspaper clipping. But while it's similarly jam-packed with electrical equipment, it more closely resembles photos I've seen of mission control centers in *Scientific American* magazine. Computers line the walls, floor to ceiling, with blinking consoles rigged out with a complex array of lights, dials, and switches. Long worktables split the room into rows, each piled high with neatly arranged contraptions and ancient-looking artifacts. Some objects are set under glass spheres with tubes and cables running to inputs on the computers.

Doc, wearing a lab coat and goggles, is working on what looks like an old arrowhead. He does not appear to have noticed our arrival, and his walking stick leans against the table beside him. Annika sees it too.

Adolf's goons seem reluctant to disturb him, so we stand there while he tinkers. He places the arrowhead inside a glass container, hooks electrodes to the lid, then flips a switch. A small burst of forked lightning illuminates the container, and we watch it light up cables as it travels through them to a bank of computers on the wall.

"Excuse us, sir?" one of the goons says.

Doc spins slowly around on his rolling chair and takes off his goggles. Putting his monocle in place, he peers at us through it. He seems pleased, but unsurprised, to see us.

"Axel said to give you this," one of the goons says, handing the diamond to Willy, who accepts it, then says, "Now go." And so the goons go. Willy is clearly not afraid of anything Annika and I might do down here, and I'm determined to make him regret it.

Ignoring us, he turns back to the table and replaces the arrowhead with the diamond. Once again, he hooks electrodes to the glass container and flips a switch. This time a spectacular, multicolored flash, brighter and more intense than the previous display, lights up the container and travels through the cables to the computers. Lights flash, dials move erratically, and all the readouts go crazy.

A small compartment door in a computer console slides open, and Willy removes a syringe full of a glowing, sparkling, foaming, rainbow-colored fluid.

"Sparks," I say, finally realizing what Doc is up to. "He wants to put them into people."

Willy sets the syringe down on a table, then turns to me and asks, "Where are the others? They will soon suffer indescribably. If they aren't doing so already."

"Spare us your lies, Wilhelm," Annika sneers. "Whatever you're doing—whatever you've done—it's *over*. We know Felix doesn't have brittle bone disease. He had X-rays taken of his entire body, and we don't think the others—"

"There is no machine in any hospital you visited that could detect the condition you have," Doc tells me. "It is true I gave you that condition. It is true I gave your friends the conditions they must endure. But you'll be happy to know that you have contributed to the greatest scientific achievement of all time."

"You are nothing but a vile and petty murderer!" Annika snaps. "All those kids at the home are dead!"

"Years ago," Willy says, ignoring the outburst, "I discovered how to extract cosmotic energy from primordial matter that still contained it, and I am studying its effects on the human body. Thus far, they are decidedly deleterious. On you, for example," he says to me, "they weakened the structure of your bones on an atomic level, leaving them unstable. Your bones, though they appear normal, and truth be told, most of the time act like normal bones, are also as fragile as blown glass. Your yearly *vaccinations* help stabilize the atomic structure of your skeleton. You are now due for your latest shot. Without it, you are gambling with your life."

"He's lying, Felix," Annika cries. "He's a pathological liar, a sociopath!"

But he *has* been experimenting on us! What if, beneath all the lies, there is some truth?

Breathe, Felix.

"You killed Charlie," I say.

"She was the first subject," Willy says. "Her infusion weakened her heart. The Discharge shot was meant to cure her permanently so that she could go live a normal life, but instead, I'm sorry to say, it stopped her heart. Progress never comes without a price, my boy."

"But everyone knows *you* never pay!" Annika rages.

"Charlie wasn't first," I say. "Your brother was."

If Willy is surprised to hear this, he doesn't show it. I see the slight raise of one thin eyebrow over the silver rim of his monocle.

"Wolfram was indeed my first true subject," he admits, "but that was long before I learned how to infuse plasma with Sparks. I'm afraid I had to use old-fashioned methods on him. Of course, he was a willing, if undependable, volunteer. Until he wasn't anymore and ran away. Oh, yes," Willy sighs, apparently still disappointed in his little brother. "He tried, weakling that he was. I had to wrap him up tightly in his favorite blanket and attach the electrodes to one little arm that stuck out of it. Wolfram wanted to participate in my experiments. Not for the reasons I wanted to conduct them, of course, but that's neither here nor there."

I cannot imagine the Wolf willingly submitting to torture, but then I remember the expression on his face after witnessing his parents' incineration. Then Willy's words came back to me, that strange threat he made right before frying the Wolf. He threatened to give him what he always wanted. And I think about the way the Wolf always talked about Seeing the Light, and the coin-op machine in his office with the blanket-wrapped figure being raised to a waiting pair of hands. "You told him your parents weren't really dead," I say. "You told him they became Sparks and returned to the Divine Light, and that you could bring them back. Or if he helped you figure out how Sparks worked, he could join them."

"The problem was," Willy says, "that as much as Wolfram wanted to be reunited with them, he just couldn't take the pain. He didn't have enough—"

"Discipline."

"Precisely."

My hatred for the Wolf is nothing, I realize, compared to what I feel toward Wilhelm Adelsberger. The Wolf, like the rest of us, was just another of Willy's pawns. I guess damaged people damage other people.

"It's a shame he's gone," Willy says, "because had he been here today, he would have seen my work finally come to fruition. But it's appropriate that you are here, Felix. I have learned so much over the years, in no small part thanks to you and your friends."

"You're nothing but a lousy Nazi!" Annika cries, her eyes narrow slits of ice-blue fury. "But not even a Nazi. You're a filthy, lowlife, Nazi-wannabe."

"The Nazis are beneath my contempt," Willy says with a condescending smile. "They failed because they thought too small. Hitler was satisfied with the Aryan race. He was satisfied with his short time to rule the sandbox. He, himself, was nothing but an unexceptional *untermensch*."

Annika and I exchanged disgusted looks. We don't know what to say.

Willy picks up the syringe, still frothing with rainbow light. "What I am about to do," he says grandly, "is imbue myself with the selfsame creative energy that weaves together the fabric of the universe itself. Do you understand what I am saying? Cosmotic energy. *Divine* energy. I will possess power over space and time. I will shape the world as I see fit. I will be a human god. I will be the Übermensch!"

"That's not what Oskar Adelsberger wanted!" Annika shouts. "He wanted to give endless energy to the world! He wanted to end war! You're betraying everything your grandfather ever stood for!"

"I am impressed," Willy says. "You are more trouble than I ever thought one spoiled little brat could ever be. But you may yet have an important role to play in this story, my precious daughter, for one must always have a back-up plan."

"I'm not your daughter!" Annika roars. "I was adopted from *across the road*, remember?"

"You came from across the road," Willy says. "But I assure you, Annika, you are my flesh and blood. Nothing is more important to me than that fact."

This takes us both aback.

Bewildered, Annika says, "But why would you adopt your own—?"

"So no one would ever know you were his *real* daughter," I tell her.

"But *why*? Unless you don't want anyone to ever wonder who my— What did you do to my mother?" Annika cries.

What about my parents? Did this ogre harm them too? Did he *kill* them? I feel weak in the knees.

"And for that matter," Annika rages on, "what did you do to your sister, Emelia? We know she didn't die in that explosion! You killed her too, didn't you? Is there *anyone* who won't have to pay the price for your so-called progress?"

This makes me realize something. "Hey, Adolf!" I shout, turning toward the stairs. "Your boss has been experimenting on you!"

Willy's expression turns ominously dark. He sets the syringe on the table again and moves toward us, menacingly. "What are you talking about?" he demands. Then he, too, turns toward the stairs. "AXEL!" he roars. "Get down here!"

"Keeping ze guard!" Axel shouts down the stairs.

"GET DOWN HERE *RIGHT GODDAMN NOW!*"

After a long silence, we hear an awful thumping as Adolf lumbers down the steps. When he comes into view, Willy stares at him expressionlessly—he looks exactly as he did when he watched his parents die at eighteen. He is a scientist observing the results of an experiment. Nothing more. Nothing less.

Adolf glares at Annika, then mutters, "I vanted to help more, Villy. I always said I vanted to help more. Nothing can stop my heart. Zis is good information, yes? Very important."

I was wrong. Adolf injected himself with Sparks, and Willy didn't know.

Willy's cheek twitches beneath his monocle as he continues to study what remains of his henchman. "Axel," he finally says. "I have been carefully, meticulously pursing my dream for nearly forty years."

"Yes, sir."

"And everything has gone smoothly, if slowly."

"Yes, sir."

"Until the last few days."

"I'm sorry, sir. But now is over. Now ve vin."

"Perhaps," Willy says. "Perhaps."

He turns toward me then, offering a grim smile. "Let's resolve this unfortunate series of misunderstandings, shall we?" he says. "We can help each other, Felix. I am in need of a caretaker for a new orphanage, and I would like you to take on the task. In return, your friends will be safe. But I need to know where they are, so that I can maintain their treatments and continue to gather data for my experiments. Perhaps they would like to assist in the management of the orphanage with you."

"He's lying, Felix," Annika says. "Don't tell him anything!"

"And I can also arrange for a reunion with your parents," he adds, his dark eyes intent on my face.

Annika grabs my hands and forces me to look at her. Her eyes, intensely blue, bore into my own. "He. Is. Lying. Felix!" she says. "It's all he does!"

"Do we have a deal?" Willy asks.

"Deal this," I say. And then I give him the Left-handed Salute.

Before Willy can respond, Annika darts past him, seizes his walking stick from where it rests against the table and cracks it across her knee. The broken pieces clatter to the floor. She shoots me a triumphant smile.

But Willy seems utterly unperturbed. A shiver runs down my spine as his thin lips turn up in a chilling, condescending smile. He raises a finger in Annika's direction, and a jagged blue bolt sparks from his hand. In a flash, it snaps across the room, striking Annika in the chest. She collapses to the floor.

"Annika!" I cry, rushing to her. A blue bolt hits me in the chest, stunning me. I remain on my feet, but my body is going rigid. Willy strikes me again and again with jagged bolts of blue lightning. My vision fills with white light, with blue sparks. The basement dissolves, then rematerializes again. I'm not in pain, but I find I can neither move nor speak. I'm trapped inside my own body.

While blasting blue lightning at me, Willy nods toward the prone figure of Annika. He tells Adolf, "Take care of her."

Adolf disappears through a door in the back of the lab, then reemerges pushing a hospital bed on wheels and pulling along a rolling IV stand.

I try to scream, to rouse Annika. But I am mute. I am a statue. I feel the energy streaming into me, flowing into my bones. I'm going to disintegrate from the inside out.

Adolf moves Annika to the bed, then proceeds to draw fluid out of a vial into a syringe.

No! No! No! I silently scream.

With the needle poised in his hand, Adolf leans down to whisper something in Annika's ear. An expression of demented glee crosses his mauled face. Gore drips out of his mouth onto the smooth curve of her cheek.

Just as he is about to insert the needle in Annika's arm, we're all startled by a crashing clatter from the stairway. Everyone looks to the foot of the stairs, where a wooden chair now lies in splintered pieces.

But it wasn't just any chair.

It was an old-fashioned wheelchair.

25.

THE UBERMENSCH

We hear rapid footsteps on the stairs, and Mila appears—*on her feet!*

Then Klaus is beside her, and Elsa is there next to him, standing erect, her eyes focused and sharp.

"I will kill you all!" Willy screams, still blasting me with blue lightning. I brace myself as the bolts streak through and around me. I feel no pain, but still, I cannot move.

In a moment too brief to process, I see all my friends together on the steps—and then they're gone.

An instant later, Elsa is snatching the syringe from Adolf's hand, and then, somehow, in a mere blink of an eye, she's back on the steps, holding it triumphantly in the air.

"Zey know—!" Adolf cries.

"Goddamn it, die already!" Willy shouts at me. His hand is still outstretched, but it trembles with the effort of continued blasting. His hair is bristling, now in tumbled disarray. His monocle has cracked, but his black eyes are narrowed with concentrated fury.

Despite his efforts, I feel nothing, only a sense that the world is quietly receding. Willy takes his syringe from the table with his left hand, keeping his right hand aimed at me. He's going to inject himself! I try desperately to scream, but I still can't make a sound.

Suddenly Mila has materialized above him—*floating* in midair! I can't believe my eyes. She reaches down for Willy's syringe, but he stabs it into his thigh.

But now Klaus is there too, having appeared out of thin air.

Mila and Klaus both fight to stop Willy from injecting himself.

"Don't let him!" I scream, and this time my voice rings out

powerful and loud. The blue lightning no longer issues from Willy's finger. He's on his knees, trembling violently. He looks possessed. The syringe, still plunged in his leg, is drained of the rainbow-colored liquid. Klaus and Mila back away.

I watch, dumbstruck, as Willy's body begins to glow blue, and I can see what looks like rivers of light pulse and throb beneath his skin. The light intensifies until his skin emits sparks and a blinding light shoots from his eyes and mouth.

"I AM THE UBERMENSCH!" he roars, standing erect, arms outstretched. His voice is nearly deafening.

"Villy!" Adolf cries. "Is it for real?"

"WE MUST MAKE CERTAIN," Willy booms.

"No!" the Freaks all cry.

Willy raises a hand and two crimson bolts streak across the room. Elsa and Mila crumple to the floor. Then Willy fires a third bolt that strikes...nothing it seems. But I hear a grunt, and then suddenly Klaus appears, and now he's down next to the girls.

Willy turns to Adolf and booms, "FINISH WITH ANNIKA."

Annika, who has yet to open her eyes, says calmly, "First, Adolf, why don't you tell Wilhelm what you whispered in my ear just now."

"I said nothing, Villy," Adolf protests. "She is lying." But his mangled face is a mask of fear.

Annika finally opens her eyes, wipes the gore off her cheek, and swings her legs over until she's sitting on the bed, then turns her attention to Willy. "Shall I share, Daddy dear?" she says, sweetly. "He said—"

"No, Villy! She is deranged!"

I slide a few feet closer to Willy and Annika, managing to close the distance between us with no one noticing.

"He said," Annika says, flashing her gleaming white smile, "and I quote, 'Just have *zis* as your final thought, you little whore. I'm going to have a go at you every day for ze rest of your life...'"

"No!" Adolf pleads, sinking to his busted knees.

"'Just. Like. I. Did. Your. Mother.'"

Willy, still glowing, still throwing off electricity like a human dynamo, turns to Adolf, breathing hard.

"It's true," Axel finally says, attempting to straighten his ruined body. "My children vould be every bit as vorthy as yours, Villy, to help our cause."

"WHOSE CHILDREN ARE THEY, AXEL?"

"I don't know," Axel says. "Zey are…ours."

At that moment, the lights in the lab explode, the dials and switches on the computer consoles flip insanely, and a shrill alarm sounds. It feels as if the air is getting sucked out of the room.

I dive onto Annika just before Willy unleashes on Adolf. The blast envelops all three of us. As I curl around Annika, I see Adolf atomized in a flash of white light.

The blast dissipates quickly, leaving only a faint cloud of gray-blue smoke. Somehow, I'm still here, still alive.

"ANNIKA?" Willy cries. His body, I see, has resumed its normal appearance. The glow, the sparking, is gone. "ANNIKA?" he screams, "I DIDN'T MEAN TO—!"

It's then that I realize Annika is no longer beneath me.

That I'm lying on a mound of ash.

A
n
n
i
k
a
Please no. Please no. Please no.

"IT DOESN'T MATTER," Willy roars. "THE EXPERIMENT IS OVER! I AM A GOD!" He sends an arcing bolt of crimson electricity in my direction. The blast hits me in the chest, knocking me off the bed. On the floor, I instinctively curl into a ball, the way he taught me to do as a child.

"DIE!" Willy roars, standing over me, blasting out electrical fire.

And now he kicks me too.

He kicks me in the head, the face, the back of the neck. He kicks me in the gut, the back, between the legs.

I decide this is right. This is how I was always meant to die.

Willy blasts more lightning at me—a barrage of blue, red, and orange bolts. Soon I will be nothing but ash, and I will be with Annika. In the Light. He keeps kicking me. Kicking and kicking and kicking.

At some point, I realize the kicks don't hurt any more than the electricity. And I begin to wonder...

Why am I not dead?

And: *Why didn't anyone shoot me when they had the chance?*

Then a fact occurs to me: *Elsa's meds made her slow. Because she's fast.*

Then another one: *They put Mila in a wheelchair. Because she can fly.*

And another: *Klaus's cream treated his skin...Because he can turn invisible.*

Finally, one more question comes: *Why was I told that I was weak?*

And one more answer: *Because I am strong.*

I rise to my feet.

"DIE, GODDAMNIT!" Willy roars, unleashing one furious explosion after another. "FOR THE LOVE OF GOD, *DIE!*"

I walk into Willy's storm like a man who does not feel the wind.

"Time to pop smoke," I say.

And I punch him in the face.

I know Willy's dead before his body hits the floor like ten pounds of shit in a five-pound bag.

Pardon my French.

Then everything stops.

The lightning is gone.

The air settles.

Several lights flicker on.

I turn to see the Freaks getting themselves up off the floor.

I feel energy coursing through my veins, and I feel strong. Incredibly strong.

And shattered.

Six hands touch my back. Then six arms wrap around my body. I feel…encased.

And I understand that wanting to hide from the world is not the only reason I climbed so willingly into the Wolf's Bags.

Something unzips inside me.

And I weep.

Annika.

Please no. Please. No.

My friends hug me. And I weep.

When I can't cry anymore, Elsa says, "We saw your message."

"It's over," I say. "It's finally all…over."

"I don't think so," Mila says, gesturing toward the wall on the far side of the lab. "Look."

The insulation that covers the basement walls has melted there. Just visible, behind the globs of dripping rubber, is another recessed vault door.

Gripping its edges, I wrench the door right off its hinges and toss it aside.

"Damn," Klaus says.

Inside the vault is, incredibly, a furnished apartment. A frail, elderly woman sits at a desk, writing in a book. She turns toward us slowly, then gets to her feet as we come inside.

She has ropy black hair, threaded through with gray.

She has Klaus's pale skin, but hers looks clammy and wasted.

She has Mila's broad shoulders, though hers slump with age.

She has my prominent chin, which quivers at the sight of us.

And she has Annika's electric blue eyes.

"This is Emelia Adelsberger," I tell everyone. "She's our mother. Adolf or Willy Adelsberger was our father. Emelia is—was—Willy's sister, and she has been his prisoner since she was three years old. Annika, her other daughter, was meant to take her place when she got old enough to bear children. I think it's time we called the police."

ONE YEAR LATER

AFTERWORD

SO MANY MONSTERS IN THE MAZE

I managed to repair Mila's old wheelchair. It's much sturdier now and moves without creaking, but she never wants to see it again. Which I can understand. I didn't think we should throw it away, though, so I brought it up to the top of my tower. I'm sitting in it right now, putting something else together, some gears for a coin-op. I found one at a garage sale down the road, a peep show game designed like a circus tent. Its front panel proclaims, *FREAKS!*

How about that?

When you drop a coin in and look through a viewer, four freaks dance by—a bearded lady, a fat man, a lizard boy, and a dwarf. Or at least that's what happened when I first got the thing. I've replaced the figures with four new ones that look just like the Headquarter Freaks. Us. When I'm done, they'll dance by the viewer, but then climb up through a hole in the top of the machine, and then down the side.

Because that's what we did.

From my vantage point up here, I have an expansive view of the mansion grounds. I see kids playing volleyball, tetherball, badminton, and horseshoes. Klaus is playing hide and seek with a group of preschoolers, who seem perplexed by the fact that he's impossible to find. Pretty close to cheating, if you ask me, but it makes him happy. Elsa, I see, is having a tea party picnic with six toddlers, who have no chance of crawling away. She zips between them, placing them back on the blanket just as fast as they escape it.

Mila is strolling with our mother, who is wearing her usual dark sunglasses and sunhat. The doctors say that she may be able to tolerate direct sunlight eventually, and they hope one day she'll be able to speak because there's nothing physically wrong with her vocal cords. Emelia may look sixty, but she's only forty-three. She decided to take her mother's maiden name, Becker. And so the rest of us have too.

I must admit that I don't understand how she can be so kind, so gentle, so positive about life after what she's been through. The poor woman was forced to give birth to babies she never saw again after bringing them into the world, babies destined to be used in demented science experiments, then discarded like trash. But she sees us now, every day, and we will never leave her side. I can't imagine what else she had to endure, but I'm slowly learning everything about her life by reading her journals. Whatever that turns out to be, I know now that not all damaged people damage other people. That gives me so much hope.

Emelia was writing in her sixty-ninth journal when we found her.

How about *that?*

I think a lot about Hannah Schmidt and her diaries. We keep them in the library downstairs, in a place of honor on a shelf with Willy's lost film and the Philosopher's Stone. All Hannah ever wanted was to know the truth about our family history. She did nothing to deserve that horrible end. The truth set me free, but it ended her life, and I don't know how to feel about that. I guess I have a lot to learn. Fortunately, I can afford all the books and magazines I could ever want now. Which is all of them.

When Mila and Emilia turn in another direction, I see that Mila's feet float an inch or two above the ground.

I wonder what kind of world Willy wanted to create and what kind of god he wanted to be. Did he want to possess *all* of the Freaks' unique qualities? What would have been special enough for him? I wish I knew why some people need to feel superior to others. I know one thing for sure: we Freaks aren't better than anyone else. Far from it.

Just to be clear, I'm absolutely in favor of self-improvement. But the world would be a much better place if people aimed to be more like Oskar Adelsberger than Wilhelm.

I set the gears in my lap, then make my hands into binoculars. I put them against my eyes and look across the road at the
ruins of Headquarters. Some partial walls and the lower portion
of a brick chimney still stand with the forest of junk looming
up around them. Headquarters, it turns out, was built to host
illegal gambling back in the day, and all those hidden stairs and
hallways were designed for easy getaways. They certainly helped
me with my getaway, although it was anything but easy. And I
gambled on someone, someone who gambled on me.

I can see phantom Sucks running roughshod all over the
place, playing games, pretending to clean their rooms, fighting,
fooling around in closets. I hope they don't know they lived to
be distractions and died for being loose ends. I hope they roam
Headquarters forever having non-Mandatory Fun.

And there's the Wolf's hungry ghost clomping through the
crazy corridors, dragging a Bag behind him. It's full, but not
with a Suck. I'm sure of that. It's more likely filled with his
helplessness, his rage, his defeats. I think he genuinely wanted
to share the discipline he discovered during his darkest hours
with his unwilling disciples. I believe he inflicted that darkness
on others in the hopes that someone would find a light inside it,
a light, perhaps, to illuminate a better way through the labyrinth
of his life. I hope one day I see that light.

There are, after all, so many monsters in the maze.

Until then, like I said, I have a lot to learn.

I let the Wolf go about his business and turn my gaze up
toward what's left of the attic, which is only a few charred floor
beams that used to sit below the diamond-shaped window.
A small stack of half-burned boxes also survived, and I see
my oldest sister, Charlie, with her long ponytail, perched atop
them. A boy with a curlicue of hair pasted to his forehead sits
on her lap.

The boy peers through his hands—a spyglass—in this direction.

And I know what he's seeing.

Not me.

He's seeing a beautiful and, yes, *fierce*, young woman with a braided auburn crown of hair and blue fire in her eyes. A young woman whose spirit can never be broken.

Annika is looking back at him. Because she is, and will forever be, the most real part of me.